A NOVEL

Mark Rogers

ISBN: 1470129604
ISBN 13: 9781470129606

Library of Congress Control Number:2012903610
CreateSpace, North Charleston, SC

For Ann, who makes my quixotic pursuits possible

ACKNOWLEDGEMENTS

To Trish Burdette who gushed when it wasn't gush-worthy.

To Brian Burdette and Rob Cunningham who took a chance and recommended me to their VIPs.

To Tom Maloy, Hong Tsun Simon, and Bill Reynolds for time spent reading and invaluable insight.

To Casey Rogers whose exuberance carried me through the low point.

To Josh Rogers who, with precious little free time, read and critiqued my book anyway.

To Linda and Curt Gillespie for the kindest words a first time writer could ever hope to hear.

To Tom Dennard for his words of experience.

To Beth Hinson for all the help and encouragement a brother could ask.

To Julia Fatou whose editing skills made this a better book.

And finally to Ann who took the brunt and stood her ground, agreeing with me only when I got it right.

In memory of Sara Ellen Lowe Rogers who was born February, 20, 1924 and died February, 16, 2012. She was forever telling me, "you can do anything you put your mind to."

Thanks Mom.

"What have you given us, Mr. Franklin?"
"A Republic, madam. If you can keep it."

Ben Franklin

CHAPTER 1

It's Thursday, past midnight in DC, and I've just undergone another fifteen-hour strategy session locked in that stress cage we call the conference room—third day in a row. My shirt's soaked, my butt's numb, my brain's mush, and I'm wrung flat. My condo's only a few blocks away but I'm doing what I always do when I'm stressed, driving through the park buying some unwinding time before going home to Annie.

It's working. The cool, spring drizzle, aided by a legion of glimmering street lights, give the city a glow all its own. The monuments and buildings, blurred by soft, sultry rain, are more reminiscent of an impressionist's canvas than the stark, angular reality of marble and stone. The view of Washington, D.C., tonight truly is that shining city on the hill.

Sometimes when I'm driving through the city this way, not another soul around, I can almost envision the founding fathers hammering out our Constitution, bestowing rights and freedoms on *we the people,* proclaiming principles and truths never before brought forth by any government in the history of mankind.

I glance in the rearview mirror and see that I'm smiling. I laugh out loud. What a crock.

This is exactly the BS I've been peddling my entire career to the naïve, the uninformed, the indoctrinated, the sheeple. Tomorrow the sun will come out and so will the players, the controllers, the spinners, the appeasers, the dealers, the shakers, the lobby-cons, the lords, and their ladies, and this city will turn back into a pumpkin and will, once more, be mine. Thank God that document we call The Constitution didn't hold up. Fortunately, our politicians and their lawyers have been able to riddle more holes in that piece of parchment than an NRA convention at a target shoot. Otherwise how could a guy like Senator Feldstone get re-elected term after term and a guy like me manage to hang on to the cushiest job in DC?

My name is Hartford Keepe. I'm Chief of Staff to the Honorable Senator Harold P. Feldstone, Chairman and senior member of the almighty Appropriations Committee. No one really knows what the p stands for. The senator claims it's for "paragon," but I don't think so. Maybe "pedantic" or "paranoid," but more likely it stands for nothing—much like the senator.

My job, my sole purpose in life, is to keep the senator in office. It's not difficult. Only once every six years do I need concern myself with it. What with the plethora of rules and regulations enacted into law by Feldstone and his cohorts, along with their House colleagues, re-election for them is about as close to a sure thing as any of us'll ever get. You see, Senator Feldstone subscribes to the incumbent's motto:

To make a difference I came,
To make a difference I remain,
And remain, and remain, and remain...

Senator Feldstone has been making a difference for thirty-five years now and is hardly in any mood to stop.

DC is, after all, a city of winners and losers. The winners stay around while the losers turn tail and run. You've got your professional flip-floppers, your double-talkers, fence-sitters, spinmeisters, and outright liars.

I know these people, I work with these people—I am these people.

If you're a quick study, agile of foot and mind, who can dodge the press and dance with lobbyists, you might stick around. If you're deliberate, principled, slow to reverse course, a true decision maker, you're likely gone.

I control two senior staffers, six junior staffers, and a varying number of dedicated interns—my own little fiefdom, if you will. You take on my Senator, you take on me. You take on me and you're going to lose. This is my town, my career, my life, and, like the senator, I intend to be here 'til the day I die.

I turn onto Madison to drive by the mall. I'm feeling better but still too wired to go home; maybe a couple more laps. I turn left again on 14th and dutifully slow to twenty—a good five mph below the speed limit. No other cars share the road so there are no blaring horns or middle fingers to break my mood. In the daytime you can do twenty over the limit and not raise an eyebrow, but go the other way and you pay hell. I cruise into another left on Jefferson and find my right hand snaking out to turn on the radio. Yeah, I know I've got buttons built into the steering wheel, it's a Beemer after all, and lord knows I use them often enough to follow the news and the unending Washington scuttlebutt during working hours, but when I'm mellowing and want my music, I use a hand-to-dial approach. As I'm twisting the tuner searching for something tight, I spot my first human.

He's sitting on a park bench with his head in his hands while the rain pelts his body. The man seems to shake and quiver as if he's cold or crying. I figure him for a war vet—probably Vietnam or The Gulf; too young for World War II or Korea. He's probably spent all his money getting up here or down here to see the wall, to find the name of that best buddy or big brother or some other poor slob buried beneath a rice field in Southeast Asia. It strikes me as the saddest sight I've ever seen.

I detect movement to my right and a park security vehicle pulls up next to me. I glance over and meet the cop eye-to-eye. He looks me over, shows little interest, and turns his attention to the ne'er-do-well on the bench. But not before I recognize him— Woody "The Sap" Kolowski, named for the ten-inch sap he carries on his belt just above his right hip. It's against regulations, so he keeps it hidden from the brass; but he pulls it out every time he makes a stop.

Kolowski pulled that crap on me eight years ago when I first arrived in DC as a junior staffer, still wet behind the ears. He got me—not for speeding, not for running a stop sign, not for illegal parking—for going too slow; a hundred-and-fifty-dollar traffic ticket for going five mph below the limit. I think he targets all the rookies just to establish his turf. I've been waiting these eight years to return the favor.

I watch him pull to the curb adjacent the sad sack on the bench. He steps out of his vehicle, grabs the leather sap from his belt, and begins slapping it against his palm as he swaggers toward the suspect.

I pull up behind him and hop out of my car leaving the engine running. I head toward the two men at a fast clip. I'm too far away to hear the words but I don't need to. Kolowski has one hand high under the guy's left arm while the other one's clutching the sap. He's roughly hustling the man to his feet using whatever force he deems necessary. It pisses me off. My stride lengthens and my gait quickens. I march right at them and block their way.

"Excuse me, officer," I say. "Is there a problem here?"

"Will be," he says, "you don't mind your business and get the hell outta my way."

I love this guy.

"I believe you've made a mistake, officer. I know this man. As a matter of fact, I've been busting my hump all night looking for him."

Kolowski, wider than me but shorter, looks me up and down. I watch him check out my Armani suit and glance over at my Beemer. I don't see any sign of recognition in his face, but his eyes show a smidgen of doubt, which is all I need.

"I represent Senator Harold P. Feldstone, Chairman of the Appropriations Committee, and this man is one of twelve military heroes flown in at the senator's behest for a special celebration to honor his service to this great country. I doubt the Senator would take kindly to finding his guest of honor sitting in a DC holding cell."

Kolowski lets go of his prisoner but tightens his grip on the sap.

"Well he shouldn't be out here on a bench at this hour." He squints and adds, "In the rain."

I move in a little closer and stand a little taller so I'm looking down at him. I had him at *excuse me officer*, I'm just playing with him now.

"This man was to meet me at the Washington Monument at eight o'clock," I say. "Apparently he became confused. Maybe the golf-ball-sized piece of shrapnel lodged in his head less than two centimeters from his brain had something to do with it. I don't know, but I'm here now and would like to get him out of the rain and escort him to his reserved suite at The Ritz Carlton."

I take the man's arm and steer him around a hundred eighty degrees. I don't look back, nor do I hear word one from "The Sap." I smile to myself, then glance over at my charge, hoping to share the moment. He looks confused. It occurs to me that during the entire performance my victim didn't open his mouth or offer the slightest resistance to me or Kolowski. Maybe he does have shrapnel on the brain.

I release his arm but continue to lead him toward my car. It's then I notice that Kolowski isn't the only one in uniform. My companion is wearing some pretty strange duds himself. Not a uniform exactly, but certainly what a citizen soldier might wear—if he were fighting the British back in 1776. In his right hand is a three-cornered hat, his pants are leather breeches, he wears a waistcoat and a vest, he even carries a rucksack on his back. I wonder if I've picked up a Tea Partier who's downed too much tea—a "Don't Tread On Me" type—but I don't think so. His clothes are old and worn.

It hits me—a re-enactor. They're forever recreating Bunker Hill or Yorktown or one of those other battles. Today's probably the anniversary of some major campaign.

"That's me over there," I say, pointing to the BMW.

"Ah," he says "a motorized cart."

These are the first words out of his mouth, and I'm pretty sure he said *cart*. I stare at him and then look back at Kolowski, who's still standing there eyeing me. I decide we should get out of here so I let the cart comment go. I quickly open the passenger door for him but before he can get in, ask if I can place his rucksack in the trunk since his clothes are already going to soak my leather seats. I want to take his hat and coat, too, but we need to move so I settle for the backpack.

He takes it off and hands it to me. I drop it in the trunk, climb into the driver's seat and buckle up. The safety alarm immediately goes off. I glance over and motion for him to buckle his seat belt, but he doesn't understand. Apparently the boys on Revolutionary Road don't do seat belts, so I reach over, snap him in place, shift into first, and hit the gas. As I pull out in a smooth, albeit rapid, acceleration, he keeps his eyes straight ahead, with something between a smile and a grimace on his lips. As is my custom, I wait for him to start talking so I can play off of his questions and control the conversation—tactics 101. But my passenger doesn't want to play. He has yet to thank me for the rescue or the ride and doesn't seem all that interested in where we're going.

Everything in life involves power, either gaining it or surrendering it. Gaining and maintaining the upper hand is my strength; silence, especially uncomfortable silence, my weapon. My passenger, however, doesn't seem to want to engage. He remains silent and appears quite comfortable, so I cave.

"What's your name?" I say.

"Thomas," he replies.

"I'm Hartford Keepe. My friends call me Hart." I stick out my hand and he shakes it. "You got a last name, Tom?"

"You misunderstand me, sir. My name is Thomas."

Well woopty doo, aren't we the snooty little ingrate? But the thing is, he doesn't say it that way; he says it as if he doesn't know who Tom is. As if it can't be him because his name is Thomas. What a funny little man.

"So, Thomas, do you have a last name?"

"I believe I must," he says, "but, alas, I cannot recall what it might be."

I start to wonder who's running this game and if I'm losing my touch.

"You don't know your last name?" I say.

"This, sir, is my unfortunate condition, yes."

His speech sounds funny. He's American but too...formal. Maybe a New Englander. I had a professor at Harvard who spoke in a similar manner—stilted, old-fashioned. It suddenly occurs to me that he's still in character. As a Revolutionary War re-enactor I'm sure they're required to speak as well as dress the part. I look over at him. As for the memory loss, I'm wondering if maybe somebody shot a cannon too close to Thomas's ear, or perhaps he got conked on the head by a flintlock during battle. Either way he doesn't appear to be too much of a nutjob, and though he's not a vet—unless you count faux wars—I'm still proud to have effected his rescue. Now I just have to find a place to deposit him. I look over again and smile. He seems so serious, so clueless—I think I might have to play with him.

"So, Thomas, where can I drop you?"

"Drop me?"

Let's lose the re-enactor bit already. "Where would you like to go?" I repeat.

"A lodging house called The Ritz Carlton, if you please," he says. "I believe the proprietor is expecting me."

I jerk my head toward him in a double-take pantomime. He's still looking straight ahead but a hint of a smile has found his face. He's not only digested everything I've said but, he's able to joke about it. Not only has he a clue, Thomas has a sense of humor.

"I don't think The Ritz will take you with no last name and no luggage," I say. "I doubt your rucksack will count."

"Then I must request you transport me to my home, sir."

I jerk my head again. "Home?" I say. "Where's home?"

"My bench." He smiles. "I believe the officer in command will have vacated the premises by now."

I smile back. "Why don't I just take you to my condo, get you out of those wet clothes, get some food and drink into you, and maybe have a little chat about that missing memory?"

I'm immediately surprised by my words. I'm not this nice. To hear Annie tell it, I'm a Hart-less bastard. I look over at Thomas. He's smiling at me as if he knew where this was going all along.

We suffer through three red lights and fifteen minutes of uncomfortable silence before pulling into my driveway. My Beemer clock says 12:51. Annie's going to be pissed.

Annie is my live-in girlfriend. When I met her I was dating a woman named Ann, no *e*. The new Anne I cleverly referred to as "Anne with an *e*," which eventually became Annie. She either likes it or hates it.

Annie and I have this running feud which has been going on since we met six years ago. To her, not calling, is crude, rude, and disrespectful, and denotes an enormous etiquette void in one's upbringing. I see it as a preservation of freedom. I've been working late all week and have no idea how long the sessions will last night to night and, therefore, I'll be home when I get there. It's the kind of attitude that keeps her uncommitted and me in the doghouse. But as I pull into the driveway, it dawns on me that tonight I'm claiming the upper hand.

Annie's always been a sucker for strays. Puppies, kittens—anything without a home. What could be better than a rain-soaked amnesiac rescued from a park bench on the National Mall? I check my smirk in the mirror. This is gonna be fun.

I hit the garage door opener and Thomas and I watch the door ride up its rails and disappear into the ceiling. Thomas seems fascinated by the disappearing act. Still, he asks no questions. I think that's what I like about Thomas, his ability to listen and observe. No one who works for me does either of those things.

I pull the Beemer into the garage, shut off the engine, unbuckle my seatbelt, and get out of the car. Thomas observes my moves and a few seconds later emerges from the passenger side. He follows me up the stairs to the first floor living quarters.

We have our living room, dining room, and kitchen combo on the main floor, along with a small powder room. It's a decent space with good light. Upstairs are two bedrooms and two full baths. It's not huge, but it suits the two of us and suffices during the occasional short-term visit by my mother or Annie's.

I pause at the top of the garage stairs staring at the locked door between us and the living room. I'm no longer smiling. I'm wondering if I should warn Thomas about the probable hostile on the other side.

CHAPTER 2

Rather than knock, I take out my key for a silent entry. I'm hoping Annie's upstairs and already in bed, which would at least delay the inevitable confrontation. I slowly ease the door open. She's in the kitchen, closing the freezer compartment door—half a Dilly Bar in her left hand, the other half in her mouth. Her hair's wrapped in a damp towel and she's wearing her shabbiest bathrobe, open in the front, with mismatched flannel pajamas underneath. Her feet are shuffling about in her ten-year-old Peter Rabbit fuzzies. All that's missing is a generous spread of cold cream on her face.

She suddenly turns and faces us—two men entering her condo unannounced. A lesser woman might startle or blush, let out a scream or a curse, and bolt for the bathroom door. Not Annie. She walks directly toward us, swallows her ice cream in a painful gulp, throws a mean frown at me, a plastic smile at Thomas, and presents her right hand.

"Hello," she says, "I'm Annie, sorry about the mess." Meaning herself, I suppose, since the room is spotless.

Thomas must be as surprised as she, since I have yet to mention a live-in girlfriend. Still, he accepts her hand graciously and kisses it, executing a wee bow.

"My name is Thomas," he says. "I am quite delighted to make your acquaintance, Mrs. Keepe. Please forgive this boorish intrusion."

Her smile remains and she doesn't correct the Mrs. Keepe part, so I almost grin before a hard glare shuts me down.

"Thomas," I say, motioning him to the couch, "why don't you make yourself comfortable and excuse Annie and me for a minute?"

He sits down and Annie grabs me by the hand, only because there's no leash, and insensitively tows me toward the kitchen. She would have preferred the bedroom, where she could berate me with volume, but parading me all the way up the stairs in front a guest is outside of her etiquette envelope. She does lead me to the far corner of the kitchen, however, where distance and the hum of the Sub-Zero will shield her tirade from Thomas's ears. She maintains a pretty good fake smile while she lights into me.

"What is it with you, Hart? What are you thinking? You show up at one o'clock in the morning, no call, no text, you bring a crazy, costumed, homeless man into our condo unannounced—Are you purposely trying to blow this relationship?" She pauses, all huffed up and red-faced, her left foot tapping the floor like a crazed metronome. She looks at the kitchen clock and takes a breath. "You have thirty seconds to get this person out of our house, after which time you shall be accompanying him."

It seems I've miscalculated on my stray puppy theory. Still, Annie can be a bit unreasonable at times—it is my condo.

"Mrs. Keepe, if I may be so bold."

It's Thomas. He's standing, facing us, but wisely keeping his distance. Annie turns toward him and produces an artificial smile which is badly betrayed by her body language.

"Your husband, Hartford," he says, "effected my rescue in a rather difficult confrontation with the local authorities. I am much indebted to him. He is quite noble, you know."

His words disarm her, since he's used *noble* and *Hartford* together in adjoining sentences.

"I see my presence has ungraciously wrested you from your bed chamber, madam," he continues, "so, with your permission, I would kindly take my leave."

She cocks her head slightly and stares at Thomas. He's a little man—five foot six, stout, mid-fifties, meek, mild, unassuming, and quite gallant; nothing like my other friends.

"Thomas," she says, "you do not have my permission to take your leave—not until you're dried off and I fix you something to eat." Her smile turns genuine and she adds, "I think I like you, Thomas."

"I see nobility and generosity runs abundantly in the Keepe family," he says.

I'm staring at the little suck-up and shaking my head. I know of absolutely no one who can get away with that kind of talk.

"Come on, Thomas," I say, breaking up the love fest, "I'll show you where you can wash up."

I direct him to the main floor powder room while I choose the upstairs bathroom. By the time I return, Thomas is still in the powder room and Annie has disappeared from sight. I sit on the couch and wait for someone to emerge. I hear a flush, but then everything goes quiet and no one comes out. Another flush and Thomas still won't appear. After the third flush I call out to see if he's all right. A few seconds later, he opens the door wearing a broad grin.

"Quite fascinating," he says.

Somehow, during all the commotion, Annie manages to reappear in the kitchen with long, wavy, expertly primped hair, minus the towel, wearing her jogging sweats and looking impossibly pretty.

"Gentlemen," she says, "dinner is served."

She's set three places, indicating a slightly more forgiving attitude and demonstrating her intention to join us. Annie normally retires to the bedroom by ten o'clock, earlier if I have a friend over. Tonight she's either lapsing or breaking tradition. I look over at Thomas. He's sitting up straight with his hands in his lap and a pleasant smile on his face. I start to wonder how I can go about keeping this guy around.

Annie brings over two steaming bowls of Campbells' chicken-vegetable soup and sets them in front of us. She then retrieves her own bowl and joins the party. We all sit in silence, trading glances, wondering who will start the conversation. I doubt it'll be me. I'm here to listen and observe.

"Well, Thomas," Annie says, "Hartford has told me nothing about you. I don't believe he's even mentioned your last name."

So now I'm Hartford vice Hart, but in a good way. The last time she called me Hartford was when I forgot our fifth anniversary, but in a bad way.

"He doesn't know his last name," I blurt, ignoring my own council.

"I'm talking to Thomas, dear." She looks at Thomas and smiles.

"This is true, Mrs. Keepe. It seems I have developed considerable memory loss and am presently unable to recall my surname."

"That's terrible," she says, looking over at me as if it's my fault. "Have you seen a doctor?"

"No, Madam, I have not. My ailment has only this day afflicted me. For several hours I attempted to ascertain the severity of my condition, when the park authorities took an interest in my presence."

"He's referring to park security," I say. "I bailed him out."

She ignores me. "What did you discover?" she says sweetly. "How much memory have you lost?"

"Apparently a great deal. I know not from where I come, nor my age, nor if I enjoy marital bliss. I have no recollection of my career, my wealth, nor my dog's name."

"You have a dog?" I say.

"I know not." He smiles.

I look over at Annie. "Thomas has quite the sense of humor."

"Do you know why you are dressed this way?" She says. "It's mid-eighteenth-century colonial-style clothing." She reaches over and feels the fabric of his waistcoat. "Do you know why you are wearing this?"

"Perhaps I am a citizen soldier," he says.

She smiles politely. "The Revolutionary War took place over two hundred thirty-five years ago, Thomas."

"Perhaps I am older than I appear."

"Told you," I say.

"How do you know your name is Thomas?"

"While wandering through the park I came upon a magnificent statue of President Thomas Jefferson, and I knew. Perhaps I was named after President Jefferson."

"Do you recall why you came to Washington, D.C., or why you were in the park, or how you got there?"

"I am truly sorry, Mrs. Keepe. I have tried in earnest to recall my past, and other than my name have been completely unsuccessful."

She turns to me. "Hart"—we're back to Hart—"We need to take Thomas to Dr. Robeson first thing in the morning. You'll have to do it, I've got to be on the road by six. I want you to call me on my cell the minute he makes a diagnosis."

"I work, too," I say.

"You're a chief of staff. You've got a gazillion junior staffers and interns to do the work. I'm sure Senator Feldstone can get by without your wisdom for a few hours. Now, I'm tired. I need to make up Thomas's bed and put clean towels in his bathroom. You need to find him some clean pajamas and a spare toothbrush—unused."

She heads up the stairs before I can retort or decide with what. Did I mention I match wits with the most powerful people on earth for a living?

"Who is Doctor Robeson?" Thomas asks.

"He's a neurologist and my cousin. He can check you out, see if you've suffered any kind of head trauma."

He nods but appears apprehensive. I can't shake the feeling that this is all an act, that he's playing me. If so, he's the best I've seen. I decide that once I expose him I'll have to hire him. Either way, I'm confident Jim Robeson will either pinpoint the memory problem or else flush Thomas out in the open where I can pounce.

CHAPTER 3

sleep relatively well, interrupted at times by Annie, who seemed to wrestle with herself most of the night. She got up once that I know of, probably to check on Thomas—out of concern, I suppose, or maybe suspicion. By five a.m. she's up and dressed and leaning over the bed kissing me goodbye. I watch as she quietly slips through the bedroom door, then immediately I jump up, grab my robe, and hurry after her. We reach the kitchen at the same time, where we find Thomas outfitted and sitting at the breakfast/dinner table sipping a glass of water.

"Thomas," she says, "you're an early riser." She sits down across from him and puts her hands protectively over his. "I wish I'd known. I would've cooked you breakfast."

Cooked him breakfast? She never cooks me breakfast. I'm always relegated to an Egg McMuffin and OJ in a paper cup. I glance at her and then back at Thomas. She likes him—no, she *really* likes him. I don't see it but he must have something. Maybe her suppressed mothering instincts are kicking in, or perhaps he's awakened a passion for tiny and meek—whatever it is, I feel just the slightest touch of jealousy rearing its head.

"I must depart your company," Thomas is saying, "gracious though it has been, and enable you and Hartford the freedom to continue the pleasures of life."

"Don't be silly, Thomas," she enjoys speaking his name. "Hartford is going to take you to the doctor today."

Hartford again. She tosses me a glance.

"You need to be there by seven thirty."

"Why? Jim doesn't get there until eight."

"I spoke to Elinor this morning, James is booked up for the month but we were able to fit Thomas in before office hours."

Great. I wonder if James—or as I have known him all my life, cousin Jim—knows about it, and if he doesn't I wonder at whom he's going to be pissed, me or the girls.

She puts her purse on her arm, stares at me, and dangles her car keys at the ready.

"I want to know exactly what the doctor says. As soon as you know anything you call me."

She brushes up against my lips with hers then looks at Thomas for a long time. She abruptly reaches for him and hugs him tight, sighs loud enough for me to hear, and rushes out the door.

"I work, too," I say, but only Thomas hears me. I harrumph and shake my head. Senator Feldstone is in session first thing this morning, with two follow-up meetings on his agenda. He'll be tied up through lunch, so, as it turns out, taking Thomas to the doctor is doable—but Annie didn't know that.

I look at my watch—five thirty. I glance at Thomas. He's dressed in his colonial outfit, without the rucksack or hat, which makes him look only slightly less inappropriate. I know we'll have to buy him new clothes, but the stores won't open until at least nine, so I decide we should head to my favorite 24-hour diner for breakfast instead.

I tell Thomas to help himself to juice or beer while I go upstairs and change—the diner's only a fifteen-minute walk. He nods and I make for the stairs. I fail to hear the fridge door open and it occurs to me that in Thomas's world refrigerators may not yet exist.

The diner smells good and I'm hungry. I begin to worry about our breakfast conversation and whether he plans to pelt me with uncomfortable questions about head trauma and memory loss, not to mention a possible lapse into overall lunacy.

After we place our order and the waitress leaves, he says, "Mrs. Keepe pursues a career, it seems."

"Yes," I say. "She's a t-shirt rep, and you can call her Anne."

"Oh no, Hartford," he says, almost in shock "I would not be comfortable with such familiarity. What exactly is a t-shirt rep?"

"She sells t-shirts for a large screen printer in Southern Maryland," I say. "She covers Pennsylvania, Maryland, and the District."

"What exactly is a t-shirt?"

I stare at him. If he's putting me on he certainly does it well—and persistently. I look to see if I have a t-shirt on under my dress shirt, but I don't.

"There," I say pointing to a large, bearded, biker type on the other side of the room. He's wearing a black t-shirt with the words *Hairdressers do it coiffed* printed across the front. Go figure.

Thomas stares at the man, then turns to me and smiles. "Underapparel proffering a message," he says. "Quite ingenious."

He doesn't ask what the message means.

"May I now inquire as to your career, Hartford?"

Hartford. So with me he's fine with such familiarity.

"I am Chief of Staff to a senior United States senator," I say proudly, or arrogantly.

"Which senator?" he says. "Which state does he represent? There is no senator for the District of Columbia."

I'm shocked. Thomas knows something. Maybe he learned about DC and the Senate while wandering the Capitol grounds and he's miraculously managed to retain it—or he's faking the whole thing.

"Senator Feldstone represents Virginia," I say.

"The Commonwealth of Virginia, the tenth state to join the union, Old Dominion. How delightful. And what duties might a chief of staff perform for the senator from Virginia?"

And I was worried about doctor questions. I spend the next thirty minutes, most of them hemming and hawing, trying to explain exactly what I do for Senator Feldstone. Thomas peppers me with query after query about the senator, his beliefs, his principles, his vision for the country. He is not pleased with my nebulous non-answers. When he starts into senior staffers, junior staffers, and interns, their numbers, their pay, their benefits, and what exactly they all do for such compensation, I start to feel not so pleased myself.

I pull out my Blackberry—6:52, thirty-eight minutes before the calls and texts start flowing in earnest. "We need to get you to the doctor," I say, "and I need to get to work."

I stand up, pay the check, and hustle him out the door. The doctor's office isn't far, but we will have to take the motorized cart. Thomas is getting less and less enamored with automobiles since we are seeing so many of them. We face an unending line of bumper-to-bumper traffic as we trek back to the condo.

We arrive at Doctor Robeson's office and step up to the receptionist's desk at exactly 7:27. The sign above the closed window reads: *We don't do Medicare any more courtesy of Mays, Polanski, and Reed—the three blind mice.* What a putz. I start to sign in and the receptionist stops me.

"Oh you don't need to bother with that, Mr. Keepe." She stands up and slips from behind the counter, extending her hand. "And you must be Thomas," she says with a giggle.

Thomas takes her hand, bows, and kisses it. She giggles some more. Word has gotten around. She turns, smiling, and opens the office door.

"Dr. Robeson will see you now."

I try to tail in behind him but Kimmie won't let me. "The doctor feels it best that he see Thomas alone," she says. "We discussed it earlier."

By "we" I figure she means my Annie, Jim's wife, and Kimmie. I wait. It isn't long—twenty minutes or so—time enough to check my messages and send seventeen texts and four emails. The office door opens and out comes Thomas, closely accompanied by Doctor Jim, who's all smiles and grins.

"Fit as a fiddle," says Doctor Robeson as he grabs Thomas's hand for a goodbye shake. "Nice to have met you, Thomas, hope to see you again soon—Let's make it socially next time." His grin broadens as he slaps his patient fondly on the back. "I would love to take you two out for an early lunch"—*it's 8:10 a.m.*—"but Hartford needs to get you to Dr. Freeman's office as quickly as possible. He's backed up, you know—going to squeeze you in as a favor."

Before I can ask, he dusts us out of the room with his fingers. "No time for talk, Hartford, go, go—drive fast."

"Right, James, but we'll talk." I put my hand to my ear phone-like. He never calls me Hartford and I never call him James. Thomas and I hurry out the door and down to the car.

"Who's Dr. Freeman?" I ask as we step out of the elevator.

"Dr. Robeson believes Dr. Freeman to be an exemplary psychiatrist, who may provide me the aid I seek. What is an exemplary psychiatrist, Hartford?"

I look at Thomas, less and less surprised by his questions. "A doctor who deals with the mind," I say. "Maybe a man with a pill that can hasten memory's return—certainly worth a try."

"It would be nice to recall my origins," he says, then hands me a piece of paper.

It contains directions to Dr. Freeman's office, which is less than ten minutes away. My phone is already vibrating every thirty seconds or so. I check my messages again—nobody's died, but the day is young. I refuse to listen to voice mail because it takes too long, and besides, everyone who knows me knows to text—the exceptions are Annie and Senator Feldstone.

Once we arrive, Dr. Freeman, like Dr. Jim, bans me from his office, opting to speak with Thomas alone. Annie calls while I'm Blackberry-ing in the waiting room. She asks if Thomas is okay and wants to know all about Dr. James's diagnosis. She then makes me promise to call her the minute I learn anything from Dr. Freeman. She doesn't ask me how I'm doing or whether or not I still have a job.

My Blackberry and I continue to interact with each other, texting and messaging. I check my unending string of calls, but if they're not from Feldstone or Annie I let them go to voice mail. After a while, my fingers start to cramp so I look at the time— 10:20; we've been here an hour and twenty minutes. My phone is now vibrating non-stop. They really want me. Suddenly the door opens and Thomas followed by the good doctor step out. There are no grins or smiles this time, no backs are slapped and no late breakfast or early lunch invites are issued, possibly because Dr. Freeman is a psychiatrist. Instead, the doctor frowns and/or scowls at me and motions me into his office. I follow him, checking the time and shaking my head. I glance behind me and catch Thomas picking up a copy of Psychiatry Today as he enters the waiting room.

The doctor tells me that there are no pills, no quick fixes, no special therapy for Thomas's memory loss. He says that the amnesia is real, not imagined nor faked, and that his memory will come back sooner or later or never. His memory could return in large chunks, in small dribbles, or not at all—it's anybody's guess. He goes on to recommend that Thomas embark on a relatively new strategy in dealing with his amnesia.

Most patients, he explains, spend their time trying to uncover bits and pieces of their past, hoping one of these tidbits will trigger a total recall. Studies have shown these methods in fact have little or no bearing on restoring memory. It would be far better for Thomas to continue with life. He should take what he knows of himself and move forward. This will give him stability and purpose and help him deal with the uncertainty and chaos in which he now finds himself. Are there any questions?

Yes, I have one. "How will Thomas know what he likes and what he doesn't like if he can't remember anything?"

By his expression, I can tell the doctor is wondering if there's someone else he can talk to.

"If he tastes ice cream and smiles then he likes it. If he sees a cat and backs up that means he's afraid of cats. If he laughs at a funny joke, it means he possesses a sense of humor. Anything else?"

I think about telling him a funny joke but decide against it. I shake my head instead.

"It would be good," he continues, "if Thomas could find a hobby. Work would be even better. A full-time job would put his mind in a forward-looking direction and give him purpose."

Before I can ask how we should go about uncovering Thomas's skills he says, "Watch him, experiment—He'll show interest and probably aptitude in something. You already know he has a feel for American history. That's a start. It would be good if he could come in contact with someone he admires—someone he can look up to, someone he can emulate. A person like that in his life, at this time, could be of immense help."

I think we both know he isn't talking about me.

"One last question," I say. "This 'starting over'—is Thomas all right with the idea?"

He looks at me like *does it really matter?* and says, "Yes."

"Okay. Well, thank you very much, Doctor, for your time and advice. We'll get him on the program immediately, right away, today. Thanks again."

I back toward the door, smiling and waving like an overanxious rube. I'd like to get Thomas out of here before Freeman can come up with twice-a-week therapy sessions for life.

We finally make it back to the car and I check the time—10:55. I need to get to work, I need to report to Annie, and I need to figure out what to do with Thomas. If I call her she'll tell me to take him to the DC Police Station, Missing Persons Department. Then she'll want me to put Thomas posters up all over the city, check all of the newspapers in the land and whatever I do, not let him out of my sight.

Normally that would fly, but not today. We're in crisis mode and the office is in chaos. When we pass each other in the halls, we don't greet, we cuss. It's hardly an appropriate environment for an amnesiac. I put my phone in its cradle out of habit, and it rings immediately. It's loud and hard to ignore. I say "Hello," activating the speaker. An oversight, since I'm not sure I want Thomas to hear the conversation.

"Hart." It's Niles, my gopher. He's calling my name without a hello which means things are desperate.

"How bad," I say.

"Feldstone's furious—nine and a half on the rage scale. He's still in session but, what're you in, a bunker? I've been calling all morning."

I say nothing so he goes on.

"Feldstone's talking about cutting off heads. You need to be here—We've got a meeting."

"I thought he was in session. What meeting?"

"He's leaving the floor early and he's cancelled all his follow-ups. The conference room—twenty minutes."

"I'll be there in fifteen." I click off.

I start the car and peek over at Thomas. He seems far more interested in how the phone works and where the voice is coming from than what we'd said. I leave the phone in the cradle but put it on vibrate.

He doesn't ask, so I say, "Thomas, I have to get to the office. I don't have time to take you back to the condo. I've got an idea, though. How would you like a guided tour of the Capitol grounds?"

I might as well have asked him if he wants his memory back. His eyes widen and a big grin lights up his face.

"George Milton," I say, re-activating the speaker. The phone beeps and clicks, and finally we hear a digital ring on the other end. After a couple of those, George answers.

As I pull on to Capitol grounds I tell George I have a special guest with me who is eager to experience the sights and sounds of DC with all its bells and whistles. George works at the Smithsonian.

He loves US history and Washington, D.C., and though not an actual tour guide, he's the best tour guide in the district. He likes nothing better than to welcome a fellow history buff into his world. He confirms that he's free for any friend of mine and urges me to bring Thomas on over.

"On my way," I say, and audibly click off. "All set," I say to Thomas. "Now we need only to come up with a place to meet afterward."

"Perhaps there," he says, pointing to a bench in the distance—the bench where I first found him.

"Perfect, I'll meet you there at three o'clock. Here, take this." I hand him my watch. He looks puzzled but takes it anyway. "Don't worry, I have my cell." I show him the phone with its digital clock readout.

He gives me a confused nod, releases his seatbelt, and steps out of the car. I point him toward the Smithsonian, wish him a good day, and speed away.

CHAPTER 4

I wade into the firestorm known as Feldstone's Compound. The halls are awash with chaos, the cubicles ripe with sweat, the air choked with profanities. I yell to Niles, who is passing me eye-to-eye so tightly wound he doesn't see me. I grab him and turn him, and stare into his face.

"Hart," he says, wild, bloodshot eyes registering recognition. "Welcome to hell."

"Tell me," I say.

"What's to tell? Internals are out, worse than we thought—favorables down five, unfavorables up six."

"For the party?"

"For the senator."

"Crap." Feldstone's already under thirty percent—the lowest in his thirty-five years.

"Heads are gonna roll."

"No," I say, thinking aloud, "they're gonna be loped off and stuck on pikes."

Niles puts a sympathetic hand on my shoulder. "Come up with a strategy, boss, or you're pike number one."

Damn. I'm glad I didn't call Annie back. Glad I didn't bring Thomas to work. Not glad my mind's oatmeal and I have no inkling of a plan.

Niles and I file into the conference room with the others and find our seats. We're sitting directly across the table and thirty-six inches away from the empty chair waiting to claim the honorable butt of Senator H. P. Feldstone.

Desperate chatter ramps up all around me while my mind sorts through the myriad strategy options acquired and discarded through the years. My one purely experimental, semi-developed, thus-far-never-expressed idea appears front and center in my thoughts, and I begin to chew on it. The room suddenly goes quiet and I shut down my brain as the senator enters the room. He stands without smiling, surveying his minions.

"Hartford Keepe," he says, glaring at me, "glad you could make it." He throws a thick manila folder down on the table and pulls out his chair but remains standing.

"Gentlemen…and ladies," he says, eying the two female interns while opening his folder, "we are in a world of S-H-I-T." The senator feels it perfectly permissible to use crude language as long as he spells it. He pauses, puts his focus back on me, and is content to just stare.

I'm not intimidated—I invented this game. I wait patiently for the silence to get uncomfortable and say, "You knew it was an anti-incumbent year, Senator. We are the majority party—this is not unexpected."

"Maybe for rookie incumbents," he shouts and slaps his hand on the table. "Not for old warhorses like me. I should not be vulnerable."

"And you're not," I say. "The people of Virginia love you."

He pulls a sheet of paper from his manilla folder and shoves it in my face.

"Is that why I'm holding negative record-f-ing-breaking poll numbers?" he yells. "Because they love me? I'm at twenty-seven percent, for god's sake. What am I missing here?" He puts his hand to his chin in mock think. "Have they got pictures of me with a male page? Did they find ninety thousand dollars in my freezer? Did somebody show up with a soiled blue dress?"

He's half smiling now, at his cleverness, so I remove my hand from my throat and say, "No, sir, nothing like that. It's the Party, it's Congress, even the president. America doesn't trust its elected officials. They find them arrogant, elitist, dishonest, some downright corrupt. They feel their representatives are more invested in self and Party than in God and country."

He waves my words away and pins me eye-to-eye. "We've got eight months until the election," he says. "Can we fix it?"

We go through more or less this same routine every six years. This time...okay, this time it's serious. The senator could well lose his seat and so could a lot of others. This time he does need to "fix it." I elect to drop the spin and go with the hard truth.

"Yes, sir," I say, standing, matching his stare, "we can, but it'll take the cooperation of the entire Party, of both Parties. This thing targets all incumbents—Republicans as well as Democrats."

He frowns big at that. They all do. Interjecting the 'R' word never pleases the senator, and if Feldstone's unhappy, everybody's unhappy. But truth is truth, and deep down in his narcissistic little heart he knows it. No one likes fraternizing with the enemy, but if that's what it'll take to re-ingratiate incumbent senators with the American voter then that's what they'll do—Democrat and Republican alike.

"Tell me," he says, and the room grows pin-drop quiet.

I allow the silence to build, take in a deep breath, and let the air out slowly. "They want to be listened to," I say. "They want to be heard."

Feldstone gets that squinty look of puzzlement on his face like he's unfamiliar with the language.

"Number one is arrogance," I go on, "followed closely by elitism and privilege. These three vices permeate the system, from the president on down. They even trump corruption. This has to change or at least the people's perception has to change. Otherwise, you and a bunch of your colleagues are going to be turned out of office to live on large pensions and short memories while the rest of us join the unemployment line."

My tablemates don't actually release a collective gasp but they want to. All their mouths have fallen open and their eyes have gone silver-dollar wide, darting back and forth between the senator and me. Feldstone is smiling. He's found my words neither insulting nor disheartening, neither dishonest nor out of line, because he's only heard one of them—*perception*. To a politician, the word "perception" means you don't actually have to change your ways, you just have to fool your constituents into thinking you did. No language barrier here—we're well within Feldstone's wheelhouse now.

"Continue," he says, his smile growing broader.

"I call it 'Listening To America,' or LTA. We invite the heads of major organizations, corporations, industry groups, unions, associations, minorities, coalitions, alliances, societies, what have you, that are near and dear to the hearts of the American people. We put these leaders on stage in front of Congress and the president. We persuade the media to pick up the event and televise it throughout the country. We let these pillars of society represent their constituents by speaking their piece, while Congress and the president listen—and the American voters watch. Listening To America."

"Listening To America..."

The senator cups his chin with his thumb and index finger and looks up at the ceiling. Three interns glance up also.

"Listening To America..."

He closes his eyes, tasting the sound, digesting the words. He takes his hand from his chin, stretches out his fingers and suddenly slaps the table with a loud bang.

"I like it," he booms. "I like it a lot." He grabs a sheet of paper from his folder and hands it to me. "Make a list—everybody we need on the planning stages of this thing. Dems only at this point. We need a small group of heavy hitters who can put this thing together quickly. You write it up and prepare a presentation. Call a meeting—party chair, Majority Leader Senate, Minority Leader House, Appropriations, Budget, you know the drill. Keep it down to ten or twelve—we need to get this thing set." He scans the faces in the room. "Everyone take your marching orders from Hart. Questions?"

"Are we going to tip the administration?" It was Julie Dragon, the lone female senior staffer.

Feldstone stares at her at length. "No," he finally says. "Let's keep this in-house until we get a read from our own." He gazes over his subjects again. "Okay, people," he says, clapping his hands together. "Lets go, let's get it on. Hart," he starts toward the conference room exit, "my office."

Senator Feldstone leads the way, and I follow a couple of steps behind as per protocol. It allows him to meet and greet, handshake, and backslap his way down the hall. But, because of the crisis, there are no takers today. Once we get past the receptionist's watch stand and into the inner sanctum, he closes the door.

He gestures for me to sit, then walks around the oversized desk to the power side. He remains standing, then, propping both arms on the desk for leverage, leans forward, his face nearly touching mine.

"Hartford," he says, almost in a whisper, "how much trouble am I in?"

I study his face. This is no drama play—Feldstone's scared. I've never seen him this way. He searches my eyes for some kind of truth then drops into his chair with a heavy sigh. A depressed smile crosses his face.

"About time for you to earn your keep, Hart," he says, chuckling at the pun. "Time to put that devious, calculating, highly irritating little brain of yours to task."

No, I'm thinking, *it's time to prop up a senator*. The man's ego, though enormous, is as fragile as a snowflake. Handle it improperly and he'll cut off his nose, and your balls, to spite his face. He'll do it just to prove you wrong and him right, in that order.

"I don't think your seat's in serious danger, Senator. It's not possible—you're a fixture around here, you've served your state for over thirty-five—"

"Did you even follow the midterms, Hart? Did you see the results? Holland lost his seat—he was a three-termer; Landis is out, he was a two-termer and expected to chair the Budget Committee. We of the old guard are gonna be next if we don't turn this damn thing around."

"Senator, you're still the party of the people. You gave them Universal Health Care. Once the American voter understands the benefits of the program they'll not only be pacified, they'll be grateful."

"Dammit, Hart, Universal Health Care was never meant to pacify the people. It was a power-play meant to keep the Democratic Party in power. The Federal Government in charge of health care. It's like Medicare on steroids. It includes, not just seniors, but everyone. It puts the whole country in a Democratic choke-hold. The voters vote against us, we claim the Republicans will take away their healthcare. It's perfect—calculated and executed as planned. Trouble is, it's not working."

"Why not," I say innocently. Not that I care—I'm busy boosting my power grid and devaluing his. My job is to get Feldstone re-elected every six years. To do that he needs to stay dependent on me. He wants to vent though, so I let him. '

"We thought we could blame it all on the last guy, Goodman." He continues. "The recession started on his watch after all. Normal recessions last, what, 9 to 18 months - this one had to go and be anything but normal. After two years of things refusing to get better the voters were looking for somebody to blame. They started to question our spending habits - the bailouts, the stimulus, the Omnibus bill, all chocked full of pork and favors. By the time Universal Health Care came along the voters were properly pissed. They didn't care about the benefits, they cared about the cost, the spending. They feared for their children, their grandchildren, generation upon generation saddled with an impossible debt."

He pulls out his chair and drops into it. "When you're broke, cost always outweighs benefits. Try buying a new car when you can't afford one. Doesn't take long for those untenable monthly payments to sour the smell of new leather and dampen that zero-to-sixty acceleration. It's the economy, stupid. We should have given more attention to jobs and spending, and we didn't. That's what happened in the midterms, Hart. That's why Republicans reacquired the house. And if we don't get our act together, in eight months they'll take the Senate and the presidency as well."

He stops talking, his head drops, and his shoulders sag. He looks up at me with defeated eyes.

"I don't want the damn Republicans in on this, Hart," he says. "Let us Democrats run with it. We can take the credit—we need the credit."

"Senator." I hate to pile on, but my job requires me to lay the cards on the table.

"The Republicans are already a step ahead of you. They're making noises about ending earmarks as well as repealing health care. Hell, the House Majority Leader has given up his personal airplane. He claims he can just as easily fly back and forth commercial and save the taxpayers money. It's all symbolic, of course, but it looks to the people as if the Republicans are listening to them. Fortunately for us, the masses have their pitchforks aimed at incumbents of both parties. Anyone who's up for reelection and deemed guilty of ignoring the American voter will be targeted despite his or her record. All incumbents need to band together to turn the tide. If the Dems try to go it alone it could easily backfire and elevate Republicans even more so."

Feldstone's vigorously shaking his head, but I won't let him speak.

"This is equally true of the Republicans," I go on. "However, if the two parties can manage to cooperate with each other, the people will glimpse a side of two-party government they've never before seen. They'll figure their government is serious about change and does want to hear what the people have to say. Why else would Democrats and Republicans, whose animus is legend, be willing to bury the hatchet and work together?"

He stares at me, through me, around me, with all ten fingers clutching his chin.

"I still don't like it," he says. Then, breaking his scowl, "But I can sure as hell see why I keep you around, Hart. Okay—but we meet with our people first, right?"

"Right."

"Good, set up the meeting. You outline the presentation—shouldn't be any problem getting everyone on board. This is good, Hart, it's very good."

He walks me to the door with his arm around my shoulders and gives me a firm, audible slap on the back as he sends me out into the reception area.

Ahh, recognition—what we staffers live for.

CHAPTER 5

A quick flirt to Jeannie, the steely-eyed receptionist, and I'm out the chamber door, through the waiting room, and into the hallway checking my Blackberry. I'm over an hour late for my meet-up with Thomas, but, knowing him, I expect he's still sitting on that bench waiting for me—all night if he has to.

I'm wrong. Thomas is nowhere in sight. I walk the length of the mall and still don't see him. I refuse to shout out his name, from embarrassment, I suppose, or arrogance. But the crowd is sparse and my charge is wearing a minuteman outfit, so how hard can this be? All the walking is starting to wear me down. I'm used to spending my days in air-conditioned surroundings, conducting meetings and dispensing orders to my staff. I spot an empty bench in front of the Smithsonian, so I walk over and sit on it.

I check my email and send five texts. I don't check my voice mail because the vibrations have slowed to less than one per minute and Feldstone's in a meeting. I could continue the search, but to what purpose? Thomas could be anywhere—the Monument, the Memorial, the Smithsonian, the White House, chatting up the president. The man needs a cell phone.

I'm thinking of giving George a call when the smell of grilling hot dogs wafts my way, reminding me that I'm starving. I haven't had anything to eat since breakfast, and my eggs were overdone.

I get up and head to the vendor's cart. I purchase two hot dogs, a bag of chips, and a Coke with ice, and then I grab a soft pretzel because I can't help myself. I pay and look around for a closer bench.

I spot a good one immediately. Thomas is sitting in the middle of it.

He seems caught up in watching the tourists stroll by, so instead of calling his name I walk over and stand in front of him. It takes him a good ten seconds to notice me. He seems intent on checking out an elderly couple walking along the mall wearing his and hers matching T-shirts. *The beatings will stop when morale improves,* they read, and there's an image of a skull and crossbones below the words. Thomas finally looks up, sees me, and smiles broadly.

"Hartford," he says.

I hand him a hot dog and he stares at it as if it's a filet mignon from Ruth's Chris.

"My appreciation, Hartford, I've grown quite famished since our delicious breakfast." He sniffs it and takes a bite, savors it, and takes another. "This is quite flavorful, Hartford, I do not believe I have tasted the like. I must thank you yet again."

I sit down next to him while he chews vigorously. "Sorry I'm late," I say. "Long meeting."

His mouth is crammed with hot dog so he just nods. Watching him gobble makes me realize Thomas has no money.

"How about a Coke?" I say, handing him mine.

He chokes down enough of the dog to manage a, "Yes, and I would be grateful for another of these," and holds up the empty wrapper. I give him my second dog, as well as my chips, and content myself by nibbling on my pretzel.

After devouring two hot dogs, a bag of chips, and a large Coke, Thomas leans back on the bench, places both hands on his stomach, and smiles in contentment.

"I guess we've discovered you like hot dogs," I say.

"Yes, Hartford, they are quite delightful. It is the first time I have tasted such a meal. Are cold dogs as satisfying?" He's grinning at me with playful eyes, so I refuse to take the bait.

"So, Thomas, what have you been up to?"

"More than you might suspect, Hartford. I have chosen a profession."

"You want to sell hot dogs."

"No," he giggles. "I would very much like to enter the t-shirt trade." I stare at him but he looks past me. "It is quite fascinating," he says, pointing over my left shoulder. "There is one that says 'Graceland.' I do not know of Graceland but it is obviously a land to which that young lady has traveled and, apparently, she enjoyed it so thoroughly she felt compelled to procure a t-shirt on which to display its name. I have seen many such t-shirts with names of towns and villages, sayings, and platitudes. Is it not wonderful, Hartford? The people are speaking their minds through their wearing apparel. It is quite imaginative."

"T-shirts," I say.

"Yes, to announce where one has traveled, or which University one has attended, or one's beliefs, one's principals, one's proclivities—moral or secular—even one's state of mind. Oh yes, Hartford, I believe the imprinted t-shirt to be quite a spectacular invention."

I'm wondering when I should clue him into Facebook. "So you've been sitting here watching t-shirts go by the whole time."

"Yes," he says without shame, "indeed I have."

"And from this you have decided you want to embark on a t-shirt career."

"Yes, my mind is filled with thoughts which I would have imprinted upon such garments. I may well become a wealthy man, Hartford."

"You know Annie is in the t-shirt business," I say.

"Do you suppose Mrs. Keepe could consult with the park authorities on my behalf? I wish to market to these people." He spreads both arms, indicating the plethora of tourists roaming the grounds "These individuals who have come to Washington, D.C., the seat of our nation's government, to take lesson and pride in the greatness of this country."

I smile and say, "Sure, and you might want to expand your base to include those who come to demonstrate, whine, grab, lobby, diatribe, demagogue, exploit, con, and demand. I'm confident a slickly worded slogan would appeal to most of them. And, if you play your cards right, you might get Uncle Sam to foot the bill."

He grins at me as if I've wholeheartedly endorsed his plan.

"Excellent." He stands up. "Shall we return home to discuss the matter with Mrs. Keepe?"

Mrs. Keepe. Christ, I haven't checked my voice mail all day and Annie doesn't text. I pull out the Blackberry and find Annie's number listed fourteen times. Maybe I should get Thomas to call her. No, I can't do that to him. Besides, her first words would be *Put Hartford on the line.*

Well, at least I've been working, not out at the bar drinking lunch with my cohorts. That should count for something. In fact, I've been busting my butt, doing my job—which, by the way, brings in most of the money—and babysitting Thomas. If I don't have time to pick up the phone and check in every five minutes then so be it.

I'm shaking my head. Here I am about to own up to the truth and it even sounds lame to me. I hunch my shoulders, hold the phone in close, and reluctantly punch Annie's speed dial. Midway through the first ring she picks up.

"Is Thomas okay?" she says.

"Yes, he's fine. Listen, Annie, I'm sorry I—"

"Nothing's happened to him, you're sure."

"Yes, he's fine, I'm—"

"Put Thomas on the phone."

I hold the Blackberry at arm's length and stare at it. I'm getting pissed and I don't know why—she's the one supposed to be mad. I put the phone back to my ear.

"Don't you want to know why I didn't call?" I say.

"You were in a meeting with your precious senator. He was in crisis mode, ranting, raving. All were atremble. You came up with a brilliant idea and saved the day. Feldstone's happy, his minions are happy, you're a hero—Put Thomas on."

"I'm not hearing any respect here."

"You shouldn't hear respect. You should hear yelling. You should have called."

"Okay," I say, "maybe we should start over."

"Okay." She pauses a good ten seconds and says, "Damn it, Hart, I've been sick with worry. You don't call. You don't call. You say you'll call. You don't call. I'm thinking car crash, mugging, terrorist attack—"

"Okay, here's Thomas," I say, and hand the phone over. Lord, I need to figure out a way to get that girl to marry me.

Thomas and I drive home in silence. I break the quiet by suggesting we stop off for pizza since Annie won't be back until tomorrow morning.

"What is a pizza?" He says.

I don't respond. I'm still upset with Annie. She has little if any respect for what I do. I mean, I'm the eyes and ears for one of the most powerful men in the country. We change lives, we make a difference. Annie would say—*has* said—we deceive people so we can keep our jobs; the same old "all politicians are scumbags" rant. What does she know? She sells t-shirts for a living. I ponder the implications. Hmmm, maybe we both could have put our degrees to better use. I turn to Thomas. He seems lost in thought himself.

"Thomas, Annie's last name isn't *Keepe*. We're not married, we're just living together." It's difficult for me to tell him this and I don't know why. "Her last name is Green. Anne Green."

"She enjoys being addressed as Mrs. Keepe," he says. "I anticipate it is a name you will share in the not distant future."

He smiles as I pull into the Pizza Hut parking lot. I bypass the pickup window and decide to go inside. Thomas is fascinated, as per his MO, by the pizza concept, and requires considerable time to choose. We're shown to a booth by Sheila and presented with two menus. After an explanation by me and much deliberation by him, we settle on the same thing: pepperoni with extra cheese. We order a large, with a couple of Cokes and four sticks of garlic bread.

Unlike this morning at the diner, I'm looking forward to our conversation. I wait until Sheila drops off our drinks before I start.

"So, Thomas, why do you think Annie and I will be married soon?"

"Why would you not?"

"It's not something to be taken lightly, Thomas. It's a big step. I need to be sure I'm ready." I didn't add, *and that Annie will have me.*

He puts his glass down and studies me. "Hartford, I should think you quite distraught should you tarry too long and lose such a woman."

"I don't know what too long means," I say.

"You will know, the day you return from work and find Miss Anne no longer residing in your dwelling." He takes another swig of his coke, pats his mouth with his napkin, and says, "This, my friend, would be a tragedy, would it not?"

Sheila comes back with the pizza holder in one hand and the pizza in the other. She bangs around the table for a clear area, puts down the stand, lays the pizza on top, then deposits some utensils from her pocket and leaves. I'm staring hard at Thomas the entire time.

He and Annie have developed quite a bond in the short time they've known each other. The depth of their friendship both amazes and irks me. He talked with her on my cell for a good twenty minutes in the park. They laughed and chatted and bantered like they had known each other for years. Annie and I never talk that way.

"So what did you two talk about on the phone?" I say.

"Why we talked of my new career, Hartford. Miss Anne seems quite energetic on the subject and has generously consented to aid me in my pursuit. She has an acquaintance to whom she will introduce me and from whom I may gain considerable assistance."

"An acquaintance," I say, "to help you sell your t-shirts."

"Yes, exhilarating, is it not?"

So it's Miss Anne now, no more Mrs. Keepe—he's playing with my head.

"Shall we now discuss your day, Hartford? From your conversation with Miss Anne, I understand it must have been quite extraordinary."

All right, finally someone who wants to hear about me. "Are you interested in politics, Thomas?"

"Very much so."

"Well, you know I work for Senator Feldstone."

"You are Chief of Staff to the senator from Virginia who stands for nothing."

"Yes, well, the senator has internal polls taken on a regular basis. The latest one shows his favorables are down and his unfavorables are up, which means—"

"He is growing unpopular with the people."

"Well, yes, and therefore he's worried about his reelection bid which is in less than eight months. It's my job to turn those numbers around. So today, in a staff meeting, I proposed a strategy that would do just that." I smile proudly.

"A strategy that would secure his popularity," he says.

"Exactly."

"Would such a strategy involve the senator changing his stance from nothing to something?"

"No," I say, "this is politics. The strategy involves giving the people what they want."

"And would they not want the senator from Virginia to stand for something?"

"No, no, they want to feel the senator is listening to them, is hearing what they have to say, is attuned to their needs."

"But he is not."

"Not what?"

"He is not listening to the people and he is hardly attuned to their needs."

"Why would you say that, Thomas? You don't even know Senator Feldstone."

"If he was listening to the people he would be standing up for the people and his popularity would not be in decline."

Thomas obviously doesn't understand politics. He's oversimplifying a very complicated issue. Senator Feldstone is standing up for the people. He's standing up to get reelected so that he can continue to serve the people of the great state of Virginia to the best of his abilities. He's been serving the good citizens of Virginia for over thirty-five years now and has certainly earned the right to continue serving them for another few terms or until he has given all he has to give.

My eyes dart around for a pen and paper—I should be writing this stuff down. I lock on the empty pizza pan, however, and say, "Maybe we should get a move on. I've got a big day tomorrow."

"Yes, and I have a goodly number of t-shirt ideas I would prepare as well."

I pull out my wallet and leave the appropriate bills on the table. I look at Thomas and shake my head. I'm talking about the intricacies and nuances of politics to a guy whose whole focus in life is coming up with t-shirt slogans. He looks back at me and smiles. Together we stroll out to the motorized cart.

CHAPTER 6

I realize as I pull into the garage that I'm exhausted. I remind Thomas that Miss Anne will be home tomorrow morning but probably not until after I've left for work. He nods in understanding, and we bid each other a good night and traipse off to our respective bedrooms—I to prepare my national "Listening To America" extravaganza and he to dream up t-shirt slogans.

I'm up by five thirty and out of the shower by six. I opt not to wake Thomas but to leave him a note: *Gone to work. Help yourself to food and drink. Miss Anne should be home by ten. Call me if you need me. Hartford.* I don't know if Thomas can work a telephone or not, but I leave the note on the table, next to the morning paper, grab some juice and head off to the Compound alone.

I walk through the office door to a hero's welcome. Grins, back-slaps, and handshakes greet me around every cubicle—hugs from the interns and butt-kissing from the junior staffers. No applause yet, but that should come at the staffer meeting. When the senator's happy, everybody's happy. Niles is waiting for me at my cubicle.

"Brilliant," he says, "abso-f-ing-lutely brilliant. Feldstone was whistling in his office—I swear, whistling 'Happy days are here again.' I swear." He holds up two Boy Scout fingers.

"Yeah, okay," I say nonchalantly, beaming inside but outwardly maintaining my cred. "Tell me about the meeting. Who's in?"

I had left instructions as to which party heavyweights were to be contacted. This was to be a short-notice, high-profile deal, which requires numerous staffer-to-staffer contacts and major scheduling rearrangements in order to pull it off. Everybody knows the drill: you go after the top of the power structure first, get a couple of prime-timers on board, and then everybody else falls in line.

"We've got Alcorn, Reed, and Polanski so far," he says, grinning.

That's the top three—Party Chair, Senate Majority, and House Minority. Plus, of course, there's Feldstone.

"It's set, then" I say. "The rest'll be chomping at the bit. You got a date and time?"

Niles gets on his beer-silly grin and then pauses for effect.

"Today. Twelve o'clock."

Jesus! Nobody arranges a meeting in a day. "Good lord," I say.

"I'm telling you, boss, this thing's huge—everybody wants in. Your problem's gonna be the ones you leave out."

That's the least of my worries. This fast track miracle Niles has just performed is about to work against me. I have yet to finish the presentation—it's little more than half done. I glance at my watch and realize I've got less than four hours to wrap it up and get it to Feldstone for approval.

"Niles," I say, "you contact the rest of them personally and stall Feldstone. I've got to get away from here and finish this thing."

"He's already asking for you."

"Stall." I grab my laptop and make for the elevator.

I'm not worried about the senator. I'm his wonder-boy, his Hart almighty. Feldstone'll take any excuse I offer as long as he gets his presentation on time. I reach the outdoors and fresh air, taking in large gulps while searching for a place to work. I spot an unoccupied bench under a large maple that's just greening up. I sit down, open up my Mac, and study the screen.

Time flies. It's quarter till noon when I get back to Feldstone's office. He's perturbed but visibly relieved to see me. Cursing my tardiness would be neither prudent nor politic, so he expels his irritation by arm-sweeping a bunch of papers from his desk, clearing a spot for my laptop.

"Okay, Hart," he says. "What've you got?"

It takes me ten minutes to go over the presentation, but the senator makes an executive decision after two. He'll do the intro, I'll do the spiel. Just give him enough time, at the end, to jump back in and take the credit—depending, of course, on how it all goes down.

"Enough talk," he says suddenly, standing up and slapping the desk. "We've got a meeting."

The presentation goes extremely well. So well, in fact, the senator finds it necessary to step in a good five minutes before I'm through speaking in order to claim credit and accept praise. I don't mind, everyone here knows the game—staffers do the work, senators take the kudos. Even the idea of pulling in Republicans garners approval. Everyone agrees for different and mostly self-serving reasons, but they all agree.

The administration had managed to get wind of the meeting and slipped in an uninvited representative. Turned out he, too, loved the proposal and left with a glowing endorsement.

So with the president on board, the only thing left to do is convince the Republicans to join us. And then, of course, to select those organizations, unions, groups, businesses, committees, movements, and so forth that will most accurately represent the thoughts and ideals of the American people. Such duties rank well above my pay grade, so, as far as I can tell, I'm done. Nothing left for me to do but go back to the office, get myself hoisted up on a couple of broad, underling shoulders, and be carried around the room to the strains of *For He's A Jolly Good Fellow*. I decide, for reasons of my own, however, to skip the celebration and go home instead.

On the way, I pass the Thomas bench and wonder what kind of day he's having. I doubt it can top mine. It occurs to me that my current run of good luck started the day I met Thomas and since then has done nothing but escalate. I want to call Annie and tell her my good news but decide against it. If I drive straight home I can surprise her in person—a chance to glimpse that elusive sparkle of admiration in her eyes. The risk, of course, is that word will have already spread and Annie will be in the midst of preparing a giant surprise party for her Superman. I elect to take the chance.

I wheel up to my driveway and see no cars lined up, no partiers dancing on the patio, no frivolity spilling out into the yard. Maybe she's limited her guest list to neighbor friends, and they're all inside hiding, preserving the surprise.

I hit the remote, pull the car into the garage, and step out, straightening my tie and running a hand through my hair. I dance up the stairs to the landing, wearing a wide grin. I throw open the door and am not greeted by the three people huddled around the dining room/conference table talking amongst themselves. There's Annie, Thomas, and a stranger—none of whom look up or notice my presence. My feelings are hurt, but I refuse to throw a tantrum.

"Hello," I say loud enough to wake the dead, "I'm home."

Annie, smiles, gets up, comes over and gives me a kiss and a hug. Thomas does the same but doesn't kiss. The stranger just stands there.

"This is Archie," Annie says. "Archie, this is Hartford."

We exchange pleasantries and then someone, Thomas, I think, says, "How was your day?"

By the time I can form my ebullience into words, they're all back at the table huddled over their paperwork. My timing is off, best to wait awhile before breaking my news. Instead of making a scene I tromp up the stairs to shower and sulk. I'm sitting on the bed, untying my shoelaces, when Annie walks into the bedroom.

"What's wrong?" she says in that tone usually reserved for three-year-olds.

"Nothing, I'm just going to hop in the shower."

"You can't. We need you downstairs. We need your help—your expertise."

Oh, she's good, this one. She knows something's wrong but doesn't want to waste her time pleading it out of me so she goes straight to my vanity spot.

"We're discussing Thomas's t-shirt designs," she says. "He has three. Each of us has chosen a different one—we need you to break the tie. Besides, I want to hear about your day."

That Annie, I told you. I retie my shoes and follow her down the stairs.

It turns out the mystery guest, Archie, is one of Annie's best customers. He owns half a dozen retail stores in downtown DC, where he sells various souvenir paraphernalia: mugs, key rings, postcards, miniature replicas of The White House, etc. But his main gig is imprinted t-shirts. He does quite the volume and buys most of his blanks from Annie. It seems Archie has, just recently, won the t-shirt lottery. The powers that be plan to sponsor an event entitled "Patriotism In The Park," which will run from April 20th through Memorial Day. There'll be all kinds of special booths scattered throughout the park, including a fixed number of kiosks selling food, drink, and merchandise. Archie, because of his retail stores, has scored the t-shirt kiosk. He's extremely excited and he figures, with the right designs, he can sell more t-shirts in two months from a kiosk in the park than he could sell in his stores in a year. When Annie asks if Thomas could work for him as a favor to her, Archie is happy to oblige. When Thomas mentions he has been working on several t-shirt design ideas himself, Archie is less so.

Archie's been in the T-shirt business for over fifteen years. There isn't a person he knows who doesn't think they have a million dollar t-shirt design idea floating around in their head. He comes up with two or three of them every week himself. He also knows that trial and error is the only way to test such designs and that trial and error costs money. Besides, in a small kiosk, shelf space is at a premium, so displaying untested ideas is a fool's game. Archie makes it abundantly clear that he has a limited time in which to move his merchandise and he plans to move a ton of it, so no untested designs will be tolerated.

But Archie has never negotiated with the likes of Annie Green, so, after all the discussing, reasoning, disputing, bickering, quibbling, and pleading, Archie acquiesces. But, to his credit, not by much. He consents to allow one unproven design into the kiosk, but only if Thomas pays for the shirts and the printing. They've narrowed the field down to the top three and are bringing me in to pick the winner.

I walk over and look at the three white sheets of paper on the table. They aren't exactly designs, they're historical quotes with a small minuteman soldier silhouette at the bottom of each sheet. The soldier wears the same outfit as Thomas only he has a rifle instead of a rucksack. I study each quote carefully, as if I have some interest in the matter.

The first one reads: *Government, even in its best state, is but a necessary evil; in its worst state, an intolerable one.*

The second: *Moderation in temper is always a virtue; but moderation in principle is always a vice.*

The third: *Those who expect to reap the blessings of freedom must, like men, undergo the fatigue of supporting it.*

"Where did you get these?" I say, looking at Thomas.

"I do not know. Perhaps I learned of them when I was quite young."

"They sound like historical quotes."

"Perhaps," he says, "but I know not who said them."

I wonder about the copyright laws, but, considering these are obviously very old quotes, I figure they're well past the statute of limitations. On the other hand, the author's name could add value. We could do a web search.

"Who picked what?" I ask.

"I went with number one," says Archie. "The voters are already pretty angry out there. Number one would play nicely into that. We'll probably sell a couple hundred to Tea Partyiers alone—if they sell at all."

"I chose number two," Annie says "It's a truism I believe in."

"I prefer the third quote," says Thomas, "because protecting our freedoms requires constant vigilance from *we the people*."

I look them over again while clutching my chin with my thumb and index finger.

"Well," I say, "I'll have to go along with Thomas. In my view, he's the expert around here."

Of course I know he isn't. Both Archie and Annie know more about selling t-shirts in DC than Thomas and, in truth, I agree with Archie. People are pissed at government, and playing into that kind of anger would certainly be the way to go. But my career revolves around assuaging the people, convincing them that government is their friend and that their friend is listening to them. I feel a slight pang in my chest for not being honest with the group, but it's nothing I can't handle. In DC you've got to be tough to survive. You can't trust anybody, and Thomas needs to realize that. In a way I'm doing him a favor.

"Okay, Thomas," says Archie. "We're only going to try one—final decision."

"I have much trust and faith in my friend Hartford," he says. "I therefore choose to proceed with number three."

Now I feel bad. This is new to me—but nothing I can't handle.

CHAPTER 7

I feel Annie shift in bed and lift her head. I know she's awake and trying to get her bearings. I feel her right hand slide over and on top of my hip finding either reassurance or disappointment. I sense her shift again and know she's sitting up, staring at the clock.

"Hart!" She says shaking my shoulder. "It's after eight—your senator's going to have your hide for a lampshade." I continue to feign sleep. She shakes my shoulder some more and then a lot more. "Hart! Get up, this isn't funny. I know you're awake. Are you hearing me? It's after eight."

I open one eye and then the other. ""Whatadyawant,"".

"You heard me. What's wrong with you?"

I prop myself up on an elbow. "Oh, I guess I thought you and Thomas were bringing in the money, now. Should I not have quit my job?"

"Hartford!" She knuckles me hard on the arm and glares at me. Her expression suddenly softens and she cocks her head slightly, bringing on her smile. She leans back against the headboard and takes my hand. "Maybe you should tell me about your day," she says.

Is she not something? So I sit up in bed and tell her all about LTA and how it carried the day. She listens without interruption and seems duly impressed, especially when I tell her I'm now out of it and have officially passed the baton. When I finish, she asks if Senator Feldstone has *officially* given me the day off. Hearing the words "not exactly," she gets out of bed, walks over to my clothes chair, goes through my pants pockets, finds my Blackberry, and throws it at me. Well, *to* me.

"What," I say, catching it on the fly and hearing it ring at the same time. I fumble it open and answer "hello" while staring at Annie's smug face. A desperate Niles is on the other end, demanding to know where the hell I am.

I dress and shave quickly, forgoing a shower. Annie rustles up some grub, toast, and juice, and hands it to me as I pass through the living room on my way to the garage. Once in the Beemer and on the road, I call Niles and, in a firm tone, because he's the messenger and my underling, demand an explanation. Before he can speak I say, "Is it the Republicans?"

"No, the Republicans are totally on board. Feldstone's been yelling for you all morning. That's all I know."

"Fifteen minutes," I say and hang up.

What the hell? I'm surely out of the loop by now—unless some power hitter is holding out, but Niles would've known that and warned me. I just can't imagine. I pass the Thomas Bench and give it a nod, then turn left into the staffer parking lot.

I enter the bottom floor of The Russell Building on the run and Niles intercepts me exiting the elevator on the second floor. He just points toward the senator's office and says, "Go." I walk into the reception area and Jeannie gives an audible sigh from her desk. She picks up her phone, makes it buzz and says, "He's here." She glares at me, making a sweeping motion with her fingers and saying, "Go, go."

I walk into the senator's office without knocking. He looks up, eyeballs me, and says, "Meeting at eleven."

I wait for more but nothing more comes, so I say, "what meeting?"

He looks up again, this time with his are-you-still-here? face, and slowly manufactures a smile. He puts down his pen and leans back in his chair while his smile turns to smirk. "Oh, I see," he says, "you thought you were out of it," and chuckles.

I know to say nothing.

"You thought you had done your part—your idea and all, let someone else put it together. Well now, you see, Hartford, it doesn't work that way around here."

Actually it does, always has, but apparently it isn't working that way today. I wonder why not—and it hits me.

"They put you in charge of finding the speakers," I say.

"Damn right they did," he yells. "No way we're going to find speakers acceptable to both Democrats and Republicans—there is no f-ing way. What the hell were you thinking, Hart? We should have never brought them in."

"Is that what the meeting's about?"

"What do you think?"

"Going to be heavies there from both parties?"

"As well as the vice-president. The Administration wants their say."

He's right. What was I thinking? There isn't a group, a movement, an organization, or even a cause—unless you count earmarks and pay raises—equally acceptable to both parties. I look at my watch. I have less than forty-five minutes before the meeting.

"I'll get back to you," I say.

"You damn well better," he says shouting me out the door. "You've got thirty minutes."

I leave Feldstone's sanctuary and find Niles just outside the door next to the keyhole. I tell him to find me six organizations hated by the Democrats and six equally hated by the Republicans, then to get me a dozen or so mildly disliked by both.

"When do you need them?" He says.

"Twenty minutes ago."

There is no way this meeting is going to settle anything, but I figure if I can threaten them with those groups they detest then maybe they'll settle for a few organizations they only mildly dislike. With politicians, sticks and vinegar trump carrots and honey every time.

The meeting was horrible. Not that my strategy didn't work, it did, much like defense and prosecution lawyers picking through jurors. You throw out the ones with intelligence and conviction and you end up with twelve mealy-mouthed pinheads who can't make the decision to come in out of the rain. That's pretty much how it went. Once the organizations, groups, and industries that meant anything to anybody were discarded, all that was left was a short list of outcasts about which nobody, including the American voter, could give a damn. The Organization For The Restoration Of Victorian Antiques, The Movement To Stop Sheep Shearing, and The Mothers Against Profanity In Soccer Sports were simply not on the top of anyone's list—except ours. When it was over, the problem still lay squarely in Senator Feldstone's lap, which meant I was still on the hook for a solution.

The good news is that the next meeting isn't until Monday morning which gives me four whole days, with the weekend, to come up with a fix. I put Niles and the rest of the staff on it and decide to go home early. I think better out of the office, and besides, Annie's home with nothing to do, so I might get lucky.

It takes me another hour to get away from work, so it's after twelve thirty when I pull into the garage. I'm mentally making plans to take Annie out for lunch and other things when I discover no one's home. I immediately call her on her cell. She answers on the second ring.

"You have got to come see this, Hart," she says. "Where are you?"

"I'm home," I say, holding back, *where you should be.*

"Get over to the t-shirt booth, you know where it is—first kiosk on the right, south end of the reflecting pool. You can't miss it." I'm silent and so she says, "Come, Hartford, come quickly."

I go.

I park three blocks away because it's as close as I can get—spring tourist season. I lock the Beemer and hoof it over to the vendor's area. She's right, you can't miss it. The first booth is packing a huge crowd and my little friend Thomas is right there in the middle of it. He's talking and joking, garnering handshakes and back pats, generally playing to the people. I figure his colonial outfit is partly responsible for the draw, but there's got to be more to it than that. I look around and spot Annie across the lawn on a hill, sitting on a bench, taking it all in. She's so focused on Thomas she doesn't see me until I'm on top of her.

"Somebody must've picked the right quote," I say.

She looks up at me, then around me, and finally motions for me to sit down and stop blocking her view.

"No, well, yes," she says excitedly. "He sold his three dozen shirts in the first ten minutes. Now he's selling Archie's stuff, mostly patriotic designs—American flags, Washington Monument, Lincoln Memorial. Thomas is very good. I think he's a natural."

I watch her watching Thomas with something like worship in her eyes.

"What's he telling them? Doesn't look like a hard-sell routine."

"No, not at all, he just discusses things with them—doesn't even try to sell them. They just buy."

"What things?"

"History, the founding fathers, the Constitution, current events..."

"And yet he doesn't know his last name."

She gives me her hands-on-hips look and says, "Your point?"

"Just seems odd is all."

"He's not faking it, Hart—the doctor confirmed that."

"I'm not saying he is, it's just, well, I don't know. Current events?"

"Yes, current events. He's become quite the news hound, you know."

No, I didn't know, nor necessarily believe. "Where would he get access to the news?"

She looks at me like I'm Natty Clueless. "Every morning Thomas goes through the newspaper word by word. Every night he watches the news, usually flicking between two or three stations."

"How—"

"I put our old TV in the guest bedroom and taught him how to use it. We usually discuss current events over breakfast."

I wonder how I've managed to miss out on all this and then realize I've been in crisis mode the last few days.

"He talks to you?"

"Yes, well, mostly he asks questions."

"Questions?" I can't remember the last time Thomas asked me a question. He's a listen–and–observe kind of guy. "What questions?"

"You know, news questions—mostly having to do with government. Thomas is very interested in government."

"I work for the government," I say too defensively. "He doesn't ask me questions."

"Well you haven't been around much lately."

This is true. Still, I keep seeing this bond between Thomas and my wife—girlfriend— strengthening, and I'm not sure I like it.

"Specifically, what questions?" I say.

"Well, let's see. Remember that case where the FBI came in and took over land from that couple in Ohio to build a parking deck? I think her name was Lansdale or something. The government cited 'Eminent Domain.' Thomas got all upset over that. And then there's the immigration and illegal alien situation in Arizona. He's forever going on about that. Oh, and he's very concerned over the oil spill and the moratorium on deep water drilling. And then, of course, the government's runaway spending spree and the size of the deficit, you don't want to get him started on that. And then—"

"Okay, okay, I get it. He's pissed off at the government. Aren't we all. That's probably why he doesn't want to talk to me. I work for the government and he doesn't want to offend me."

"Yeah, Hart, that's it. Thomas is worried about your feelings. Aren't we all."

I'm sensing sarcasm here, but I hold my tongue.

"No," she says, her eyes back on Thomas. "There's more to it than just disfavor with government. There's a kind of sadness in his eyes when he talks about it, a disappointment, a spirit broken. After we talk he always says the same thing."

I watch her watching Thomas, and I see sadness in her face also.

"He always says, 'It was never meant to be this way,' and then bows his head. It's like he senses an inevitability with our country and our way of life. Like we've screwed it up one time too many and are fast approaching the point of no return." She looks over at me with tears in her eyes, "I sometimes feel that way myself."

It takes her a minute to get hold of herself. She pulls a Kleenex from her purse and dabs her eyes. A few more sniffles and she bucks herself up enough to glare at me.

"So, Hartford, why are you here?"

"You told me to come."

"No, why are you off work? It's a bad time to get fired."

"I took off early because we were stalled out, we're at an impasse. Monday morning, however, the onus is back on me to come up with a solution."

"I thought you were out of it. I thought you had 'passed the baton,' remember?, your words."

"I know, so did I, but they tossed it back in Feldstone's lap and he threw it—"

"In yours," she completed. "What's the impasse?"

"Who represents the people. In other words, while Congress and the president are listening to America, who's doing the talking?"

"Wouldn't the bigwigs be deciding that? Didn't you say the president was involved? Let him decide." She's shaking her head now, ever bemused by government's inability to make a decision.

"I would love to. They tried, they had a meeting."

"Oh goody," she says, "a meeting."

"It's not that easy, with both parties involved. You know the drill. They want a handful of spokesmen," I look at her, "or spokes-*women*, to represent America. The Dems won't buy into someone from the NRA, the Republicans won't permit anyone from the teachers union. Finding representatives acceptable to both parties is damn near impossible."

I stare ahead. The Thomas crowd has more than doubled in size since I've been sitting here. The tourists aren't just milling around, they're buying, asking questions, laughing, chatting, shaking hands, and posing for pictures with Thomas.

"So what you need," she says, "is someone who appeals to everybody—an everyman American." She nods her head toward Thomas. "Someone like that."

"Yeah," I say. "I just don't think an unknown t-shirt hawker with no last name and no memory is going to fly with the boys in the back room."

We both go quiet while our eyes focus on Thomas and his escalating enterprise.

CHAPTER 8

I wake up Friday morning to my condo all a-buzz. I look at the clock and see the little red digital numbers blinking out 6:27. I hop out of bed, quickly throw water on my face, and brush my teeth. I think about getting dressed but the bustle of excitement below won't allow it, so I grab my robe and hurry down the stairs.

Thomas is placing plates and silverware on the table while Annie's frying up bacon. They're cackling back and forth like hens at a social. It isn't current events that has them charged up, it's t-shirts.

"Hartford," Thomas says when he sees me, "Miss Anne and I are going into town to retrieve a cargo of t-shirts." He stands all proud and smiley.

"Well, I hope you sell them," I say, bee-lining it to the coffee machine.

"Oh, there can be no doubt of that. The tourists that visit our Capitol have been most accommodating thus far."

"How many shirts?" I say, wondering how much money we're fronting on this deal.

"Four hundred thirty-two t-shirts we have on order," he says proudly. "One hundred forty-four of each design—is it not exhilarating, Hartford?"

"Four thirty-two," I repeat, looking at Annie, "three designs."

She shrugs. "Thomas has a gift."

"And therefore," Thomas says, sitting down at the table, "we shall first ingest a hearty meal and then shall we, all of us, be off to work."

"You seem overly happy," I say.

"And should I not be? I have embarked upon a promising entrepreneurial career with my two dear friends speeding me along the way." He sits down all grins and delight.

Friday is not a big news day in Washington world. All the reporters and cameramen who normally invade the halls of the Capitol are nowhere to be found. For this reason, stealth legislation, covert bills, and unpopular executive orders are usually passed and signed on Friday.

I arrive at work late, a little after nine, and find no signs of the chaos that had invaded the halls less than twenty-four hours ago. Niles is on his computer playing solitaire while most of the other staffers are tying up personal odds and ends and getting ready for the weekend. Through the glass, I can see the flat screen television in the conference room. A senator is speaking from a podium somewhere in flyover country, but it's muted so I don't know what he's saying. The TV's been placed there, not for entertainment, but for the staffers to follow the news. I'm happy to see we aren't watching Nickelodeon.

"Any breakthrough on the LTA front?" I say loudly. They all look at me in confusion, most just now becoming aware I'm in house.

"What?" says Niles.

"Listening To America," I repeat, "the campaign."

"Not yet, boss, still working on it."

Which means they have yet to get serious.

"Conference room, ten thirty," I say. "We need solutions, people."

I don't much like the fact that it takes a crisis to push us into action. For once I'd like to be just a tiny bit prepared before the catastrophe strikes. Looking around at the faces staring back at me, I don't see that happening anytime soon. I squint at them à la Clint Eastwood, and they all scurry back to their PCs, frantically surfing the web for someone to speak for America. I go outside, find a bench, and open up my laptop. I click on my LTA folder and double click it open. There's not much there. Realizing I don't have anything to add, I close the folder and scroll down to my last solitaire game and attempt to complete my run.

I wonder how Thomas is doing with his new career. He's so damn excited about his work. Selling t-shirts, for god sakes. I try to remember the last time I felt that way about my work—the last time I felt that way about anything. And then there's Annie. She's almost as excited as Thomas, supporting him, cheering him on. I try to remember when she last did that for me. Hmmm. I think about walking over to Thomas's kiosk and catching some positive vibes when I glance down at my watch—10:25. Oops. Meetings 'r' us.

I take my time reaching the conference room. Everybody's already there and waiting. I don't know if I'm pulling a power-play here or just wanting an extra breath of fresh air. I walk into the room and note the lack of enthusiasm on each and every face. Niles has a folder in front of him but his expression says there's little inside. I stand behind my chair refusing to sit, knowing this meeting will likely be short and sour. I begin to speak and immediately pick up on the palpable lack of focus by my staff. Their eyes keep shifting past me; it's distracting if not rude.

Finally, exasperated, I yell, "What!"

Niles lifts his right hand and points a finger over my left shoulder. I turn and look. The television, still muted, shows a man in a three-cornered hat being interviewed by an attractive female reporter. A mob of exuberant tourists surrounds them both. I walk over and turn up the volume as the cameraman zooms in.

"Tell me, Thomas," the reporter says, motioning the cameraman to scan the crowd, "to what do you owe this amazing response to your t-shirts?"

Before he can answer, another voice says, "It's not just the T-shirts, it's Thomas." The camera zeroes in on Archie and a microphone is shoved in his face. "He speaks to the people," Archie continues. "He talks with them."

"So Thomas is an ace salesmen, then," the reporter says, missing the point. "A man who knows how to close the deal." She smiles, showing extremely white teeth.

"No," retorts Archie, refusing to relinquish the mike. "He doesn't sell at all; he just talks with the people."

"About what?" she says, genuinely interested now.

"About the government, the country, the founding fathers, the Constitution; he talks about his love for this country and its history. I think he must have been a history teacher at one time."

"That *is* interesting," she says, turning back to ask Thomas about this new twist but finding him out of range, swallowed up by the crowd. "Well, that was Thomas, history-professor-turned-t-shirt-salesman, down here at the mall. A pretty interesting fellow, after all. Back to you, Jason."

I click the sound back to mute and look around at my staffers. They're up milling and murmuring, an air of expectation lighting their faces.

"What," I say, "you think we need a guy like that?"

Niles takes a step forward. "Not a guy like that," he says, "that guy."

Nods of agreement bobble their heads.

"He's an unknown," I say, "no one knows anything about him."

"So was Joe the Plumber," somebody throws in.

"Yes, and he was a Republican hero...until we dug up the dirt and ripped him to pieces."

"Boss," Niles again, "this guy's perfect. He's into history, a teacher, possibly a professor—that brings in the Democrats—and he has a successful all-American entrepreneurial venture going— that brings in the Republicans. He's what we've been unable to find: an asset to both parties. He's perfect." The nods and murmurs increase.

I catch my reflection in the front glass and find my head nodding as well.

"You want me to do the background," Niles says.

And there lies my problem—no name, no background. This train is already off the tracks. And then there's Thomas himself—how would he handle the media circus, the vetting process, not to mention the speech itself in front of three hundred million people? Could he possibly pull that off—or even want to?

"No," I say, "I'll do the background checks. I want everyone else into a major brainstorming session in case this thing doesn't work out."

They don't like that—they've gotten nowhere thus far, and now this big, fat, sugarplum of an opportunity falls in the middle of their collective laps. Having it not work out is like hitting a grand slam and watching it go foul. It's doubtful you're gonna get another chance. I stare at them. I feel their pain, but not really.

"Now, people, now!" I say, clapping my hands. "Time's a-wasting."

I have a lot on my mind. Number one is getting out of the building and over to check out that t-shirt booth. I need to see what kind of airplay Thomas is really getting. I don't want to try for something that can't be had. I watch my staff form into groups and head for the conference room. I wait until they settle in and start their discussion before departing the office. I hate to leave them unattended, but I have no assistant substitute.

Once outside, I notice my pace picking up and realize only decorum prevents me from breaking into a sprint. If this thing is as big as the cameras make it look, and if I can persuade Thomas to go along—which is my forte (and besides, he owes me)—this could prove quite the proverbial feather in my cap. I turn the corner, giving me a clear view of vendor row. The crowd around Thomas' kiosk is huge—at least three times the size it appeared on TV.

My mind is spinning. My face breaks into a super grin. If Thomas can electrify this large a crowd he should have no problem speaking before Congress. I see the two major DC newspaper vans,

The Times and The Sentinel, parked at the curb. This means every senator and congressman in town will know about Thomas by dinnertime. They all have staffers and interns whose entire workday consists of following breaking news stories, regardless how big or small.

I find, as I close in on my target, that I'm unconsciously licking my lips. Convincing the heavies is all but in the bag. And the beauty of it is that Thomas is my guy, my houseguest—nobody's going to be snatching him out from under me. The whole thing will be completely contained within our camp; Feldstone's gonna go ape. I keep my hands confined to my pockets as I get closer. It wouldn't do to be seen rubbing them together and licking my chops at the same time.

I glance across the lawn and see Annie sitting on her same bench with a smile on her face. I walk toward her and, as before, she fails to see me until I'm on top of her.

"Staying out of the fray?" I say.

"Hart," she looks surprised, "I didn't see you."

"Our boy's business seems to be going gangbusters."

"Two network television stations, three cable stations, two newspapers, and the senator from Delaware have been by," she says proudly. "Who knew?"

I sit beside her and watch the show.

"The crowd has grown steadily all day," she says.

"This keeps up, you're going to need a bigger booth."

She smiles. "I'm so proud of him, Hart. He has such a way with people."

It's the way she says it, the way she smiles, how her eyes light up when she looks at him.

Maybe she has father figure tendencies toward him. Maybe I was all off on my stray puppy theory. I stare at her then look down at the kiosk. She looks happy. The shelves look bare.

"Archie must be doing a heckuva trade," I say.

"Oh, he sold out an hour ago."

"No more t-shirts?"

"No, they're gone."

"So why are all the people still there?"

"They're listening to Thomas."

I look back at the crowd. Sure enough, Thomas is speaking and the people are listening, mesmerized. Listening to Thomas— Listening to America. I think my grin might break my face.

"You should go down and listen, find out what you've unleashed."

I stand up, take a few steps, stop, and look back over my shoulder at her smug expression. She wants to say, "Double dare you," but she doesn't.

I carry on, walking across the lawn toward the kiosk, planning to meld with the crowd. At six foot three, it won't be easy. I want to get close enough to hear Thomas's words but not so close he can spot me. I work through the throng from the rear until I'm only three rows from the front. I stand behind a large man, almost my height but twice as wide. With my head down, I sidestep ever so slightly to my left and slowly raise my eyes. They lock directly onto Thomas's, who says, "Hartford, how nice it is to see you."

My eyes immediately dart to the crowd. The reporters are no longer recording and the cameramen are no longer filming, they're all listening to Thomas. But now that he's outed me, they grab their gear and make a charge in my direction. Fortunately they're all on the other side of the perimeter and don't get a clear look at me. It gives me the precious minutes I need for my escape. I execute a crisp about-face and make a serpentine dash through the people, across the lawn and toward Annie's bench, walking not running. Sneaking subtle back-glances along the way, I arrive cleanly without a tail. My face is flushed and my breathing is hard, but I still manage to sit down next to Annie wearing a victory smile.

"Wow," she says, "you sure know how to bust up a party."

I look back at the crowd. Sure enough they're breaking up. Archie's putting away empty boxes and locking up the kiosk while Thomas, by his body language, is concluding his remarks and dismissing his audience. I look over at Annie.

"Learn much?" she says.

"Have you ever actually heard him? You're always way over here on this bench."

She smiles. "He talks to me—over breakfast, in the evening, sometimes at lunch or in the middle of the afternoon. We have lots of talks. I believe I have a pretty fair idea of what he says to the people. You should talk to him, Hart, you might learn something."

"Learn something?" I say. "He should be learning from me."

"Look, Hart," she continues, "I don't know from where he comes, or what he's done in the past, or even who he is."

"Neither does he," I say.

She glares at me, wondering why she even tries, and then she keeps trying.

"But I do know that he has a genuine love and great passion for this country, and he believes that our government is systematically—knowingly or unknowingly—managing to destroy it."

"Annie, those of us here in DC, those of us who actually play the game. We are the best and the brightest, the movers and shakers, the power brokers. We make the difference—we make it all work. We lead and shape the world."

"I believe that's his point."

"What is?"

"You make it work but you make it work poorly. You lead but in the wrong direction. You shape the world, but you shape it in your own arrogant image and for all the wrong reasons. Your competitiveness, your victories, have everything to do with gaining and maintaining power and nothing to do with what is best for this country."

"He said that?"

"Not in those words." She pauses. "Hart, it goes deeper than that. It's what you have become—what Feldstone and his House and Senate cronies have become, what our president and all his men have become."

"Which is?"

"Men without conscience. Men without character. Men whose word means nothing, who say and do whatever is necessary to stay in power. Men who serve not their country but themselves. Men who lie and cheat without reservation. Men for whom the ends always justify the means."

"Are these his words or yours?"

"They're mine. Thomas's words are more refined."

"As in..."

"He speaks of the absence of a forthright manner, the lack of nobility, truthfulness, purpose, the scarcity of God-fearing men, men of courage, gallantry, boldness, those who command respect—terms we don't hear much anymore."

"You realize he calls cars motorized carts."

"Quit it, Hart, listen to what I'm saying, to what Thomas is saying—for once in your life."

I nod for her to continue, afraid to speak.

"Change is not always good. Progress is not always positive. Winning depends on what you do with the victory. If we win the arms race but lose our conscience and humanity in the process and use our nuclear weapons to, say, control world population, then we have done an evil thing. You've heard the saying 'evil triumphs when good men do nothing'? Where are the good men, Hart?"

"So you and Thomas think our government is evil."

"Not evil, but perhaps not so very good either."

"How does he come up with this stuff? He's been an American, in a sense, for less than a month."

"Maybe that's how. Maybe he, unlike the rest of us, can see things from a fresh perspective. Maybe that's what makes him special, worth listening to."

"So from this fresh new perspective, Thomas wants to save the world."

"Not the world, the country. And he points to one thing in particular."

"Please," I say, "enlighten me."

"The politics of personal destruction, the demonization of one's opponents, character assassination—Thomas thinks it's a tragedy." She pauses, looks away, then stares back at me with hard eyes. "If you don't like someone's views, you go after them with both guns—the party, the president with his bully pulpit, even the media jump in with full force. Using innuendo, exaggeration, and downright lies, you go after a person's character. It's so vehement, so hateful, so persistent. Tell me, Hart, who do you know that could withstand such an assault? Not me, not you, not even a President Goodman. What have we become? Past presidents never used to criticize sitting presidents. Sitting presidents never criticized past presidents. Never were failures blamed on the guy before them or after them. The office and the man holding it was respected especially by the men who had been there. Not anymore. How would you feel about the Washington Nationals' manager blaming his season on the man who preceded him? Does the term *sore loser* come to mind? Yet we let these politicians get away with this practice all the time."

"It's the game," I say. "You do what it takes to win. It's always been that way, always will be."

"No, Hart, it hasn't always been that way. Just as in ballgames, where there are rules, along with umpires and referees to enforce them, in politics there's decorum. Fair play, honor, with a supposedly free press to expose the rule breakers. At least there was. Now the media collaborates with the politicians and the officeholders, at least the ones they favor, and they join forces with the party of their choice, as well, to participate wholeheartedly in the dirty-tricks business. The Free Press was envisioned, by our founding fathers, to expose the lies and the corruption of government, not to join forces with them. As Thomas likes to say, it was never meant to be this way."

"Well, whether it's meant to be or not, it is what it is, and the fact that we're winning is all I care about. That's my job. If Thomas thinks he knows better then let him say so. In fact, there are some who want to give him that chance."

That stops her short. She's glaring at me now. "Hart, why are you here?"

My eyes shift away from her and down toward the grass. She nods her head slightly and leans back on the bench. She flicks her little finger at me and says, "You want something. You want something from Thomas."

"I was positive it was you," came the words from just down the hill.

We both look up and find a grinning Thomas heading our way. I stand up, quickly scanning the landscape for reporters or cameramen. Coast is clear. I continue standing, waiting for Thomas to arrive. He reaches us, grabs my hand, and shakes it vigorously.

"I am quite pleased to see you, Hartford. I have much to tell."

"Yes," I say, watching the vestiges of his audience trail away. "Looks like you've had yourself a big day."

"Oh yes, indeed, I believe we have a highly successful enterprise on our hands. We have managed to sell all of our t-shirts, every one. Archibald is quite pleased."

"I'll bet he is," I say. "I think he's hired himself an ace salesmen."

"Well...ah...yes, it seems perhaps my background does involve sales and trade. Miss Anne thinks I excel in such matters."

I glance over at Miss Anne and she seems none too happy.

"I notice you spend a lot of your time talking to the people," I say.

"Yes, they ask many questions and I try to answer them. I have queries of my own, and they respond in kind. We converse with each other."

"The crowd seemed very attentive. From here it looked like you were giving a speech."

"Oh no, no, Hartford, this is not so."

He goes quiet and so I wait for more, but no more comes. So I remain quiet and just wait.

"A gentleman from Missouri asked about the First Amendment, specifically freedom of religion," he finally says. "I expounded on the thoughts and visions of our founding fathers on the subject. I believe I appeared quite passionate at times."

"And how would you know the thoughts and visions of the founding fathers?" I didn't say, *when you don't even know your last name.*

"Why it's all there, in our history—letters, documents, essays, diaries, memoirs. The founders made their thoughts and visions quite clear for anyone to read and study. I am quite surprised at the limited knowledge of most Americans I have spoken with. Do the children not study their history in school?"

"Well, of course they do, it's just, well...it's complicated."

"No, Hartford, it is not."

"Not what?"

"It is not complicated. It is all there for the teaching and the learning. I fear that someone is not properly performing his job."

"Perhaps we can discuss this later," I say. "Right now I'm famished and thought I might take you two out for a nice steak dinner."

"I should very much like to join you, Hartford, but alas, I must help Archibald secure the booth, and then we must go into town and replenish our inventory for tomorrow's work day." He pauses and bows his head slightly. "In addition, I must embark on an important errand for one of my customers."

Annie weighs in. "Thomas, why don't you and Hartford run your errand and I'll help Archie close up shop? We can put off our t-shirt pickup until tomorrow morning before you open. Perhaps you two can talk."

A big smile lights his face. "Thus can we rejoin here, where Hartford will treat us to a delicious steak dinner? I think this a fine plan, Hartford, and you?"

"A fine plan," I say.

Thomas gives an excited clap with his hands and says, "Then let us make haste, for I, too, am famished."

CHAPTER 9

Thomas starts out across the lawn toward the east. After a few steps he stops and looks back at me. "Hartford, this way, if you please."

I follow, picking up my pace. "We're walking, then," I say. "So what is this errand?"

"A favor for one of my fellow countrymen."

We round a restroom out-building and top a small knoll. I scan the area.

"Where exactly are we going, Thomas?"

"There," he says, pointing at the Vietnam Memorial Wall, its ebony marble reflecting the golden glow of a setting sun. This is getting interesting, if not incomprehensible. I stay with him.

"What favor would this fellow countryman have you do?"

He's striding purposefully now, directly toward the midsection of the wall. "His only son perished in the Vietnam War," Thomas says. "Mr. Connor would have me locate his son's name and offer a prayer for him. He wished to know if his son has died in vain."

I stop walking. "He asked you that?"

Thomas keeps going and says, "Yes."

I wonder why a complete stranger would ask Thomas if his only son died in vain. I've been around Washington, D.C., for ten years and no one's ever asked me that. Senator Feldstone's been around for over thirty years and, as far as I know, no one's ever asked him that. Why Thomas? And, just as fascinating, what had he said?

I look down at the wall. Thomas has joined several dozen others searching the names engraved in the black marble. Small flags, photos, bracelets, and other keepsakes litter the ground below; tangible memories retrieved and stored each night by park rangers. I continue toward the memorial at a more reverent pace. I see Thomas pause, reach up and rub his fingers across a name. I watch him bow his head and close his eyes, mouthing silent words. I reach him as he finishes his prayer.

He looks up with tears in his eyes. I want to say, *Thomas, you don't even know this guy and you barely know his father,* but the mood of the place overwhelms me so I stand there in silence. I look at the names engraved on the wall and then at the people who have come to pay their respects. These soldiers, I wonder, did they die in vain—did they die for nothing? It's a sobering thought. One, I'm ashamed to say, I've never had before.

My father didn't go to Vietnam, although he was of age. I never asked why. I know he didn't participate in the war effort except to complain now and then about the cost. I was pretty sure he didn't burn his draft card or move us all to Canada—I would have remembered that. We just never talked about Vietnam, and to this day I don't know why.

As I stand here I'm surrounded by the stillness of the place, the grief, the disappointment, the emptiness, the futility. Even I can't escape the overpowering sadness in the air. A pang of guilt stings at me for never having volunteered for military service, never even having the thought. I was perfectly willing to let the gung-ho, macho, gun nuts take that role. I always felt I was meant for more intellectual pursuits like making a difference in the political sphere, helping to transform the country into a better place for all.

I'm shaking my head. What's wrong with me? Here I am justifying myself with the same BS I peddle to everybody else. Is that why I'm feeling guilty? My eyes fall on a brass plaque with the words "served their country" engraved in the metal. It refers to the men and women whose names are listed on this wall. These men did serve their country, and in doing so, paid the ultimate price. Senator Feldstone and his cronies talk incessantly about serving their country—*I am proud to have served my country and my state for over thirty-five years, blah, blah, blah.* They no more serve their country than an assembly-line worker serves Ford. Less so, since congressmen are better paid, with huge pensions, cushy offices furnished to the hilt, staffers to do the work, and generous allowances for everything under the sun. They serve no one but themselves.

The soldier, on the other hand, is paid a pittance, to trudge through mud and snow and desert sand, sleeping in tents and trenches in freezing cold and stifling heat. He risks his life on a daily basis for a pension which, if he lives to collect it, falls somewhere between poverty and broke. These men, these women, *they* are the ones who truly serve their country.

The pang of guilt stings me again. It comes from the way I've often used soldiers as political pawns in my advice to the senator. Urging him to vote to fund the troops on some occasions and then encouraging him to deny such funds on others, all in order to position himself more conservatively or more liberally as dictated by the polls. It never ceases to amaze me how easily the American voter lets us get away with it. Our hypocrisy is astounding, and unless there's a sexual scandal involved, we always get away with it—sometimes *because* there's a sexual scandal involved.

I shake my head again, this time vigorously. This place is bad for me. I'm beginning to think negative thoughts, thoughts detrimental to my job. I need to get out of here, back to my office, back to my people, back to my version of ends and means. I turn around and walk back the way I had come. I decide to wait for Thomas at the top of the knoll where there's less discomfort in the air. As I approach higher ground I feel a nice breeze. I take in a deep breath and I feel better.

After a full minute of deep breathing I turn around and look for Thomas. He's still studying the names on the wall. I think about Annie, about all those things she said about our government, my government, my job. She's never shown much appreciation for what I do, but lately her disrespect is getting downright mean-spirited. The things she said today struck me more as her words than Thomas's.

I glance at him down there still studying the wall. The man is so damn amiable, so mild-mannered, so easy to get along with. I know he's passionate about his country and its history, which makes it even more unlikely he would badmouth its government. The words from Annie could certainly be interpreted as overzealous. No, I think I was hearing Annie's displeasure with me and my job and that she was merely using Thomas as her scapegoat.

I look back down the hill. Thomas is starting toward me now with a big grin on his face. This is the Thomas I know—pleasant, mild-mannered, polite to a fault. I smile back. I see absolutely no downside to offering him the Listening To America gig.

10

We end up at Outback Steakhouse. There are several other restaurants I would have preferred, but neither Archie nor Thomas is dressed appropriately and would have probably been intimidated by the wine list. So Outback's fine—it's been years since I've been to one.

My mission to uncover the enigmatic message Thomas conveys to his fans is still on going. Any attempt by me, however, to lead the conversation in that direction is either unintentionally or purposely rerouted by Archie. The talk always leads back to t-shirts and the phenomenal success Thomas's presence is having on sales. Archie thinks it's the new slogans with the minuteman logo, so he's been advocating for more of the same. Annie believes it's Thomas's salesmanship, as well as his outfit. Thomas is unsure and graciously humble about the whole thing, though also quite proud to be part of a successful entrepreneurial enterprise. They don't inquire about my thoughts on the subject, as though they could hardly expect an honest answer. I'm naturally incensed but then wonder how I can use that perception to wrangle the information I want from Thomas.

We leave Outback at ten thirty. Archie's in his van, so after agreeing on an early morning t-shirt pickup time with Annie and

Thomas, he drives away. We three settle into my Beemer and head to the condo—Annie sits up front and Thomas takes up the rear.

"Thomas," I say, turning right onto Independence. "The man whose son died in 'Nam, the guy who asked you if his son had died in vain—what did you tell him?"

I'm thinking this might lead into a discussion of the kind Thomas has with his t-shirt crowd, but the minute I say it I know it won't. In fact, I fear it might lead us to a place I don't want to go. The silence extends for such a long time I wonder if I should withdraw the question. Maybe he didn't hear me, or maybe he just doesn't want to answer.

"I know not the history of the Vietnam war, Hartford," Thomas says.

This, in itself, seems strange to me, since he had to be about the right age for the draft when the war started. But then again there's that amnesia thing.

"I know from Miss Anne," he continues, "for we have previously discussed it, that this war did not reach a successful conclusion. I also know that it was fought to stop the spread of communism— the 'domino effect,' I believe it was called. I informed Mr. Connor that his son died to keep us free. Communism has not overtaken us. We are still a democracy. His son died for this. God bless him."

I want to say, *Yeah but we lost—Communism didn't continue to spread because the domino theory and the brain trust that thought it up were wrong. South Vietnam in fact did fall to the communists, and those people suffered greatly.* But I don't.

I'm still trying to stake out his political views, but this discussion isn't giving me much. I know Thomas has a passion for preserving freedom, but everyone's for that. I need to know if he's a liberal or a conservative or a moderate, a libertarian, or what. It would not be good for my career if I push him into my Listening to America campaign and he comes up a John Bircher.

I'm about to try a different approach when Annie, completely silent thus far, shouts, "Ice cream!"

We're coming up to *I Scream For Ice Cream*, her favorite dessert spot of all time, located not two blocks from the condo. Two scoops of double-rich chocolate in a cake cone reside there. Failing to stop would be heresy. I pull into a parking space and we all exit the car.

Fifteen minutes later we're back in the BMW. Thomas has mimicked Annie, chocolate ice cream in a cake cone, and I've gone more exotic—rum raisin in a cup with a spoon. There are two kinds of people in the world: those who fast-lick cones, risking shirt stain and brain freeze, and those of us who are civilized. My car mates are going at it fast and furious while I watch, hawk-like, fearing for my beige interior. Everyone seems happy—ice cream will do that to you. So I'm thinking, *What better time to ferret out Thomas's views?*

"Thomas," I say, "what do you think of politics?"

"Politics."

"Yes, more specifically, the government."

"The American government."

"Yes."

"It's founding or what it has become?"

"Our government today," I say.

Thomas pauses and I watch his expression sadden.

"Hartford," he says, "it was never meant to be this way."

Well this sucks. Less than a block from home with no time for elaboration, and I'm stuck with *Never meant to be this way.* What does that mean, anyway? He doesn't like the way they redecorated the oval office? The Tea Party gets on his nerves? Can't understand why Bill Clinton is still hanging around?

I decide not to push it. Probably best to have this discussion without Annie present anyway. I reach out and turn on the radio, dialing up some Mariah Carey. I glance at Thomas by way of the rear view mirror. He's sitting back in his seat all mellow and smiling.

Who are you, little man?

I notice I'm smiling, too. I nod to my reflection.

I will find out, my friend. Your time will come.

I turn into our driveway and press the remote.

CHAPTER 11

Each morning as I drive to work and each evening as I drive home, I pass by the Thomas Bench. It's become a symbol to me, like the Washington Monument or the Lincoln Memorial. Pretty ridiculous, I know, but unlike the Monument or the Memorial, the Thomas Bench has had a direct impact on my life. I found Thomas on that bench a month and a half ago, and since then things have changed—Annie's changed, I've changed. I sense more changes on the way. Something's out there—building, intensifying, fomenting. Whatever it is, it's about to surface, and when it does, I see Thomas smack in the middle of it.

I've still not totally decided on whether to try and sell the higher-ups on Thomas as the voice of LTA—a lack of courage, I suppose. If I convince the party powerful to go with my guy and he fails, it's going to come back on me hard. Feldstone'll have no problem making me the scapegoat. I'll lose my job, be blackballed from polite political society, and probably lose Annie in the deal. I mean, why would she stay?

On the other hand, if Thomas shines I could well write my own ticket. There isn't a political party or major campaign in the country that wouldn't pay top dollar for my services. My career would be made. Not only could I rightfully claim credit for the whole LTA strategy, I could wax obnoxiously as the man who discovered

Thomas: *the voice of America*. But, more importantly, I could provide Annie the status and lifestyle she deserves. I mean, how could she say no?

I pull into my reserved space in the underground parking garage of the Russell building and exit the BMW. I enter the garage elevator and press "one." In the lobby I enjoy, as always, the transition from stainless steel to waxed mahogany and polished brass. I enter the nearest lobby lift and press two. I look at my watch—8:37; the big meeting goes down in less than an hour. I suddenly have that stupid thought about today being the first day of the rest of my life. The elevator door slides open and I walk out into the corridor where I'm immediately accosted by Niles.

"Have you seen it, boss?" he says, handing me a newspaper. "The guy's on the news, the papers, TV, blogs, everywhere. We've got to find him. Look," he taps at the newspaper in my hands, "look."

I look. There he is, my Thomas, staring back at me from the top fold of the Washington Times. You can bet they're out there, right now, scouring every nook and kiosk in the city for him. Fine, they may find him, but only I can deliver him.

I doubt my grin could have grown any wider without doing damage. How perfect is this? They've gone and discovered my boy on their own without any selling or cajoling from me. All they need now is someone to wrap him up and bring him in—my political payday at hand. This is gonna be fun. I reach my cubicle and send Niles away so I can call Annie.

"Are you on the bench?" I ask once she picks up.

"No, we just pulled in. We're about to unload the t-shirts."

"Annie," I pause long enough to imply seriousness, "I need to ask you a favor."

"Yes?" Her tone says, *as long as you don't expect me to grant it.*

"I need you to get Thomas out of there—now."

"I'm going to need a bit more," she says. "I think you know that."

Of course I do. The only reason she's still with me is because she learned early on not to trust a word I say. She sure as hell knows not to grant me a favor without full disclosure. So I play to her protective instincts.

"People are coming," I say, "they may already be there."

"What people, reporters, cameramen—"

"No, staffers, handlers, maybe a senator or two, they—"

"Hart, what have you done?"

"It's not me; they saw him in the papers, on TV. They might want him to speak before Congress. I'm not sure he's up to it."

There's a long silence, then, "Why Thomas?"

"I told you: newspapers, TV—people know about him."

"Only in DC," she says.

"He has the look," I say.

"It's for your campaign, isn't it. Hearing America."

"'Listening to America,' and yes, it is, but I didn't put him out there—they found him on their own." She goes silent again so I say, "Why would I warn you? If it was me I would have brought him into work myself."

"Okay," she says, "but Archie's going to be mad. Where to and for how long?"

"I'll call you when I get out of my meeting. Take him to breakfast. He loves bagels."

"You haven't had your meeting?"

"No, I told you, I'm innocent here."

"I see them—must go," and she clicks off.

I click off, too, returning my Blackberry to my pocket where it rings again.

Jeannie says, "The senator would have a word with you, Hart." She pauses a beat. "That would be now," and hangs up.

I look at my watch—9:18, twelve minutes before the meeting. I head down the hall and am immediately ushered, eyes-only, by Jeannie, into Feldstone's office.

"Good morning, Senator," I say standing before him. I smile pleasantly but he doesn't return it.

"Hartford," he says, "we need to find this Thomas."

I want to play dumb, I want to make him spell it out, I want him filled with anxiety, pleading and begging so I can come riding in on my white stallion and save the day, but time is short so I say, "We will."

He studies me, reads me, then raises an eyebrow. "You know where he is," he says.

It really would be fun to game this thing, draw it out and wallow in it, but the clock's ticking so I play it straight up. "Yes, sir," I say, "I do."

He stands abruptly. "Hartford, you SOB, I should've known," he shakes his head back and forth. "I should've known. You're on top of this, aren't you, boy. You've got this one in your pocket." He puts on his big grin. "Hartford, Hartford, we're gonna bust some chops this time, gonna prick us some egos we are." He puts his arm around my shoulders and walks me to the door. "Oh yeah," he says, "get me to the meet—we're gonna have us a fine time this morning."

That's the way the senator talks when he's been dealt a political happy-hand, and right now he's holding aces.

The meeting is set to begin once everyone is here, and—everyone is here. Republican and Democrat bigwigs, all in attendance, as well as the administration's chief of staff. Three or four newspapers are lying on the conference room table, with Thomas's picture staring out from the front page of each one. I look over at my senator. He's smiling like he's just digested the canary. I suddenly realize why there wasn't enough time for me to bathe in my moment; it was so the senator could bask in his.

"Gentlemen," Feldstone says, grabbing the reins, "I believe we have found someone to listen to."

Chuckles and murmurs start making the rounds when Senator Halyard, from Georgia, says, "Yes, Senator, but can we find him? The press has no last name, no address, and no phone number."

"And he's not at his t-shirt booth today," says Joel Murphy, house member from Ohio.

"Well now," Feldstone says putting his hand to his chin, "am I hearing we're all on the same page here? Am I to assume that we're all in agreement on this man..." he reaches over and pulls one of the newspapers to him and reads, "Thomas?" He looks up with a smile. "Should we locate him, that is?"

The nods are vigorous and unanimous.

"As long as he gets through the vetting process," says the president's man, making himself known.

"Of course," the senator says, "understood. So. If we can locate him and he's properly vetted then he's our man. Hands?"

Everyone in the room raises his hand.

"Good," he says, "because Hartford Keepe, my Chief of Staff, and Thomas are like this."

He holds up two fingers meshed together and gives us his Cheshire Cat smile—so named because when deployed, it's the only part of him you can see.

There's not so much a gasp as a collection of under-the-breath profanities, as his colleagues realize Senator Feldstone & Co. have just taken over command and control. Listening to America has neatly fallen under the imposing thumb of the senior senator from Virginia, making him the major recipient of all the political capital it will garner.

The meeting breaks up with faux handshakes and back-slaps and the onus on one Hartford Keepe to bring in the elusive Mr. Thomas. I'm smiling and laughing as well, enjoying the fake kudos and artificial "attaboys" while a chord of uncertainty keeps twisting around in my brain. What if Thomas doesn't want to be the man? What if he refuses to be the man? That's silly, of course. I'm Hartford Keepe, master manipulator, premier persuader, Mr. Perceptions-R-Us. Besides, I rescued Thomas, put a roof over his head, fed him, and found him a job. He owes me.

I swagger into the condo at six p.m., announcing my presence, and I get nothing. I glance at the counter and then at the breakfast table and see no note. I want to call Annie but would prefer to meet her face-to-face. I've already come down against Thomas's participation in this thing, citing his welfare as the reason, now I'm going to have to do a one-eighty and sell the job. I doubt Thomas will be the problem, he's such an agreeable fellow, but my Annie's a different story. She learned long ago, from me or because of me, not to trust anyone. She's always been a tough sell. The fact that Thomas has chosen her, instead of me, as his bonding mate adds to the difficulty. Still, I am Hartford Keepe.

I hear the garage door motor and listen to the metal wheels clank up their rails. I look out the window in time to see the tail of Annie's red Audi disappear into the garage. I stretch my neck right and left, front and back, to take the kinks out. I roll my shoulders back and forth, getting rid of the tension. I shake my hands and arms vigorously to loosen the muscles and free up blood flow. I turn toward the entry and smile. Showtime.

They walk through the door talking, giggling, BF's forever, so full of themselves they don't see me. I have to exaggerate my throat-clearing a second time to get their attention.

"Hartford," Annie says, "you're home." Always Hartford, now, especially when Thomas is present. Her eyes grow cautious or suspicious and she says, "How was the meeting?"

"Great," I say, smiling large.

I walk over and hug her. She stays stiff, and on release takes a wary step backward. "What's happened?" she says.

"Nothing's happened, everything went great." How did she get like this?

She stands there with her hands by her sides but wearing her hands-on-hips look.

"Thomas," I say, turning his way, "good news."

I swear he seems to sidle her way and mimic her expression. If he were four he would be behind her skirt, peeking out, sucking his thumb. What am I, the enemy? These two were about as dubious a pair as I've seen. I decide persuasion by charm is out of the question, and elect to tell it straight.

"They have selected you, Thomas, to be the voice of America in their 'Listening to America' event."

Okay, it's out there. No clapping, no cheering—fine. I figure Annie to go off on me about now but, uncharacteristically, she stays mute.

Thomas says, "Whom do you mean by 'they,' Hartford?"

"Why, Senate and House leaders, even the president's on board. You've been selected by the most powerful men in the country—in the world. It's quite an honor, Thomas." Still no cheering.

"Should not the voice of America be selected by the people of America?" He says.

"Would not a poll suffice? I have read about polls in your newspapers. They are conducted most every day it seems. Why not conduct a poll to discover America's choice for a popular representative?"

I look over at Annie—for what, help? She's sitting on the couch flipping through a house magazine. Her face shows a subtle grin. I assumed I'd have to go through her to get to Thomas, but here she is stepping aside voluntarily, leaving me easy pickings. The magazine flipping is her way of saying, *He's all yours.*

"Politics is complicated, Thomas. The winner of a poll might not be acceptable to both parties, or either party, for that matter. In such cases we would have to start all over again, perhaps several times. But you, you've already been accepted and approved by both parties. You are a winner, Thomas." I step forward with my right foot. I want to extend my right hand and say, "Ta-daa," but I don't.

"I believe I do understand," he says. "It would seem, though, that if our government finds the representative chosen by the American people unacceptable there would be no need to start again, for there would be no reason to continue with the 'Listening to America' program. You would thus save taxpayers time and money alike."

I look over at Annie's smug smile and then back at Thomas. "Scrap LTA? Why on earth would we want to do that?"

"If our government finds the choice made by the American people unacceptable then clearly our government has no intention of listening to America."

I look over at Annie again. She's still flipping but also trying to stifle a giggle. I look back at Thomas. Enough of the polite palaver. I need to finalize this thing.

"Thomas, the government has already made its decision. It has chosen you. It's a wonderful opportunity—a once-in-a-lifetime opportunity. You'll be famous. Your t-shirt sales will go through the roof. You'll be able to make your words and thoughts known to the most powerful people on earth. But time is short. I need to know, now, if you're in or out."

In my experience, the hard sell stops the BS and pressures the deal to a close. It's a proven tactic that's worked every time I've used it.

"Hartford, you make a compelling case. However, I must decline your generous offer. I feel I would not be able to represent the American people in proper fashion. I would, in truth, only be able to speak for myself."

I stand stunned, unable to find my words. I look over at Annie still flipping pages and smiling. She raises her eyes to mine and her smile disappears. Standing, she comes over, puts her arms around my neck and hugs me. "I'm sorry," she whispers, "I could have told you."

I stiffen and step back. I look at her and then at Thomas. Okay, round one—been here before. This isn't over. I see the pity in their eyes, which only cements my resolve. I glance down at my watch—7:15. I recover quickly, as is my talent, smiling and clapping my hands together.

"How about we all go out for a nice dinner?" I say. "Thomas, what are you in the mood for?"

It surprises them. Thomas is silent for a moment, then says, "I did very much enjoy our Outback Steakhouse experience."

I look over at Annie. She nods and cocks her head, wondering what I'm up to now.

"Then Outback it is," I say. "Let me get washed up." I charge up the stairs to my bathroom, leaving them dazed and confused.

Our Outback meal is excellent once again. Thomas seems to really take to the shrimp griller while Annie, bless her weight-watching heart, brings on the wedge with blue cheese. I, of course, opt for the steak—it's a steakhouse. Nothing about Listening to America is mentioned, by me or my doubting duo; hence, it's another pleasant dining experience.

We're on the way home, chatting about the mundane, as I turn onto our street. The side opposite my condo is lined with news vans and SUVs. The grass area in front is filled with reporters, cameramen, equipment techs, TV anchors, and anyone else who can squeeze into our postage-stamp-sized lawn and driveway. The yard is in chaos.

Annie jerks her head toward me and I shrug my shoulders. Even she realizes this is not my fault—why would I leak our address when I could easily bring Thomas in myself? Who, then? It could have been anyone in that meeting. The minute Feldstone linked me with Thomas he set this thing on course. I should have seen it coming.

I'm more upset than I should be. As a full-time politico and chief of staff to a senior senator I know this stuff goes with the territory. It's just that now it's in *my* territory. I consider speeding up and going past, but I realize if we don't take care of this now we'll just have to face it later. These people aren't going away until the story runs to ground. So I turn in.

I brake to a stop and the Beemer is immediately surrounded by microphones and cameras. I push the remote and as the garage door rises along its rails I watch at least two dozen people fill the limited space inside. The car isn't going anywhere.

I turn toward the back seat and say, "We might as well get this over with—they're not leaving."

Instead of the wild-eyed, panicked reaction I expect, Thomas sits there calmly with a half smile on his face nodding his head. Annie is more discombobulated. She doesn't say anything but her head swivels erratically while her hands clutch her purse tightly to her chest.

"Thomas," I say, "you and I will get out. Annie, best you stay in the car."

I unlock the two left side doors and Thomas and I step out onto the driveway. The expected camera and microphone surge happens quickly, all of it directed at Thomas. Faster and more forceful than I figured, reporters, cameramen, and their equipment ram into us. A protective instinct I didn't know I possessed takes over and I throw my large frame in front of Thomas with my arms and hands extended. Thomas is immediately and helplessly wedged between the car and my body.

"Back off!" I yell. "Back off!" But nobody does. "Back off, people, or we'll go inside and you'll get nothing." It helps to know the language.

They back off—but just a fraction. They stand in mob posture wearing mob expressions. If my words don't work they'll likely send for the rope.

"Here's your statement," I say, shifting to my left. "First of all, this is Thomas," I indicate the little munchkin trapped behind me while cameras whirr and flashbulbs flash.

He looks overly small and intimidated but basically unhurt. Still, it makes me angry. I'm not sure which words I was planning to use but I'm pretty sure they aren't the ones that come out.

"Thomas has been offered the job of spokesman to represent the American people in the 'Listening to America' event. He has respectfully declined the offer."

Lord, I might as well have told them Kennedy had been shot or that global warming is a hoax. Another hundred reporters seem to appear from nowhere with another hundred microphones in their fists, all pushing and shoving for position, smashing me back into Thomas and Thomas back into the side of the car. There's lots of shouting and yelling—most words unintelligible but one seems to dominate the fray: *why?*

"Back off," I shout again. "Back the hell off!"

I have both arms out in front of me, pushing as hard as I can. I pray Thomas hasn't been flattened or suffocated. I'm finally able to shoulder us a little extra space and subsequently feel movement from behind me signaling signs of life.

"I'll tell you why," I yell and that sort of shuts them up. I stay silent for a while longer, enlisting proven tactics, and that quiets them even further. When I start to speak I use a low, normal tone which easily penetrates the hush.

"Thomas loves this country," I say, "but he feels he cannot speak for the whole of the American people. He can speak only for himself."

A multitude of questions are immediately hurled at me, but the pushing and shoving are held in check. It seems to me this interview is over. Thomas is out. I've confirmed it to all of America and to my everlasting chagrin. It's now time to move on and let the fallout begin.

I'm wrong. A reporter for CBS manages to get close enough to stick a microphone in Thomas's face and yell a question which is heard by everyone on the scene.

"Thomas," she says, "if you *were* allowed to speak to the United States Government, for yourself, what would you say?"

The yammering dies out immediately, as if sock gags have been shoved into their collective mouths. Several more microphones find their way into Thomas's face, allowing him no room for escape. A look of serenity and then sadness takes over his eyes.

He stares directly into the nearest camera and says, "I would tell them that it was never meant to be this way."

This time there's a long pause before the cacophony resumes—maybe they're digesting his words or maybe they've run out of questions. I don't know, but it deals me the pause I need. I quickly open Thomas's door and shove him in the back seat, then I open mine and jump in behind the wheel. I start the car and without flattening anyone drive into the garage as they all scatter. I hit the remote just as I clear the sensors bringing the door down nicely without trapping anybody inside. I scan left and right, then look into my rear view mirror and watch my lips curl into a smile. No one gets out of the car, so I look back at Thomas and then over at Annie. They're both smiling—at me.

I stare again at my reflection in the mirror and find I'm slowly shaking my head and mumbling under my breath, "Who the hell are you and what have you done with Hart?"

CHAPTER 12

Once inside the condo, I check my messages and see the number forty-two blinking in red digits, indicating the answering machine is full. I immediately unplug the phone from the wall then grab my Blackberry and shut it off. Calling Senator Feldstone with a heads-up is clearly out of the question. Taking a call from him could be worse. The conversation would likely turn into a rant with me saying something to get me fired. I decide instead to pull out my laptop and come up with a plan B.

Annie's already in the kitchen clinking dishes while Thomas is perusing the evening paper. I'm wearing my nervous smile and thinking about tomorrow. I'm tired and I'm agitated. I look at Annie and then at Thomas and realize that I really don't want to get into a discussion with either of them tonight. So I bid each a good evening and head up the stairs to the bedroom.

After showering and getting into my Jockey shorts and t-shirt, I climb into bed and open my notebook, intent on pursuing the elusive plan B. I hear unintelligible mumblings from downstairs and figure Annie and Thomas are well into it. A pang of jealousy hits me hard. I sometimes wish I was in the loop—perhaps I, too, need to bond. I think about all of the friends with whom I've enjoyed a strong bond over the years and come up with none. I think about all of the people whom I could even consider good friends and come up with one—Thomas. I've known him for less than a month. I lay back against my pillow and begin to ponder how pathetic a life I'm leading, and I promptly fall asleep.

Sunlight invades the bedroom, forcing my eyes open and directing them to the clock next to the bed—6:45. I sit up and wonder why a phone isn't ringing or a Blackberry isn't vibrating, and then I remember I shut them both down last night. I decide they should remain that way, allowing me a leisurely shower and a stress-free breakfast before reestablishing communications with the world.

By the time I get down to the bonding/breakfast table, it's 7:20 and Thomas and Annie are huddled together in deep conversation. I say hello, which stops the talking and evokes looks of conspiratorial silence.

"Good morning," I try again.

Annie good-morning's me back, abruptly standing and making her way to the stove, saying something about scrambled eggs with pepper jack cheese, my favorite.

Thomas, also standing, says, "A very good morning to you, Hartford," a little too loudly.

I pull out a chair and sit down, but he doesn't.

"Hartford," he says, "I would be most grateful if you would allow me the honor of accompanying you to work today."

I suddenly become aware of his dress. He's wearing khaki pants, a white long-sleeve shirt, and a blue-and-white-striped tie. It's the first time I've seen him out of uniform.

"New duds," I say.

"I wish to accept your kind offer," he says. "I wish to become the voice of America."

I'm sure my mouth has fallen open, so I'm hoping there's no visible drool. I look over at Annie, who continues to scramble with her back to me, but I'm pretty sure she's either smiling or smirking. I wonder if this is her doing. I look back at Thomas and stare at him, dumbfounded, unable to ask what has changed his mind.

"Because," he says, "you have asked me to do this thing and you are my friend." He extends his hand.

I stand up, grab him, and pull him into a giant bear hug. When I'm done, I take a step back, wondering what the hell is happening to me. Annie comes over and places two plates of scrambled eggs with pepper jack cheese, crisp bacon, and buttered grits on the table. She returns to the stove, retrieves a third plate, and joins us. We all sit down and enjoy an excellent breakfast. I decide not to spoil my meal or theirs by communicating with Senator Feldstone and the rest of the political world. I elect to take Thomas to work with me instead.

By the time I reach the parking garage it's past nine. I've been out of touch for eight hours but I'm not worried. With Thomas in tow I figure I'm prepared for the worst kind of onslaught. I'm not. The senator himself meets me at the elevator. Most of his staff stand behind him, like jack-booted storm troopers aching for battle. From the looks in their eyes and the weapons in their hands, I believe they plan to beat me into submission with staplers and cell phones. Had someone not noticed Thomas's presence and shouted his name, I'm certain they would've stapled me to the floor and covered me head to toe with Blackberry bruises.

Thomas's presence creates the hesitation and subsequent confusion I need. It enables us to step from the elevator into the corridor unmolested.

The senator, however, stands firm. He glares at me, at Thomas, then back at me and says "My office." He turns and strides down the hall while the staff parts like the waters of the Red Sea, each man throwing his backside smartly against the wall, lining both sides of the corridor. The action allows the three of us to pass by a dozen, red-faced, rage-infested minions, un-accosted. Nobody spits or cusses, although I think Niles tries to trip me. This is getting fun.

My merriment is short-lived. Once we enter the senator's chambers, he closes the door firmly, marches to the power side of the desk, and mounts his chair, leaving us standing. He continues to glare before finally speaking.

"Hartford," he says, "is he in or out?"

I look over at Thomas, who seems neither intimidated nor uncomfortable, and answer, "He's in."

The senator lets out a sigh, louder than he intended, and relaxes his posture. He motions for us to sit, then leans back and loosens his tie.

"We're starting to look like fools around here," he says.

"I know, Senator, and I take full responsibility, but, as you recall, when we selected Thomas for the job it was left up to me to make the offer. I did, yesterday evening, and he turned me down."

The senator switches his stare to Thomas and hardens it.

"When Annie, Thomas, and I returned from dinner last night," I continue, "my yard was filled with reporters. There was no getting past them without a comment so I told them the truth. Someone at the meeting must have leaked to the press."

Feldstone looks a little sheepish but quickly recovers. "And—?"

I look over at Thomas then back to the senator. "And then he changed his mind," I say.

The senator almost winks, but Thomas is present, so he says, "Good job, Hartford." He stands up, extends his hand to Thomas, and says, "Welcome aboard."

Thomas doesn't understand the terminology because he sees no ship, but he shakes the senator's hand anyway and says, "Thank you, sir."

"Okay, Hart," Feldstone says, "call a meeting, ASAP—majority leaders, both houses, minority leaders both houses, committee chairs, and better include the administration. I want them to meet Thomas. We also need to call in the press and set the story straight." He stands up, props his hands on the desk, and leans forward. "This thing's going to happen fast, Hart. We've got a small window, so once we're given the go-ahead we've got to be ready to move. There'll be no second chances. Capiche?"

I capiche, and he suddenly stands up straight and sticks out his hand to Thomas.

"Again, my boy, welcome aboard." Thomas shakes his hand a second time.

We leave the senator's office, walk through Jeannie's reception area, and turn left into the staffers' complex, where I introduce Thomas to the two junior staffers on hand. I get them going on meeting prep and then lead Thomas into my cubicle, where I proceed to make an endless series of phone calls. After about fifteen minutes of nonstop telephone chatter, Thomas, sitting in front of me, slides a piece of paper under my nose. It reads: *With your permission I would tour the halls of this magnificent building.* I nod my head, and Thomas leaves the cubicle. He wanders out into the reception area where I hear him say hello to Jeannie but hear no reply. After that I hear nothing.

My calls take longer than I figured, and by the time I hang up with Senator Crosby from Florida, the clock reads 10:33. The meeting is set for 12:00. We're billing it as a drop-everything-and-be-there affair, which to most means postponing lunch. Everyone is nailed down except the chair of the Republican Party, and he's sending a representative. The administration's weighing in heavy, sending the vice-president, signaling their intention to ratchet things up. Word has already spread on Thomas's reversal, so everyone's positively giddy to meet the man.

I finish my last call, lift my head, and look about the cubicle for Thomas. He's not there, and panic sets in. I find his note and let out a breath. I need to give Feldstone a progress update but decide it would be prudent to find Thomas first. Stepping out into the reception area where Jeannie's on the phone, I hold up twelve fingers (no easy task) and silently mouth the words "Meeting, twelve o'clock." She shakes her head vigorously, mouthing "No, wait" as I back out the door.

Thomas is neither to my left nor my right, but there's so much traffic in the corridor I can't see more than twenty feet. I turn left and pick up my pace. Soon I'm traveling as fast and as furiously as everyone else but still have no bead on my protégé. The meeting is to be held in the Capitol building, so I have less than an hour to find my charge. I know he's not shy about his wanderings, so he could be anywhere. At least I know he hasn't fallen into enemy hands since the Republicans are in on this. At the end of the corridor I come across a door that says "Stairs"—one I've never seen or used before. I walk through the doorway, choose down over up (due to the exertion factor), and emerge into a long hallway at the bottom of the Russell building. I turn right for balance and increase my pace. I'm starting to jog and sweat when I pass an open door on my left.

"Hart," comes a recognizable voice, "you slumming?"

It's Jonathan Wheeler, a fellow Harvard grad, butt-kisser, and yes-man, whose sole ambition in college was to be me.

I stop without skidding and say, "JW," which he hates, "have you seen—"

"Thomas," he completes, and nods to his left.

There, just inside the door, lounging in a cushy, brown, leather chair, is my lost Thomas, drinking hot tea.

"Hartford," he says, "so nice of you to come by. Would you have some tea?"

Another pang hits me. These two have known each other for less than fifteen minutes and Thomas is offering me his tea. Thomas, to this day, won't enter my house without permission, and he lives there.

"No, Thomas," I say, "we have a meeting—we can't be late."

"Oh yes, the meeting, I am remiss. Perhaps I am losing my memory." He smiles, puts down his cup, and stands up, shaking Jonathan's hand. "Thank you, Jonathan, it was very nice to make your acquaintance. I must now attend an important meeting."

He tails me out the door while I launch into a fast walk or slow trot, hearing hard breathing from behind as he struggles to catch up.

"Jonathan keeps tea on hand for the Tea Party people," he says between short breaths. "Do you know of the Tea Party people, Hartford?"

We make the meeting three minutes early. Senator Feldstone's there, chatting easily with the VP, so I know things are in hand. I pause and let my breath out slowly. I'm free. I have no duties here. The senator will take charge, do the introductions, and conduct the meeting as only he can. Had Thomas not changed his mind, I would be taking the floor in shame and humiliation, conducting an apology party and trying to explain myself to my betters. Instead the mood is all smiles and nods, with me grinning broadly along with the rest. But my apprehension is growing. Thomas, after all, has yet to open his mouth to any of these men. They know absolutely nothing about him.

"Gentlemen," Senator Feldstone says, now standing, after everyone else has taken his seat, "welcome—and we are especially honored to have with us the vice-president." He indicates Harvey Medville, and the VP stands up. No one applauds because everybody here belongs to the club.

"We are here today to confirm what you already know, that Thomas," he motions to Thomas with a nod, "is—by the way, Thomas," he says, "what is your last name?"

And so it begins. I was really hoping to delay this bombshell a bit longer, but this is politics and in politics you seldom get what you want. *Crap.*

The senator continues to stare at Thomas, employing a very slow downward nod of the head signifying that it is perfectly acceptable for Thomas to speak and to please not let his overblown ego and unabashed pomposity intimidate him.

"I'm afraid I do not know, sir," Thomas says with a smile.

Senator Feldstone stands a little higher on the balls of his feet, then rears back on his heels as if he's been slapped. I know from experience the senator's next words are going to turn this thing nasty.

But before he can speak or I can intervene, Thomas says, "I am afflicted with a severe loss of memory, Senator. The medical doctors have labeled my malady amnesia."

Senator Feldstone rears up and back and up again and then swings his massive head in my direction—the shelling is about to begin. I shrug apologetically, thinking maybe I should have mentioned the amnesia thing before the meeting.

This is the worst position in which a chief of staff can put his senator—an unexpected circumstance requiring him to make a spot decision in front of his colleagues, not to mention the vice-president. I scan the faces in the room and watch as one by one their perplexed frowns turn into smug little grins. I quickly realize as their political brains do the math and their expressions unfold that this is the best thing that could've happened.

The VP sees the amnesia as a way to muster up the sympathy vote. The Dems see Thomas as a man easily molded and manipulated into their image. The Republicans see him as a blank slate to be filled in with conservative talking points. The only one without a greasy smile on his face is Senator Feldstone, who's still standing and staring at me, desperately in need of a bailout. Again, before I can come to the rescue, Thomas backs his chair out from under the table and stands up. He takes a tentative step toward the senator, with his head down and his eyes on the floor. The senator nods, quite comfortable with subservient posture.

"I have been contemplating a proper surname for some time, sir," he says, raising his head to look the senator in the eye. "One name in particular has come to my liking. What think you of the surname Feldstone?" Thomas lets his serious expression morph into a smile.

The senator, not so quick on the uptake, hearing the chuckles and seeing the smiles and nods from his colleagues, finally realizes this formal little man possesses a sense of humor and is using it on him. Far from angry, Feldstone is pleased.

He steps forward, puts his arm around Thomas's shoulders and says, "Now, son, you had me going there, yes you did." He shifts his gaze and smile in my direction and says, "I like this little fellow, indeed I do. I believe this thing is gonna work out right fine. Yes, I do."

The balance of the meeting is filled with senators, congressmen, and committee chairs asking Thomas questions; all softball and all to do with his amnesia and his impression of their fair city. As the meeting concludes, no one has even a smidgen of doubt as to Thomas's acceptability for the LTA gig, nor any inkling as to his political views or speaking qualifications whatsoever.

CHAPTER 13

The press is a horse of a different color, different shape—it's a different animal altogether. Feldstone had forgotten to mention they'd been called, so as we file into the hallway the cameras and microphones take us by surprise. The media's still under the impression Thomas has declined the LTA offer, and so the minute they spot him, they're all over us. Feldstone's the last man out, but as he enters the hallway he sees the cameras and is drawn to them like a preacher to his pulpit. The questions fire nonstop.

"What is Thomas doing here? What was the meeting about? Has Thomas changed his mind? Is Thomas in or out? Is his last name Feldstone? Sir, is he really your son?"

DC can leak meeting details quicker than a Senator can flip-flop his principles. I can only imagine how Feldstone plans to handle that last one. Then I realize why the senator is the senator—he ignores it.

Feldstone embraces the half dozen microphones thrusting at his face with his Cheshire smile. "We have important business here today," he says. "I want to introduce you, the media, and all of America to—Thomas." He motions Thomas upfront with both hands. "Thomas has consented to be the voice of America and will speak before Congress and the president at the 'Listening to America' event on a date yet to be determined." He turns toward

Harvey Medville. "Mr. Vice President, would you like to say a few words?"

I find myself viewing the fanfare as a bystander rather than a participant, and from my angle I realize something's out of kilter. I'm trying to put my finger on it when Thomas's earlier words finally register in my brain. He was right. The politicians, not the people, are doing the selecting here. They're doing the introductions, setting the stage, taking the credit, with Thomas as their pawn.

Isn't what's happening here akin to allowing the fox to design the henhouse? And is there not a single member of our illustrious press able to ferret out and question such shenanigans? I shake my head in disgust. I watch as the media feeding frenzy continues unabated, right out here in the open.

The VP is taking questions from the floor but not answering them. He's effusing what a grand undertaking the "Listening to America" event is going to be. I suppose I should be proud, my brainstorm and all, but my immediate concern is getting us out of here. I see Feldstone and two senior chairmen lining up behind the VP, waiting their turn. It's obvious they aren't going to let Thomas anywhere near a microphone, but neither are they going to let him out of their sight. I would've been long gone already except there's no way I'm leaving Thomas here, alone, with this bunch.

The press conference finally comes to an end and I'm able to cut Thomas from the pack. It's 1:37 so I figure there's enough time for us to get a bite to eat and for me me to get a handle on Thomas's view of things. He agrees, but reluctantly so, since he's quite anxious to return to his t-shirts. Here's a man about to become the most recognized face in the country, and he's worried about t-shirts.

After eating a couple of roast beef sandwiches at Arby's, I deliver him back to his kiosk, where the crowd is sparse and the reporters nonexistent. I'm not surprised. Who, in this town, would imagine Thomas actually returning to work? His t-shirt booth could be the perfect hiding place. Still, the press never got a chance to question him, what with all the foxes in protective mode, so I figure they'll eventually revisit all of his haunts and, in time, turn up here.

Thomas makes me get out of the car and walk over to the kiosk to see his new designs. He has a half dozen or so new slogans, with his silhouetted minuteman logo at the bottom of each one. I ask again if he had come up with the sayings himself, and again he shakes his head, saying he must have memorized them a long time ago. (And he still can't remember his last name.)

By the time I return to my car I see Thomas has donned his leather vest, his breeches, and his three-cornered hat, and I see the tourists already gravitating toward the kiosk. They move like zombies after fresh meat. I do wonder what he says to them.

I crank up the engine and drive off. I have to get back to the office and set up the vetting protocols. It'll happen in two parts: one, the FBI will come around and talk to everybody Thomas knows or has ever known—which in his case, will be me, Annie, and Archie. They'll then conduct a detailed interview with Thomas. A report will be prepared and issued to those with a need to know. The second part involves the Senate and House intelligence committees. This will require filling out numerous forms and answering detailed questions. Each committee will then conduct informal hearings with the subject in order to fill in any holes. On completing the process successfully, Thomas will be granted his fifteen minutes of fame.

I reach my office, round up Niles, and instruct him on how to start the ball rolling. Next I drop by the senator's chambers to make sure things are still copacetic. Jeannie makes me wait an extra few minutes, as punishment for earlier transgressions, and then ushers me into the sanctum. The senator is at his desk on the phone. He motions me to sit then carries on a long, senator-to-senator conference call about fishing. Once he hangs up he stares at me in silence, wearing his serious, eye-to-eye game face. He slowly shakes his head back and forth and then breaks into a patronizing smirk.

"Amnesia," he says, "you didn't think that pertinent?"

"I was going to tell you, Senator. Time was short."

He nods, turning his smirk to smile. "Did you notice no one asked about his politics or what he was planning to say in his speech?"

"I did, sir. They seemed more concerned with comforting his affliction than afflicting his comfort," I smile. "Thomas Paine."

He laughs heartily and I join in. He then goes quiet and focuses on me. "Well done, Hartford," he says, "well done."

It means my golden boy status is still intact. I leave the reception area with a wink not to but from Jeannie, and high-horse it out the door.

CHAPTER 14

'm back in my cubicle and it's half past four. I've run out of things that need to be done yesterday, so I decide to knock off. I consider running by the kiosk just to see if Annie's there and what kind of crowd Thomas is pulling in, but I need and deserve a break, so I head for home instead. I might even take a nap.

I pull into my garage and step out of the car, knowing immediately that something's different. I cautiously walk up the garage stairs and, as I enter the house, realize what it is—Annie's home alone. I key the door lock noisily so as to alert and not frighten her and find her sitting at the breakfast table sipping a cup of hot tea.

"You're home," I say, fantasizing my nap idea into something better.

She puts her cup down, gets up, walks over and gives me a soft, warm kiss, heightening my expectations.

"Hart," she says, "we need to talk."

That cartoon bubble over my head, the one picturing lascivious thoughts, suddenly goes poof and disappears.

"Sit down," she says, "let me get you a beer."

I'm disappointed, but I like beer. She fetches me a cold brew and sits across from me behind her teacup. She takes another sip then looks into my eyes. I try to appear winsome but doubt I'm carrying it off.

"Do you know why Thomas changed his mind?" she asks.

Oh good, it's about Thomas—who knew. "Yes," I say, "because I'm his friend."

"Yes, yes," she says waving it off, "but do you remember why he rejected your offer in the first place?"

"Of course I do. As I told the press, he said he could only speak for himself."

"That's right," she says. "Thomas feels he can not speak for three hundred million Americans but can speak only for himself."

That's what I said—why this conversation is more important than me getting afternoon delight, I don't know.

"Something happened earlier that day," she continues. "Something that made him change his mind. I think I know what it was. I believe you need to know also."

I'm thinking, *Sex or talk, sex or talk—*.

"Hartford!"

"You mean now," I say.

"Yes, now, this is important."

"Okay then, yes, I need to know."

"Good," she's only half smiling now, but fully exercised. "Earlier that day I ate lunch with Thomas. We had hot dogs on the bench across from the kiosk—Thomas loves hot dogs. Once we finished our lunch, he gathered up our trash and went to the nearest litter bin. A groundskeeper was there emptying the trash barrel and I heard him call Thomas by name. I assumed he recognized Thomas from the newspapers or TV, but the thing is Thomas seemed to recognize him also. The man said he thought Thomas would be the perfect choice to speak for America. This was before anyone even knew he was being considered. Thomas told the man the same thing he told you, that he could only speak for himself. The man, *Whitfield* it said on his shirt, said 'Thomas, do you love this country?' And Thomas said 'Yes, more than my words can express.' 'Then speak for those people,' Whitfield said, 'speak for those who truly love this country.'" She stops talking and stares at me for a response.

"Lots of people love this country," I say.

"And lots of people don't."

"Well I love this country and everyone I work with loves this country. Senator Feldstone loves this country."

She looks at me a little cockeyed and says, "We'll see."

"We'll see?"

"I'm not going to get into an argument with you, Hart. I'm just explaining to you why I think Thomas changed his mind."

"Okay, fine, can we go have sex now?" I don't really say that.

"This next part," she continues, "is a bit, well, undefined."

"Undefined?"

"Well, nebulous."

"Nebulous?" Oh, I do not like where this is going. Annie is usually a very pragmatic woman, almost to a fault, but she has her moments. This may prove to be one of them.

"It's about Thomas," she says.

So not about the vices of chastity.

"There's something about him, Hart, something, well... special."

"How about odd?" I say. "The way he talks, the way he dresses, the way he remembers some things and not others—"

"An excellent example. His erratic memory, the quotations he comes up with for his t-shirts."

"I know, remember? I chose the winner."

"Get over yourself, Hart. He's added eight or ten more slogans to the line since then, all historical quotations and all selling like there's no tomorrow. Have you read the quotes, Hart?"

"The one I chose, yeah, very catchy."

"Do you know where he gets these sayings?"

"Makes them up?"

"They are all quotes from Thomas Paine, and no, Thomas didn't make them up or look them up, he came up with them from memory."

She stares at me for a response but I know better. She suspects I'm playing my power game, but I'm not. I just don't know what to say.

"How does a man who can't remember his last name," she says, "come up with nine quotes from two hundred and twenty years ago, word for word?"

"And your point?"

"I don't know, it's just that Thomas appears on the scene from out of nowhere, a complete unknown to everyone including himself, and the next thing you know he is chosen to appear before the US Congress and speak on behalf of the entire country. Is this not amazing? Do you not think some kind of destiny or fate or providence is at work here?"

I chuckle because I can't help it. "First of all, I came up with the 'Listening to America' strategy, I chose Thomas for the gig, and I sold him to Feldstone and the boys. The only divine power at work here is me, trying to keep the Democrats in power, the senator in office, and me in my job—Your Hart-throb in action."

I grin big, while she has *What an ass* written all over her face.

"Hart, you didn't attract those huge crowds to the kiosk, and you didn't call the TV and newspaper reporters and order them to put Thomas in front of America, and you didn't cause the people to fall in love with him. There is something very special about this man—his words, his ways, his heart—and I think the things that have happened and all the things yet to happen are truly meant to be."

I'm thinking of bringing up her abnormal bonding issues and her latent father figure tendencies, but how stupid would that be? Besides, something *is* happening here. I just believe it to be conceived by man, strategized by man, executed by man, and destined to result in a huge, man-made success. And that man is me.

There's a knock at the door and I jump to my feet, ready to be done with this conversation. I open the front door to a smiling Thomas decked out in his colonial uniform.

I stare at him. Maybe he is a ghost from the past come to make things right—lord knows we could use a savior. He looks awfully natural in his breeches and three-cornered hat. I don't know anyone else who can pull that off. Manifest destiny, divine providence, or just dumb luck—I haven't a clue. But watching this thing play out, I do agree, is going to be a hell of a show.

"Thomas," I say, "come on in, we were just talking about you."

Annie quickly gets up, goes over and gives him a hug—the bond. Not that I'm jealous. Okay, a little jealous, but not of him, of her. Bond or no bond, sometimes I want to hug him myself.

Thomas takes off his hat and waits for me to ask him to sit—all politeness and manners, this one. Annie fetches him a cup of tea and me another beer, then joins us with her own cup and we all sit down. Thomas waits patiently until she's taken her first sip before taking one of his own. I've downed half my beer by then.

"I trust your work day was agreeable, Hartford," he says.

I sometimes have to catch myself from mimicking his speech. It would be fun but would surely evoke The Look from Annie, which would be less so.

"Very agreeable, Thomas. I've been put in charge of scheduling your vetting process."

"Vetting?" Annie says, raising her eyebrows and lowering her cup. "What vetting?"

"Yes," I say, keeping my eyes on Thomas, "vetting and confirmation hearings. You will be vetted by the FBI tomorrow morning at eight o'clock in the conference room." Thomas gazes back at me, smiling, enjoying his tea, showing little concern. "They will ask you questions about your background, about any trouble with the law, and so on. They will ask about your friends, business associates, and others. I have apprised them of your amnesia, so you should answer their questions as best you can. I am not allowed to be present during your interview."

He seems to take all this in stride, while Annie, now standing, is shaking her head vigorously and miming unkind things through her body language—almost as if she thinks this is my fault.

"The confirmation hearings," I continue, "will be held at three o'clock on Friday."

"Confirmation hearings," Annie says, "what is he being confirmed for?"

"I know," I say, my words still directed at Thomas, "bad terminology, but that's what they're calling it. Maybe 'oversight hearings' would be more accurate. It's just a chance for the Lords of Congress to find out a little more about you, Thomas. There will be two senators and two congressmen from each party in attendance. I will be there also."

"They want to know his politics," Annie says.

"In a nutshell, yes."

She glares at me and I turn to face her.

"Well," I say, "they're not going to let just anyone into the Senate chamber to address Congress as well as the president and the entire country—some kind of discovery is going to take place." I'm louder and more defensive than I need to be, but that Annie is just so protective of her Thomas. She doesn't respond but seems to accept my reasoning.

"Do you have any questions, Thomas?" I say, shifting to him.

He doesn't, so they go back to their teas and I go to the refrigerator for another beer.

After that, I go to bed alone while Annie and Thomas hold their nightly discussion around the dinner/conference table. It's been this way all week. Sometimes they have a newspaper or magazine between them, sometimes Annie's laptop, most times they just talk. I've thought about joining them but am usually too tired and doubt they'd have room for me anyway.

CHAPTER 15

I wake up in the middle of the night and discover it's morning. The clock says 7:15 and, above that, Tuesday. The big event is Friday, and that's simply too soon. Why Friday? And then I remember—Friday was chosen because it was the only day available on the Senate chamber calendar; every other date was booked for months in advance. I leave the bed for the bathroom sink where I splash my face with water.

Friday—does it even matter? The buzz on this thing has been nothing short of phenomenal. We could stage it on a Sunday morning at two a.m. and the whole country would still be watching. The largest viewing audience in political history, that's the prediction—bigger than any State of the Union, bigger than any Super Bowl. I just wish we had given ourselves more time. I don't know if we're ready. I don't know if Thomas is ready—if I'm ready.

I step from the sink into the shower, using the blast of hot water to jump-start my brain. I think about my priorities. Getting Thomas to his vetting session on time is number two. I get out of the shower and dry off moving back to the sink. Feldstone wants to see me in his office first thing; that would be number three. I pick up my toothbrush and I brush, rinse, and spit, and then gurgle too much mouthwash. I put on my clothes and race down the stairs to find Thomas to make sure he's still on board and to make sure he stays that way. This is my number one priority.

When I reach the living room landing, I nearly run him over. I take a step back and look at him. He's dressed in his khaki pants and a white, long-sleeved shirt—his tie has tiny white stars on a blue background and he's wearing black socks with dark brown bucks. I see neither vest nor hat. I check my Blackberry—7:26. I grab his arm and hustle him past the kitchen where Annie's cooking breakfast in vain. We wave, step through the door, charge down the garage steps, and jump into the BMW. I manage to just clear the garage door as it rides, too slowly, up its rails.

I'm barely able to keep my speed under forty as I enter Capitol park grounds and take too sharp a right onto Grant Ave., nearly flattening a group of pedestrians crossing the street. I break to a stop, glaring hard at eight young, excited college kids paying more attention to me than I deserve. I manufacture a smile to mask my frustration as I wait for the last one to clear my fender. They suddenly stop walking and begin waving and pointing and yelling frantically. My passenger smiles broadly and waves back. Only then do I notice they're all wearing Thomas tees. As we ease past them I begin to scan the park for more.

There are more, lots more. Nearly every other tourist is wearing a Thomas t-shirt. I look over at my little entrepreneurial wunderkind still with the smile on his face—he must be doing blockbusters. I wonder why he possesses only two sets of clothes. Studying him, taking in his patented, all's-well-with-the world expression, I decide I want to be a Thomas.

We get inside the Russell Building and are riding up the elevator before I ask if he has any questions on the vetting process. He says no and I don't press it.

Two FBI agents wearing dark suits with imperceptibly thin pinstripes are already in place by the time we arrive. They're carrying their badges in their fists but sprout no curly wires from their ears, nor is either one talking into his cuff. Introductions are made with laconic candor, making it clear that this is all about Thomas and that I should leave. I wish him luck then quickly walk out the door toward Feldstone's office. I figure once Thomas proves unable to answer even the most basic of questions they'll have little choice but to pull out their water-boarding equipment, and I hate torture.

As I enter the reception area, Jeannie gives me the go-on-in with a conspiratorial nod. The senator's on the phone but he motions me to sit—always a good sign. He talks another ten minutes then hangs up.

"Hartford," he reaches across for a handshake, "we've got work to do." Which means he has a problem so *I* have work to do.

After the shaking I sit, silently waiting for the next shoe. Feldstone pulls out a sheet of paper from a secret desk place and hands it to me. I look at it briefly, catch the two title words— "Talking Points"—and raise my eyes to his.

"Hart, this has come down from on high—very, hush-hush, for our eyes only." He does the two-finger-point to his eyes and then to mine. "Not even the DNC is in on this one." That catches my attention, since the DNC is in on everything. "I have assured the higher-ups that we, you and I, can handle this."

That means me. My eyes immediately go down to the sheet of paper, where I count ten talking points.

"You need to work these into Thomas's speech."

Deep furrows form between my brows.

"Am I going to have trouble with you on this, Hart?"

He's using his don't-make-me-come-over-there tone, which means, *You do this or I'll find somebody who will.* Golden boy status is a very fragile thing.

"Senator, you realize that Thomas is the one writing his speech—I have nothing to do with it."

"My point exactly," he says. "I've already contacted Rosa Rodriguez and Robert Whittington to help out—you know their reputation. We're lucky to get them."

I start to speak but he holds up his hand.

"Don't worry, funds already allocated."

"Senator, all I can do is approach Thomas with your proposal. I honestly don't know how far along he is."

Come to think of it, I don't even know if Thomas has started on his speech—that's scary; the event's just over a week away. The senator stands up, stares at me, then reaches over for a dismissal handshake. I fall for it and he grabs my hand, gripping it painfully tight. He holds on and looks me in the eye.

"Hartford, first of all, it's not my proposal it's *our* proposal, and second, you are the best persuasion man in the business—you should have no trouble bringing our little Thomas on board. If you need backup, you have me." He smiles ominously and nods me toward the door.

I guess I should have seen this coming. An address to the entire country? How could the Dems keep their fingers out of that pie? I have to admit, I expected Thomas to ask me for help or at least let me read over his speech and offer some pointers. He has yet to mention the speech. I wonder if he even knows he has to give one. Maybe he thinks Congress is going raise its collective hands and take turns asking him questions.

My pace picks up as I head toward the conference room. If Thomas is still vetting, maybe I can elicit some answers from him during the water-boarding phase.

By the time I reach him, Thomas is shaking hands with his inquisitors. He's smiling, they're not—I doubt it's permitted. They stride past me without words or recognition and disappear through the door.

"Well?" I say.

"Well?" he repeats.

"Well, how did it go?"

"Oh, that would be impossible for me to determine, Hartford. The agents asked many carefully considered questions."

He says nothing more, so I prompt him with, "And?"

"And I could answer but few."

I stare at him. He looks dry.

"Why don't we go out for an early lunch?" I say, fingering the sheet of paper in my pocket. Thomas nods vigorously. "Something other than hot dogs," I add.

I choose a deli-style eatery attached to and run by The Science and Space Museum. I tell Thomas the food is out of this world. He fails to laugh, which I attribute to water on the brain. I settle for ham and mayonnaise on pumpernickel, and Thomas goes for the roast beef on a baguette. I get coffee, he orders Coke. Chips come with both meals. We find a booth in the corner, sit down, and eat.

Thomas really enjoys his food. I wonder if food was a rarity where he grew up—in the Northwest raised by wolves.

"So, how is your speech coming?" I say once we're down to chips and drinks.

He raises his head and his expression says, *What speech?*

He actually says, "Quite well, Hartford. Thank you for inquiring."

"I wonder if you might need some help."

"Miss Anne has been kind enough to provide informative answers to all of my queries. She has been most gracious."

Long talks at night, afternoon discussions, early morning chitchats, of course—Annie's helping Thomas write his speech.

"I would love to read it," I say.

He smiles uncomfortably. "I have not set pen to parchment, Hartford."

Pen to parchment. "You mean you haven't written your speech." I close my eyes and press my fingers against my temples, trying to remember if I ever formulated a plan B.

"I have but words and phrases, reminders, if you will, placed on small notecards provided to me by Miss Anne."

Opening my eyes but keeping my fingers to my head, I say, "An outline, then."

"Yes, my thoughts on notecards."

"Perhaps you would like to recite it, to practice it. I would love to hear your speech. Maybe I could throw in some pointers."

"Indeed not, Hartford, my words and my thoughts must remain mine alone, influenced by no one. Otherwise how can the words I speak, on behalf of the American people, remain pure?"

"You plan to give your speech before hundreds of millions of people unrehearsed?"

I stare at him and he stares back, undeterred. From his demeanor, I sense no talking points of ours are ever going to find their way into any speech of his. Feldstone can try all he wants, but I see a total impasse. My cell phone rings.

"Where are you?" Annie says.

I tell her.

"Is Thomas with you?"

"Yes."

"Is he safe?"

"Of course."

"Don't bring him home, Hart. They're back, the news crews, they're everywhere— twice as many as before and they're mad as hell about something. I had to shut off the house phone, the doorbell won't stop ringing, I can't go near a window. You keep him safe, Hart, just don't bring him home."

She hangs up and I stare at my cell. It rings again.

"Is Thomas with you?" The senator says. "You two need to get back here ASAP—use the back way. How long will it take?"

"Ten minutes."

"Okay, hurry up, and watch out—they're gunning for you." He hangs up.

I put the cell back in my pocket and look around for somebody with a gun. It's easy to surmise the situation. The press is after Thomas because they can't find any background on him and that makes them suspicious. Feldstone and the higher-ups can't afford to have him fall into the media's hands before they decide the best way to spin the amnesia story.

Getting Thomas from the restaurant back into the Senator's office will be easy. Leaving him alone and defenseless with Feldstone and his ilk, not so much. I figure catching the Metro and holding up in some no-name bar might prove the wiser move, but provoking the Senator's wrath never ends well, so I decide it best to come on in, olly-olly-oxen-free.

Fifteen minutes after I click off my Blackberry, we're walking into the reception arena and confronting Jeannie. It's 1:43 p.m. She's frantic, which means the senator is somewhere between tearing out his hair and ending Niles's life. She won't let us go into his office, signifying someone important is in there. She won't let us wait in my cubicle, either, because she doesn't trust me. We're relegated to the two brown leather chairs in front of her where she can keep an eye on us.

After a few minutes we hear her speakerphone say, "Where the hell are Hart and Thomas?" She smiles our way, hits a button and tells the senator what he wants to hear. With a nod, she bids us enter chambers.

We walk in on the senator and the president's man, not the VP, but the president's chief of staff, Rollie Studdeman. No one does introductions or shakes hands or makes small talk. We just stand there and wait for someone on the outside to shut the door. It happens quickly and the senator starts in.

"The press has gone rabid," he says, "have you seen the news?"

Thomas and I shake our heads in unison. He stares at us like we're Laurel and Hardy. (I'm Hardy.) At a time like this it's best to let him get it out, so we remain silent while he rants and paces.

"I thought we could hold them off. I thought we could stall them until after the address, we can't." He glances over at Studdeman, who's leaning back on the corner of the couch, picking lint from his coat lapel. The senator shakes his head. "They found nothing—no dirt, no background, no nothing. So now they're pissed and coming after us, citing the Freedom of Information Act, threatening subpoenas."

He's in my face now—we're almost touching noses. This is the point where I'm supposed to offer up a solution. I clear my throat and take a step backward for separation. I glance over at Studdeman. I don't like Studdeman—nobody does. I look back at Feldstone.

"Senator," I say, "I suggest we call a press conference for eleven o'clock Monday morning. We tell them they can ask Thomas anything they want."

He lets go a theatrical sigh, shaking his head in a just-can't-find-good-help manner, and says, "Hart, they don't even know about Thomas's handicap. They'll destroy him."

"Senator, he has his confirmation hearings Friday afternoon at three o'clock. Let the amnesia question come up then. If he's approved by the oversight committee, and he will be, he garners the sympathy vote—a man who has overcome incredible odds and is still selected, overwhelmingly, to be the voice of America. We have the whole weekend to set our spin."

Feldstone, with his eyebrows fully arched, his head slightly cocked, shifts his stare from me to Studdeman. He receives a nearly imperceptible nod. The senator turns back to me, wearing a broad smile. He sidles around to our side of the desk, puts his arms around both our shoulders, and leads us to the door.

"We'll announce the press conference immediately," he says. "But you keep Thomas away from those boys. I don't want him seen or talked to by anybody until Monday at eleven. You understand?"

I do. So Thomas and I walk out of the office and straight past the reception desk, heads held high, chins up. Jeannie flashes me a radiant smile along with a flirtatious wink, making me wonder if the senator's office is bugged.

CHAPTER 16

Once we escape Feldstone's office suite I turn to my companion.

"Thomas, we can't go home. Annie says the yard's packed with reporters again. Any suggestions?"

He has one. Thomas wants to take a tour. He wants to see the original manuscript of the Constitution, he wants to see the Declaration of Independence, and he wants to visit the National Museum of American History.

This is perfect—no reporter I know frequents any of those places. I hope I can find them. A day tour with Thomas has an additional benefit—it gives me another chance to flush out his views and push Feldstone's talking points.

We start with the American history museum since it'll consume the most time. Thomas is very excited. He wants to walk instead of drive, taking his pleasure in exercise and fresh air, much like two tourists on the hunt.

Thomas enters the museum as if treading on hallowed ground. He softens his voice to a whisper, and for a minute, there, I think he might take off his shoes. There are few people inside, highly unusual considering the time and season. Thomas walks quietly but proudly, wearing the expression of a six-year-old at Disneyland. Instead of going toward some of the inventions that made America great—the electric light, the automobile, the computer—he heads straight to the World War II exhibit. First Vietnam, now this—I think he must have a thing for war.

When I catch up to him he's reading blowups of various newspaper headlines from the 1940s: 30,000 casualties on Guadalcanal; 81,000 Americans killed/wounded/captured at the battle of Ardennes; 58,000 casualties on Okinawa; D-Day, Battle of Normandy, 209,000 Allies killed/wounded/captured. It goes and on and on. When he turns to me, tears fill his eyes, as they did at the Vietnam Memorial.

"Is this not the fight, Hartford? Are these not the heroes, the men and women, who truly serve their country?"

"You mean World War Two," I say.

"All of the wars since America's inception—all of the brave men and women who fought for our country, who fight for her today. Should they not be revered? There will be more."

"More what. Wars?"

He stares at me. "Iraq, Afghanistan, North Korea, Iran—always present are those who would do us harm, Hartford, those who would take away our freedoms."

"Now, Thomas, the only reason we're over there in the Middle East is for the oil—it's purely a money thing." I rub my thumb and forefinger together for effect, then wonder if he knows what that means. Like most, Thomas is overly patriotic and extremely naïve. I need only to set him straight.

"And yet," he says, "after liberating Kuwait and defeating Iraq, we have taken none of their oil and Afghanistan has no oil to take. Why would we spend this money," he mimics me by rubbing his thumb and forefinger together, "and forfeit the lives of our citizens for no gain?" He glares at me and I say nothing. "Are these battles not fought against those who would harm us and threaten our way of life? To protect our freedom, is this not why we fight? We should all be participants in such a fight, Hartford. Today, I fear this is not the case. Many of our countrymen are merely citizen observers who would relinquish our freedoms with but little thought. Others are anti-Americans who, as a thief, would steal our freedoms or allow them to be stolen. As our country vacillates, our government plays a game within itself. It pits its Democrats and its Republicans against one another in a game of power, each hoping to emerge the victor. You yourself play this game, Hartford. My dearest hope is that one day you, and others like you, will relinquish your childish play and join us in our fight."

Wow, these are by far the most words Thomas has spoken to me; maybe he does have the ability to give a proper speech. His jingoistic prattle, however, leaves me little room to segue into the senator's talking points. His passion makes my job near impossible. I might indeed need to pass him off to Feldstone.

We continue through the museum and Thomas does pay homage to the great inventors and the inventions that shaped the history of this country. We then walk through the Hall of Presidents. He seems to know a lot about our presidents. Some he reveres, some he discounts, and a few he disparages in no uncertain terms.

We eventually come to colonial America, which features our founding fathers and the Revolutionary War. Here we stay until it's time for us to go. This area of the museum is like a shrine in Thomas's eyes. He knows everything about everything. It disturbs me. He considers George Washington the greatest general and most cherished president we've ever had. I try to bring George down a notch by telling Thomas that the cherry tree/can't tell a lie story was a myth. He glares at me as if he's about to serve me up a slice of pummel pie. He launches into such an impassioned tirade I worry about the security guards hauling us off in handcuffs.

He goes on to explain that the cherry tree story was indeed a fabrication created by small minded men to illustrate the impeccable, lifelong veracity of a great man. And that George Washington was a man of honor and integrity his whole life long. He was incapable of being anything else. Our Congress did him and us a great disservice when they compromised his birthday, once a national holiday. How this could happen in America greatly upsets Thomas. He considers this one of the many grave errors our government has committed while turning this country in the wrong direction. Hearing his impassioned point of view makes me even more uneasy.

From the museum we walk over to the National Archives Building and head to the rotunda. Here lie The Charters of Freedom: The United States Constitution, The Bill of Rights, and The Declaration of Independence. All three documents are encapsulated, under glass, in special deterioration-proof cases. Thomas strides straight to the cabinet holding the constitution and is immediately disappointed. I guess he thought he was going to be able to pick up the document, page through it with his fingers, touching and feeling the words so meticulously laid out by James Madison. He walks over to the Bill of Rights and finds it similarly untouchable, so he goes back to the Constitution. He accepts the barriers with equanimity and stands perfectly erect, his head slightly bowed, reading every precious word before him.

When he's finished he moves to the Declaration of Independence. The parchment is significantly faded despite its encapsulation, but Thomas hardly seems to notice. He reads each word in reverence, and when he reaches the end, beckons me over.

"There, Hartford," he says pointing to the signees. I step closer and look down at the fifty-six signatures. "You understand," he continues, "that such men, such patriots, were declaring their independence from a country possessing the most powerful military in the world. To defy such an army was deemed, by most, as lunacy. Affixing their names to this document was akin to placing their heads in a noose and condemning their families to lives of squalor or worse. These patriots risked everything on a revolution which even they believed could not be won. Whomsoever serving our government today would do the same?"

I have no answer, so I remain silent.

"Whomsoever among our citizenry loves this country enough to do such a thing? I believe such people exist to this day, Hartford. I believe we must endeavor to seek out these citizens and bring them to bear. We have great need of such people."

He looks up at me with more tears. I begin to feel he's in danger of becoming a crybaby; still, none can deny Thomas's love of his country. I wonder if there are others like him. I work with all kinds—congressmen, senators, administration officials, staffers, advisers—and I have yet to meet one.

We step out of the Archives Building and into the cool, evening air, walking in silence toward the Russell Building. I don't see this as a good time to discuss the talking points, so I bring up the oversight hearings instead.

"Thomas, I thought I might go over some of the things you can expect at Friday's hearings."

"Certainly," he says, "if you feel it necessary."

"Senator Feldstone will be there, along with three other senators and four congressmen. Half of them will be Democrats and half will be Republicans. Their questions will be designed to determine your views, your leanings."

"Oh yes," he says, "much like the hearings held for Judge Eleanor Katzen in order to approve her for the Supreme Court. That went quite well."

He wears a smirk at the end.

"You're joking," I say. "You know about Judge Katzen?"

"Miss Anne and I followed the hearings quite closely on your television screen. It was most amusing."

"Amusing?"

"Yes, one group of senators, your Democrats, spent quite a lengthy time reminding the committee of all of Judge Katzen's splendid accomplishments and trusted that through her appointment there would follow many more. The other group, the Republicans, challenged these very accomplishments as errors in her judgment and remanded her with many criticisms and posed many specific questions which Judge Katzen chose to ignore. If the object of the hearings was to determine the views or, as you put it, the leanings of Judge Katzen, I believe the inquisitors failed in their task. Miss Anne and I knew no more about Judge Katzen after the hearings ended than we did before they began. I found it quite amusing. Is this what I am to expect, Hartford?"

I decide not to answer his question right away, and the silence seems not to bother him. I never feel in control when I'm with Thomas. It's always as if he's playing head games with me, which I find extremely troublesome, since I consider that my turf.

We enter the underground parking lot of the Russell Building and I spot the BMW forty feet away. I hit the unlock button on my remote and hear the click of the door lock. I motion for Thomas to get in and I do the same.

I start the car, gun the engine, and wheel out of the parking garage. Taking a sharp left on Independence, I accelerate to forty mph.

"Your hearing will be a lot different than Judge Katzen's," I say. "For one thing, it'll last only an hour or so—for another, no one will disparage your past accomplishments and achievements because no one knows what they are."

"Nor do I," he says.

"So they'll most likely dwell on your views and what you are planning to say in your speech." He nods but says nothing. "They'll bring up various issues—abortion rights, gay marriage, illegal immigration, even Judge Katzen and her hearings might come up. They'll want to know your thoughts on these subjects. They'll probably preview their questions with their own views, expecting you to agree with them. How you answer is up to you."

I'm surprised to hear this last come out of my mouth. I reach into my pocket and feel for my talking points list, then withdraw my hand.

"Will I be required to take a litmus test?"

"Litmus test?" I stare at him until I have to look back at the road.

"In Judge Katzen's hearing," he says, "there was much talk of a litmus test—how she must take one or how they couldn't force her to take one. I cannot help but wonder if I must take one."

I'm pretty sure he's messing with me again so I say, "You're not taking this very seriously, are you, Thomas."

"Hartford, you are the architect of my selection," he says with a straight face, "thus, I take such procedures much in earnest. A great honor has been bestowed upon me. I am to speak before the entire United States Congress and millions of Americans. If I take sport with you and some of your colleagues then please forgive me. Perhaps it serves to settle my nerves."

I again look over at him and for the first time today, he isn't smiling. Maybe he is taking this seriously, maybe he is nervous about his speech. Good—I mean, how could he not be? I slowly let out my breath. I'm sure Feldstone and his cohorts will ferret out the info they need from Thomas during the hearings and probably be able to add a number of talking points in the process. That should get me off of the hook, leaving the press conference as my last obstacle before the big dance. If I can get him through that in one piece we just might pull this thing off.

I ease into my driveway, hit the remote, and watch the garage door climb its tracks. I look over at Thomas, now laid back and smiling, as always. I don't think he's nervous at all.

Annie is happy to see us. She gives giant hugs to Thomas and me, in that order. She says that the reporters cleared out all at once just before five o'clock and that she was afraid someone had spotted us and had passed the word. She's glad to see us safe and sound. I tell her about Thomas's press conference on Monday and suggest the media probably went home to sharpen their beaks. She looks over at Thomas, concern covering her face. She walks over, puts her hand on his shoulder, and turns to me.

"Is he ready for them, Hartford? Can he do this?"

"He is and he can, right after he gets through the hearings on Friday."

"Hearings," she says. "I forgot about the hearings."

"He fields a few questions from Senate and House leaders, no sweat. The press should be a cinch."

"Hartford, Thomas is not a professional politician. He's a kindly, middle-aged man with amnesia. Those jackals will tear him to pieces. How could you let this happen?"

Thomas remains silent. His eyes dart back and forth between us like a young fan at a tennis match.

I stare at him. "You can jump in at any time."

He loses his wide-eyed look and smiles. "Miss Anne," he says, "Hartford has kindly spent the entire afternoon enlightening me on the deceptive ways of him and his government colleagues. I feel I am fully prepared to entertain all challenges."

She adopts a sympathetic half-smile, nods her head at him, then turns to me and whispers, "Those jackals are going to tear him to pieces."

I spend the rest of the day and into the evening not bolstering Thomas—who has retired early to watch the national news and, presumably, work on his speech—but reassuring Annie that he'll be fine. She and I also retire early. She tosses and tumbles all night and at one point wakes me up just to make me promise I'll take care of him no matter what. I think about her words as I attempt to reconnect with the Sandman, and suddenly I discover I'm no longer jealous of her bond with Thomas. I realize I've formed one of my own.

CHAPTER 17

I t's eight a.m. and Annie and I are in the kitchen, wondering about Thomas. I'm about to go up and check on him when I hear a creak on the stairs. He comes down, bleary-eyed, saying he had become engaged in a rather provocative news analyst program that had kept him up past midnight. Annie says nothing. She's acting uncharacteristically anxious, running around the kitchen cooking too much bacon, too many eggs, and enough toast for a small platoon. Neither Thomas nor I are very hungry, but we eat anyway out of gratitude or fear.

At 8:35 I say, "We have to go. The senator wants us in his office forty-five minutes prior to the hearing."

Annie stares at me for more while Thomas butters another piece of toast.

"He just wants to help Thomas feel at ease," I say, "to reassure him."

Annie doesn't accept the explanation, and why should she? It's not true—the senator wants to ensure Thomas has received his ten talking points and has dutifully inserted them into his speech. (The senator is going to be disappointed.)

We walk into Jeannie's reception area at exactly 9:10. Her expression is an inscrutable half smile, half squint. A casual toss of her head directs us toward Feldstone's office door, with no indication as to his mood. We enter chambers finding the senator wound tighter than a hangman's noose. He's on the phone, yelling at some poor intern who brought him his chocolate glaze doughnuts without the sprinkles. I take a deep breath, reach into my pocket, and pull out the talking points list. Thomas looks over at me and smiles. The senator suddenly stops talking and slams the phone down hard. He stares at us at length then motions us to sit.

"Damn terrible morning," he says, "damn terrible." He spots the sheet of paper in my right hand and his face immediately morphs into his meet-and-greet. "Ahhh," he says, "I see we're on the same page, Hartford—good, good."

"No," I say inverting his smile, "we're not."

He glares at me, then at Thomas, then back at me. He pauses a beat before starting his diatribe.

"Thomas has already completed his speech, Senator," I quickly insert.

"Well that's good," he looks at Thomas, "let me see it. I'll pass it along to Mike and Rosa so they can punch it up. I'm sure it's good but it can always be better." His smile is back.

Thomas remains mute so I say, "Thomas feels his speech should remain in his words only—it's a purity thing."

The senator's expression shows neither anger nor comprehension because the word "purity" isn't in his vocabulary.

"So," he says, ignoring me, "get me a copy and let's get this thing going."

"There is no copy, Senator, Thomas's speech is in his head."

Again, no comprehension, but his face starts to grimace, grow taught, and turn red, and I realize he's about to blow. I stand quickly and pull Thomas up with me.

"My god," I say, "look at the time—the hearing's in ten minutes, we'll barely make it." I turn Thomas around and bum-rush him through the door.

"We're not done here, Hart," Feldstone yells to my backside, "you hear me—we are not done!"

We make it to the hearing with three minutes to spare. Senator Feldstone is already there, complements of the Senate underground railroad, but it doesn't change his mood; he's as pissed as Pandora. We walk in to smiles and greetings from the other six most powerful men on the planet and the one most powerful woman. They're all over Thomas, as he has yet to utter a single word to any of them. I start to wonder if I'm going to have to play defense attorney and carry him through this entire ordeal. Maybe I can sit next to him, have him whisper his answers in my ear, and then interpret and relay the information to the committee as I see fit. Or I can just grab him by the shoulders and serve him up some slapping to bring him into focus. I'm getting paranoid. My plan goes moot when they sit Thomas in the chair of honor/inquisition and me way across the room in the chair of silent observation.

Thomas isn't facing a bevy of microphones because he doesn't need them—everyone's up close and in tight. The senators all sit on one side of a long, beautifully polished, mahogany table in eight plush leather chairs facing Thomas, who is placed in a straight-back wooden chair behind a small, square, pine table four feet away. Eight sets of pearly whites attempt to blind him—had I brought a camera, I wouldn't need a flash. But there are no cameras, no TVs, no press. This function is designed to be unrecorded, purely a he-says they-say event. I wonder if Annie is right. I wonder if these jackals are about to tear him to pieces.

Without warning, the lone woman in the group produces a gavel and raps it loudly on the tabletop.

"This hearing will now come to order," she says. The smiles and teeth all disappear as the congressmen study their notes, clear their throats, and prepare to posture.

Thomas swears to tell the truth, the whole truth, and nothing but the truth, God help him.

"Mr. Thomas," the chairman, Sheila Hardbauer Kennedy, says, "I would first like to thank you for coming here today and to reassure you that these hearings are merely a formality and not to be taken as a judgment or an interrogation. You have been selected to speak for all Americans, and therefore our goal here today is to challenge any extreme or out-of-the-mainstream viewpoints. Have you any questions before we—oh, uh, please excuse me."

A man in a three-piece suit with short blond hair and excellent posture enters the room and approaches the chairwoman. Though I'm stuck in the back corner, I can easily hear their conversation—everybody can.

"We're in the middle of a hearing," she says.

"I know that, ma'am. I'm sorry to interrupt, but I was told to personally hand you this report."

"Told by whom?" she says, taking the folder and flipping it open. Before he can answer she adds, "Oh yes, very good, thank you." She turns back toward Thomas with a smile. "Mr. Thomas, I need to confer with my colleagues before continuing. It will only take a minute."

Thomas, ever agreeable, smiles back.

After several minutes of huddled murmurs, whispers, and nods, the lady chairman turns back to Thomas absent her smile. I take this as a bad sign. She holds out a piece of paper and directs her stare at the guest of honor.

"This is the FBI vetting report, Mr. Thomas," she says. "It shows you have no arrests, no felonies, no outstanding warrants, no citations, no warnings of any kind. This section," she points to the bottom half of the paper, "shows there is no record of your schooling, employment, competence, achievements, marital status, or any kind of background at all."

She holds up her hand to stop Thomas from responding, which from his expression, is unnecessary.

"We know about your amnesia. We also know you are able to somehow recall your first name and have retained a memory of eighteenth-century American history. However, I honestly do not see how we can allow you to speak for the American people when we know so little about you."

"Senator Kennedy," it's Feldstone rising to his feet, "you do realize the event takes place one week from today."

"Well, yes, Senator, of course, perhaps we could propose a post-ponement and then reschedule after—"

"Madam Chairwoman," Feldstone takes an aggressive step in her direction, then stops abruptly, turns, and walks around the table to stand by Thomas. "May it please the committee, an inordinate amount of time and resources have already been expended on this event. Television feeds to our troops, stationed all over the world, have been put in place. Hundreds of millions of Americans have demanded an audience with their government through their chosen representative, Thomas, here." He puts a hand on his shoulder. "Newspapers, radio, and television have been touting this event since its inception—and you want to cancel it? Not because of some disqualifying skeleton found in his closet but because we are unable look into his closet. His background is somewhat murky, I'll admit, but that's no reason to disqualify him. We are here to uncover the content of his character, not the context of his life."

Feldstone raises up on the balls of his feet and peers at the chairwoman over the top of his glasses, as if he had some on.

"Well, here he is, sitting before us, eager to answer each and every question posed to him. I say we stop wasting his time and ours and start asking."

Feldstone smiles at Thomas, squeezes his shoulder, then turns and walks back to his seat. The chairwoman appears disconcerted. To kill a highly anticipated event with the pounding of her gavel would win her few friends and fewer votes. Incumbents are already in trouble. To stall this thing would be political suicide. She knows it, the committee knows it, and I know it. She sighs, then cleverly lays her gavel on the table in capitulation.

"Thank you, Senator. It is true we are all present, as is Thomas, to conduct a hearing. We would be remiss if we failed to do so in a proper and thorough manner. Senator Feldstone, would you like to begin?"

I note that we've been here an hour already and Thomas has yet to open his mouth. Senator Feldstone gets up and walks over to stand beside him again. He places his hand protectively on Thomas's shoulder.

"Thomas," he says, "how far back does your recent memory go?"

"To the third day of April in this year of our Lord, 2012."

"Is that the day you first met Hartford Keepe?"

"Yes, Senator, it is."

"And before that you remember nothing."

"I am aware," says Thomas, "of much American history during colonial times."

"Yes, yes, and we'll get to that, but I'm more concerned with recent events. Since April third have you learned much of current events?"

"Yes, Senator, I have been much intrigued with television news accounts, especially those pertaining to our government. I peruse several newspapers daily for information on political occurrences. Miss Anne and I discuss political dilemmas and their solutions each evening and oft times during the noon meal. I have learned much of Hartford's vocation, providing me uncommon insight into the seat of our government."

"I see, and the American people—what do you know of the American people?"

"I speak with many of my fellow Americans as I sell my t-shirts. I converse with tourists from every state in the union on a daily basis, all having come to delight in their nation's capital. Most evenings I must bid them leave much earlier than I would wish, since Archibald and I are required to close the shoppe prior to the fall of darkness."

"So it seems you have brought yourself up to date on current events and have enjoyed more contact with average American citizens, in the past three weeks, than my colleagues and I have had in the past year. Thank you, Thomas, I have nothing more."

He smiles broadly, pats Thomas on the back, and returns to his seat.

Nicely done. Feldstone has just soft-balled Thomas into a position of credibility, leaving his colleagues to launch hardball questions at their peril. The Honorable Congressman from Pennsylvania is next.

"Mr. Thomas," he says, "it must be very difficult for you to cope with your memory loss. I want you to know that each and every one of us on this committee feels your pain. If there is ever anything I or my staff can do to help you prepare for your address please do not hesitate to contact us."

And that's how it goes all the way down the line. There isn't a hardball in sight. There aren't more than a dozen actual questions put to Thomas, and those have more to do with his feelings than his views.

So, after a little over two hours of political posturing and feigned empathy, the hearings come to an end. Everyone is glad-handing one another as if their team has just won the Super Bowl and their star player, Thomas, has scored the winning touchdown. I'm sitting over in my little corner, wavering between amazement and disbelief.

I check my watch—one o'clock. Thomas and I need to get out of here; we need to grab some lunch and we need to celebrate. We've earned ourselves an entire weekend to prepare for the press conference. There won't be any softballs there. When it comes to reporters, "snarky" is in their job description; besides, they're mad. They've been kept in the dark for weeks—quite a feat in DC—so they want answers and they want them badly. If they can't get them through verbal demands, they'll likely try to beat them out of us. We've been extremely lucky so far. These hearings went far better than I could ever have dreamt. I expect the next event to be the press conference from hell.

Thomas and I still need to lay low. Piss-angry reporters are out there sniffing the air and scratching the ground and I don't want to run into any of them before Monday's press conference. So we travel offsite and find a Subway sandwich shop tucked into a strip mall a mile and a half north of the White House. We no sooner land in a corner booth, laden with subs and drinks, than my cell goes off.

It's Jeannie wanting us there, now. I tell her we're sitting down to lunch.

"Hartford!" Feldstone comes on the line loud and gruff.

I pull the phone away and mouth an "oh crap." I figure he's going to push me on the talking points.

"Hartford, are you there? Can you hear me?"

I put the phone back to my ear. "Yes, Senator, very clearly, Thomas and I—"

"How'd you like the show?"

I pause. "Fine, terrific, great setup, Senator."

"That b-i-t-c-h was about to pull the plug—you believe that?"

I smile—this isn't about talking points, this is about performance. He's looking for applause.

"Yes, she was, Senator. Had it not been for you she may well have gotten away with it."

"Ain't that the truth, and we'd have all been up s-h-i-t creek."

"Senator, I have to say, I thought you were brilliant. Not only did you cut her legs out from under her, you put Thomas up there on a pedestal where nobody could touch him."

"Nobody even tried," he says and chuckles. "Is he with you now?"

"Yes, sir, we're just sitting down to lunch. I thought I'd brief him on what to expect from the media on Monday."

"They're burning up, Hart. They're out for blood. Can he handle it?"

I look over at Thomas. He's stuffing a foot-long pepperoni sub into his mouth and has two bags of chips and a large Coke waiting in line. I'm not at all sure what he can do.

"He can handle it," I say.

"Good, good, you stay close, Hart. This press conference is gonna be all over the news. We need our boy to shine."

He hangs up. I glance at Thomas devouring the last of the chips and washing them down with a biggie-sized Coke—not a care in the world, this one. I can't stop Annie's words about *jackals tearing him apart* from echoing in my head.

CHAPTER 18

Monday morning comes early, with Thomas, Annie, and I sitting around the table helping ourselves to a hearty breakfast of oatmeal, scrambled eggs, raisin toast, and slightly burned turkey bacon. Annie's quizzing Thomas on current events, specifically the latest Labor Relations Board power grab and those free-enterprise-loving Americans still bold enough to stand up to it. I'm sitting here trying to figure out why our butts weren't consumed by the flame.

The weekend started out badly. Ignoring my admonitions, Thomas had stubbornly gone to work anyway. Feldstone found out about it and threatened to get rid of me—not fire me, *get rid of* me. And late Friday night I caught Niles cleaning out my cubicle in preparation for his promotion. By Saturday morning I had a blanket of trouble wrapped around me so tight I couldn't move, wiggle or breathe.

I felt sure reporters were on their way to Thomas's kiosk to corner him, brand him, and make him squeal. With his forthright manner they would easily uncover his amnesia problem and his lack of any background to be probed and would then go about destroying his credibility before he ever had a chance to gain any. The Monday morning Times would show Thomas looking ridiculous in his short breeches and three-cornered hat while the headline read,

"Man Chosen For LTA Event Doesn't Know His Last Name." The project and my career seemed set on a fast track to oblivion.

But this is Washington, D.C., where pitfalls and bailouts go hand in hand. Our deliverance came from Tony W. Skinner, a three-term House member representing the great state of New Jersey. Tony decided Saturday afternoon the perfect time to get caught soliciting young girls on the internet with naked photos of his aging body. His blunder guaranteed reporters and camera crews camped outside his condo on the corner of third and fifth or stalking the halls of the Rayburn House Office Building all weekend. The press had not come anywhere near Thomas's and Archie's t-shirt kiosk.

The scandal should also ensure minimal coverage at today's press conference, meaning fewer gotcha questions and less hostility. I doubt the story's legs are long enough to reach into Thomas's big speech on Friday.

I abruptly slide my chair back and stand up. Annie and Thomas, still quizzing, hardly notice.

"I need to get to work," I say. "I have to tie up some loose ends before the press conference. Thomas, I'll pick you up at two. Annie—"

"I'll drive my car," she says. "I'll meet you there."

Annie doesn't do well with backstage waiting and anticipation—she gets nervous. She likes to appear at an event just as it's about to begin. Sometimes she doesn't show up at all. No chance she'll miss this one, though; her Thomas is performing.

I drive away thinking about the real reason I have to go in—to reassure Feldstone that Thomas can handle the press. I also want to check out the venue and get a feel for turnout, media and otherwise. Thomas has the day off, so no worries there. He'll be content sitting with Annie, studying his current events, all the way up to press-time.

I don't arrive back at the condo until after three. They're both in the driveway waiting for me. Thomas seems ready, wearing his khakis, a new blue blazer, and his eternal smile while Annie seems overly anxious. I pull in, get out of the car, walk over, and hook my arm through Thomas's elbow.

"You look good," I say.

"You take care of him, Hartford," Annie says, hooked in from the other side.

"I will." I start to move out but Thomas doesn't budge because Annie won't release his arm. "He'll be fine, Annie, he can do this. It's his destiny, remember?" Not that I'm buying into that, I just don't want a tug-of-war.

After a long hug, she releases him and we get into the car. I glance at my watch—we'll be on time but we're cutting it close. The conference is to be held on the front steps of the Capitol Building, so I opt to approach from the rear, avoiding the crowd should there be one. I pull into the space reserved for the guest of honor and begin to prepare myself for the circus ahead. I look over at Thomas: he looks ready. I catch my reflection in the mirror: I look ready. We step out of the car, the picture of confidence, and enter the building from the rear.

We're walking through the great hall, halfway to the front door, when Niles comes sprinting toward us. He's gesticulating in fast-forward, elbows and hands all askew, words erupting in unintelligible babble.

"Niles," I reach out and put a hand on his shoulder to quell the bounce, "calm it, man, calm it."

He downshifts to hyper and says, "There's gotta be five hundred of them out there, Hart—they've been there for hours."

"Five hundred what—tourists?"

"Media, Hart, media—reporters, camera crews—maybe a thousand by now." He tries to catch his breath. "Tourists, too. Onlookers, protesters, Tea Party people, what have you—there's got to be another two thousand of those."

Niles is panting so hard I take a step back. That's crazy—there aren't a thousand media types in the entire city. I start walking toward the front entrance then stop and look back at Niles.

"Do they know we're here?"

He's bent over with his hands on his knees trying to catch his breath. "No," he says through his shallow panting, "they think you're driving in from Independence—They're watching for you, though, they know your car."

"Good." I walk up to one of the front windows, part a curtain, and peer out. "My God!" I say it in a whisper, but Thomas hears me because he's right behind me.

There's a podium about halfway down the marble stairs, with at least a hundred microphones attached in helter-skelter fashion as if somebody had gotten hold of a ten-year-old's erector set. Cameras and cameramen are everywhere, checking equipment, angling for position, dueling with the sun's glare. On the bottom landing are more reporters and anchors than I've ever seen—four or five times the number camped on my lawn. And then, as Niles had said, an absolute mob of onlookers. A few signs are being bandied about, but not many. This isn't your typical activist crowd. I put the number of non-media types at three thousand and spot maybe eight to ten cops.

"This is a bad," I say, shaking my head. "We're not ready for this."

"Yes you are. You have to be." Niles rushes up to me, putting his face an inch from mine and pointing his finger at Thomas. "He has to be, too."

I look at Thomas. He's calm, unfazed, peering out the window I just left. He finally closes the curtain, turns to me, and says, "Hartford, we must gird our loins."

I stare at him a few seconds. "Thomas, are you being funny?"

"I do hope as much," he says.

I laugh and so does Niles, although I think he's just mimicking me. Still, it eases our apprehension. There's nothing I can do or say at this point to make things easier on Thomas, or me, so I put my right hand on his shoulder sweep my left hand forward and say, "Shall we?"

He nods and we march through the center door, out onto the landing, and toward the podium, together.

It takes a few seconds for the crowd to recognize him, so by the time they do we're already at the top of the stairs and starting down. Someone shouts Thomas's name and the whole place turns to bedlam.

The entire reporter brigade, armed with portable mics, cameras and cameramen surge toward us. We have to stop short or risk injury. We're immediately surrounded by a gang of loudmouthed reporters mercilessly pelting us with unintelligible questions. Even if Thomas or I wanted to respond no one would hear us, so we stand and take the verbal assault until their voices run hoarse.

The cops seize the lull to spring into action with equal parts persuasion and intimidation, herding the media back down the stairs and into their stalls. A pair of park police then escort Thomas and me safely to the podium. We stand there while a few diehards continue to shout questions and demand answers. When Thomas fails to respond they eventually go quiet. A strange silence envelops the arena. It's quite extraordinary—five thousand people waiting silently for Thomas to speak. I look over at him, wondering if I should make an introduction or offer an explanation, since no one in the press knows of Thomas's amnesia. But after studying the calm, cool, collected little man beside me, I see no need.

Thomas steps boldly to the podium. He looks out over the crowd and in a firm, steady voice says, "Hello, my name is Thomas."

All but the press, immediately break into deafening applause. I look at Niles, he looks at me, and our expressions say, "What the hell?"

Thomas has to wait a full five minutes for the hand-clapping to end. During that time he neither backs away from the podium nor looks to me for help.

When the noise abates he says, "Before I respond to your queries, I feel I must reveal something of myself of which you are unaware."

The crowd goes pin-drop quiet.

"I came to your fair city these two months past, on the third day of April, in the year of our Lord 2012. I do not know in what manner I arrived, nor from where I have come. I do not know my surname, my marriage status, my previous occupation, nor my date of birth. I know nothing of my life preceding my arrival here in our nation's capital. I have contracted an ailment known as amnesia. Much of what I know of our government, its politics, and its history, I have learned in these two months past. There is but one peculiarity to my affliction. I have managed to retain a strong knowledge of this country's founding and its early struggle for independence. The doctors purport this aberration to be not without precedent."

The media continues with their silence though Thomas has stopped speaking. The pause is short-lived. Before he can ask for questions they fire forth, non-stop, in quantity and volume. Thomas stands erect both smiling and mute. Once the reporters catch on, they back down to a low simmer.

"It is quite impossible," he says, "for me to respond to more than one query at a time. For assistance I would ask my friend Hartford Keepe to come forward."

I step to the podium and receive a bright smile from Thomas but no applause from the crowd. He turns to his audience.

"Please register your questions by signal of hands. I would ask Hartford to select each querier in turn while I attempt to respond in kind."

I can tell by their expressions that Thomas's overly formal way of speaking leaves the press confused and skeptical. They're trying to figure out if he's putting them on or if he actually talks this way. They're not worried. They assume their impending interrogation will easily ferret out the real Thomas and hold him to account.

I scan the crowd and spot Randy Lawson from CBS, a fairly reasonable guy, so I point to him and hope for the best.

"Thomas," he says, "Randy Lawson, here, CBS. Why the flip-flop—why did you decline the LTA offer and then turn around and accept it?"

I look around at the other the reporters, they're all smiling, some licking their lips. I look over at Thomas—he looks tentative.

"I cannot possibly speak for the whole of the American people. For this reason I declined the gracious offer to do so. Subsequently, I found myself in conversation with a member of the grounds maintenance service, a Mr. Whitfield, here in this very park. He posed to me a query which prompted my reconsideration."

Thomas falls silent and steps back as if the question has been fully answered.

Someone from the crowd yells, "What query?"

Thomas looks surprised. He scans the faces trying to spot the questioner but can't, so he steps back up to the podium and says, "Mr. Whitfield asked me whether I loved my country."

The questioner, a citizen not a reporter, steps from the crowd and shows himself. "And what did you say, Thomas?"

"I said, 'More than words can express.'" The man stands his ground obviously wanting more so Thomas continues, "Mr. Whitfield then said to me, 'Then speak for those Americans—speak for the people who truly love their country.'" Thomas stands more erect and perhaps a bit taller and says, "This I believe I can do."

Instantaneous applause pours forth from the onlookers but not from the media. As the noise dies, hundreds of hands shoot into the air. I pass over CNBC, MSNBC, and ABC, and choose Digby Buckingham of Fox News. Though too much of a Republican, Digby's not a gotcha guy and I love his English accent.

"Good afternoon, Thomas," he says. "Digby Buckingham. I would have you clarify something for me, please. Are we to understand that your current memory retention encompasses only the past two months, and other than some knowledge of colonial history, you have no memory at all?"

"That is correct, sir."

"Then please tell us how, with such a formidable obstacle in your path, you can possibly speak for the American people, love of country or not."

Crowd displeasure begins to escalate but before it can get a foothold, Thomas says, "Perhaps I cannot." He pauses only seconds and then, "it is true, I have come to this country almost as an immigrant to newly discovered shores. And though in my heart resides a great love for this nation, and in my memory resides a most vivid recollection of its beginnings, my mind has had but two months to observe and to learn—an odd affliction indeed. Because of my condition, some may pronounce me quite unfit for the task at hand," he pauses and smiles, "while others, due to this very malady, may consider me a most perfect choice."

Wild, raucous applause fills the air. Again it comes, not from the media, but from the three thousand onlookers. It continues with whistles and shouts and then morphs into a mantra, starting low and finding strength—"*We want Thomas, we want Thomas.*" It lasts several minutes then ends in more applause. Thomas remains behind the podium, standing at attention and smiling broadly at his audience. Once the noise diminishes he continues.

"I have spoken to many fine Americans. Possibly to some of those gathered here today. We have exchanged views of America as she was in times past and as she is at present. We have discovered our differences as well as our agreements. On two items we have forged an unbreakable bond: we love our country and we expect our government to do right by her. That road, I believe, is not the one on which we travel at present."

The crowd erupts again, louder and longer, breaking into their "we want Thomas" mantra. I look at the press—they're agitated. Perhaps they see the makings of a new political rock star and aren't sure they approve. But more likely they see a man who can win over the people, a man who has just boldly criticized a left-leaning government and drawn applause. They're probably out there analyzing the situation and putting together their strategy. A guy with only two months of memory in his brain can't be very smart or very savvy. A man of the people, to be sure, but not smart and not savvy. If he was a woman he'd be Sarah Palin—they have no choice but to tear him apart.

I look at my watch—we still have forty-five minutes to go. Madelyn Crosby suddenly takes three steps toward the podium, her arm wildly thrusting into the air, her girth dominating the yard. The cameras are rolling so I have no choice but to point to her.

"Madelyn Crosby," she says, "MSNBC news." She's managed to acquire her own microphone so her shrill, amplified voice irritates everyone at once, quickly shutting down random murmurs. The crowd turns toward her, anticipating act two.

"Mr. Thomas," she says, "you are a most impressive speaker."

She pauses long enough for a, "Thank you, madam."

"I was wondering if we of the press are to receive advance copies of your speech?"

"No, madam," Thomas says.

Her demeanor shows that she expects this and just wants it on record.

"I hope you realize, Mr. Thomas, that this is quite unorthodox. Normally a speech of this magnitude would be distributed to the media beforehand."

Not true, but Thomas probably doesn't know that. She waits at length for him to respond. The other reporters want badly to jump in but they will their hands to their sides, enjoying the cat-and-mouse.

"No, madam," Thomas says, "of this I am unaware, however I have nothing to distribute. My speech, alas, has not been penned to parchment."

An audible gasp shakes the air. I look at Madeline's face and watch a nasty grin take shape. Apparently, she's about to hook that which she's been fishing for.

"You'll be using a Teleprompter, then," she says.

Suddenly I know where this is going—where else? Credibility, or the lack thereof. Thomas has been part of the modern world for less than two months. How could he possibly put together a speech of this magnitude in two weeks time and how could he hope to deliver it without the aide of a teleprompter. Madelyn wants her revelations to knock a dent or two into Thomas's white knight image and maybe blow a few holes through his independent, man-of-the-people, persona. I shift my gaze to Thomas. He's smiling back at Madeline, but without the nasty.

"I am unfamiliar with this term 'Teleprompter,'" he says. "My speech is not laid to parchment because it comes from here," he touches his head, "and from here," he touches his heart.

"Did Senator Felstone and Hartford Keepe write your speech for you, Thomas?" Madelyn yells. "Is it laced with Democratic talking points, Thomas?

"No, madam."

"Then," she says, "it must be an awfully short speech with mighty little substance. What could you possibly have to say to the United States Congress, the American president, or to the American people that would be of any consequence whatsoever?"

A collection of boos emanate from the onlookers and even from a few media types who feel the man deserves a chance. Her outburst has its effect. People don't like their illusions shattered.

A hundred new hands immediately go up and I point to one. A man steps forward while I'm looking at Thomas and feeling better than I thought I would. We have thirty minutes to go and this bunch is so busy trying to back Thomas into a corner on personal matters that no one has thought to ask him about current events. I want to keep that string going.

I look down at the man I've selected and—oops—in my haste I've mistakenly pointed to the snarkiest of all gotcha reporters, Gruden Franks. On closer inspection I realize I didn't select Gruden, I pointed at Jeremy Lister standing next door. Crude Grude took Lister's turn by stepping in front of him and claiming the stage. In addition, someone's armed him with a microphone, probably Madelyn.

"Gruden Franks from ABC," he says. "We have a southwestern state that shares its border with Mexico. Our government is suing said state, correctly I believe, over its recently passed, racially charged immigration law. Would you share your knowledge and opinion on this matter?"

Terrific, right into the bowels of current event insolubility. I wonder if Thomas knows of Arizona or even where it's located. I stare at him. He looks confused.

"Mr. Franks," he says. "I know not the content of the Arizona law. I do know that we are a country of laws, and, unlike King George III, who could proclaim, at will, any directive on any citizen he so desired, our laws pertain equally to all. I also know that the states of this great union were proclaimed, in the Constitution, to be sovereign so long as they don't infringe on federal law. If this be the case, the federal government oversteps its bounds. This is not what our founding fathers had in mind."

Another boisterous applause rings forth from the onlookers. I almost clap along with them but then remember I work for a Democrat. I stare at Thomas. Maybe they won't tear him to pieces. Maybe they can't. I blithely point to Ruben Claxton of CNN—I'm getting cocky.

"Thomas, Ruben Claxton, here, CNN. How do we solve our debt crisis?"

What kind of question is that? The man's not running for president. He's speaking for the American people.

"This situation is quite perplexing to me," Thomas says. "The people have little employment and so they can pay but few taxes. The government has little money yet it spends as if it has much. If this predicament is not reversed how can the end result be anything other than disastrous?"

"Reverse it how?" demands Claxton.

"Why, stop spending the people's money and reduce taxation." He doesn't say *Duh,* but I think he wants to.

"And how would you propose we pay for such tax cuts?"

"I do not understand."

"How would the government make up for its loss of income?"

Thomas stands in silence, perplexed. Suddenly a smile finds his face and he actually chuckles. "I believe I do understand," he says. "When the people find themselves in financial difficulty they must tighten their belts and exist on less. Should not the United States

Government be required to do the same? Must government ever expand, year after year, in feast and in famine? No citizen nor private enterprise can operate in such a manner. Was not our government formed to serve the people? A government which exists on excessive debt and borrowing does quite the opposite, does it not? It was never meant to be this way."

Applause after applause, in standing ovation, defines the conference as current events take center stage and by its light does Thomas shine.

I feel the vibration of my Blackberry and realize it's twelve o'clock and our time's up. I'm about to call it when Thomas points to the next questioner. It's Forrest Gladden from the New York Times. The man's relatively honest but highly ideological. I wouldn't have chosen him, because he's more likely than anyone to turn the conference uncomfortable. Thus far, things have gone rather smoothly. I really don't want to end it on a sour note. I slide over behind the microphones and say, "Ladies and gentlemen, Mr. Gladden will be our last questioner."

"Thomas," Gladden says, "present day America operates on a two party system, Democratic and Republican. Third parties come into existence now and again—The Libertarian Party and The Green Party to name two. And then there are activist organizations who rear their heads from time to time—Occupy Wall Street, Evangelicals, the global warming crowd. Since you lack all memory of any allegiances or affiliations you may have had in the past, can you tell us which party or organization you might be inclined to join today?"

Well there it is. Tossed right out into the center ring for all to see. Thank you Forrest. No matter which way Thomas goes, he's about to alienate half of the country—more if he chooses a fringe group. I desperately want to charge up to the microphone and call time but I'm pretty sure I won't get away with it so I cross my fingers and hold my breath instead.

Thomas appears pensive but doesn't lose his smile.

"Your Democratic Party enjoys spending the peoples money recklessly in the name of the poor and the unfortunate. Your Republican Party enjoys spending the peoples money recklessly in the name of protecting American interests throughout the world. I would imagine most third parties and activist groups would have their own ways of squandering the peoples money.

My party of choice would be one which would not spend the peoples money recklessly but would allow we the people to spend our money as we so choose."

Thomas steps back from the microphone and I let out my breath. Okay, that works. I think we're good.

"Have you a party or organization in mind, sir?" Says Gladden. *Damn.*

Thomas briefly hesitates, then steps forward and leans in.

"In my recollection, our founding fathers had great affinity for a group called The Sons of Liberty. These men, along with other likeminded souls, participated in a tea party on December 16, 1773 to dishonor King George the Third whom, they felt, abused the tax system of their time. I believe there exists today an organization called The Tea Party whose members strive to stem the taxation and overspending of our present day government. If this be so, then it is to this organization I would wish to affiliate."

The crowd goes wild, whistling, clapping, shouting, obviously dominated by Tea Party people. I look at Gladden. He's not happy. I look at the media. They're not happy. I should have called time.

CHAPTER 19

t's over—that's all I could think. *It's over*. Thomas is standing there basking in the limelight, surrounded by his well-wishers—hell, his idolizers, worshipers. The media, save a dozen or so, have gone away to write their stories, meet their deadlines, and lick their wounds. By six o'clock tonight this thing'll be all over the airwaves, and by tomorrow morning it'll be dominating the front pages of every newspaper in the country. Something big has happened here today and only time will tell how big. If I were a betting man, and I am, I'd say we've created a phenomenon—a phenomenal man of the people.

By the time I break Thomas loose from his groupies and hustle him back through the Capitol building and into the car, it's after two. I start the engine, pause before hitting the accelerator, and look over at him.

"Annie's gonna love this," I say.

"Ms. Anne was not present?" he says, surprised.

"She's funny that way. She gets anxious, not for herself, for those she loves. She doesn't want to see them fail."

I pull out of the parking garage and onto Independence. It takes longer than I figure, lots of starts and stops, trying to maneuver around an animated and slowly dispersing crowd. Thomas has been silent the whole time. I look over and see him rubbing his eyes trying to stop tears from rolling down his cheeks. What is it with this guy?

"Thomas?"

He holds up his hand, and shakes his head.

Finally he says, "My apologies, Hartford, you must think me overly sentimental."

"Nah." He's worse than every woman I've ever known.

"It is most probably the release of tension brought on by the completion of the press conference," he tries.

I nod my head, knowing full well that's not it. He knows and I know it's that bit about Annie and the people she loves. I still don't see the crying. He has to know she loves him. Everybody loves him—hell, I love him.

"Thomas, have you ever considered going into politics?"

"In what manner, Hartford?"

"I don't know—president?"

We both laugh—me longer than him.

"Hartford, I must now ask you to kindly transport me to the shoppe and drop me." *Drop me*, this is new. Thomas is trying on some present-day lingo. "I must confer with Archibald," he continues, "who has graciously attended the shoppe, alone, these two days past, proving me quite remiss in my duties."

Here's a guy about to give an address to the entire nation in less than a week, a man who probably could be president one day, and he's worried about his t-shirts. It occurs to me this may be the reason he could be president one day.

I turn down Washington toward the t-shirt shop. I find myself staring at him again. It makes him uncomfortable. I don't know if it's the staring or my lack of focus on the road. I look ahead and say, "Thomas, do you even know how good you were today?"

"I believe the people thought me affable, while the Free Press found me objectionable."

Well that's true. Even though the people loved him, the press, for the most part, will go negative on him because of his Tea Party remark. Though the whole thing was extensively filmed, I'm sure the selectively edited, thirty-second soundbites will dwell on that. It's shameful and it's unfair. Here's Thomas about to make this momentous speech on Friday night and most of those watching will, because of a liberal, main stream press, tune in holding unfavorable attitudes. Thomas will have to overcome indoctrinated ideology just to break even. It's not right. Our press might be free but they're far from objective.

"There is Archibald," Thomas says, pointing in the direction of the kiosk.

I pull over to the curb and he gets out. Archie's sitting on a bench, bent over, his head in his hands, his body shaking as if he's crying. He's not. As Thomas approaches, Archie looks up with a big smile covering his face. I step out of the car and start across the lawn while I watch the two of them embrace like long-lost brothers. By the time I arrive, Archie's pulling the canvas back from the kiosk revealing completely empty shelves.

"All gone—sold out by noon," he's saying, "nothing left."

"That was before the press conference," I say.

"I know, I know, what's up with that? I'll bet I turned down a thousand—no, two thousand people."

Thomas just stands there and smiles; shocked, I guess. I know I am.

"They'll be back," Archie says. "All those who got here late. They said they'd be back tomorrow. I put in an order at noon and then decided to doubled it an hour later. Davis said they'd have the shirts printed by six this evening. He said if we need more that they'd work all night if they had to."

Thomas looks over at me, then says something to Archie in a whisper.

"All taken care of," Archie says.

"So, how many shirts did you sell today?" I ask.

"Fifteen hundred, maybe more; I'll have to check the receipts."

"Impressive."

"Yeah, it's been a gold mine." Archie can't keep the grin off his face.

"So what are they buying?"

Archie glances over at Thomas who, I swear, is blushing. "They're buying the Minuteman T's," he says. "They love the quotes, and the Minuteman logo has become a status symbol of sorts—we're like the Polo of political wear. It's all I'm ordering."

"Archibald," Thomas says, "I am ready to attend to my duties. Please forgive me for my absence."

"'Attend to your duties?'" I say. "You do realize today is Monday and that your speech is on Friday."

"I do, indeed. This is why I must toil when I am able."

"You can't toil tonight, you can't toil tomorrow or the next day."

"Can I not?"

"No, you have to prepare, you have to rehearse, to get ready. What would people think if they found out you were out here selling t-shirts?"

"They would think me gainfully employed and performing my duties, Hartford."

"They would think you insane. You're the celebrity of the year, the decade, the century. You don't need to be selling t-shirts. You need to be preparing for your speech."

"Am I thus to be compensated for my speech then, Hartford?"

"No, not in money."

"I am indebted to you and Miss Anne for my sustenance and my shelter, Hartford, therefore I must toil to earn my keep, as must we all."

"You'll be mobbed by reporters if they find you."

"Then you must alert no one to my whereabouts."

He's right, no reporter in the district will expect him to be at work. This is the last place they'd look. Still, I'm aghast. While everyone in the country is anticipating the most momentous speech ever undertaken, Thomas will be out here selling his t-shirts.

"Okay," I say, "but I'll be off—I've got preparations to make even if you don't. You're sure you want to stay and toil?"

"I must. We must secure the shop and then journey into town to replenish our supply. Our shelves, as you can see, are quite bare."

"Today," I say. "It has to be done today."

"Indeed, our new t-shirts are being freshly printed even now. We must recover them and in addition we must deliver a sampling of t-shirts to the auditorium."

"Auditorium?"

"Yes, Hartford, it seems Archibald is determined to expand our already thriving t-shirt enterprise. We will display our shirts at a show-of-trade where proprietors of shops from all over the nation come to select their merchandise. We very much hope they will choose from our Minuteman designs."

I look at Archie who shrugs and smiles. I smile back wondering when Thomas's speech goes south because he refuses to prepare and therefore gets me fired, if I might join their t-shirt empire.

I'm anxious to check on the fall out from the press conference so as soon as I reach the office I head straight to the conference room and turn on the TV. I flick to channel twenty-one, MSNBC, for the worst case scenario. I'm greeted by host Chuck Mathison's smiling face. Chuck usually reserves his bristling sarcasm for all things Republican but right now he has it aimed at Thomas.

"This was certainly a press conference for our times," he's saying. "Senator Feldstone's mystery man has finally been turned loose to parry with the media on pressing issues of the day. And with the match over and the results in, we're all eagerly asking ourselves the same question—what have we learned?"

Chuck laughs and then answers.

"Well for starters we've learned that the man chosen to speak before the entire country has no memory. That's rights, folks, he has amnesia. Oh, yes, the citizens in attendance seemed to like him well enough but tell me Senator Feldstone, if you're tuned in, what exactly can a man with no memory possibly have to say that's worth listening to? Does anyone else out there see something wrong with this picture?"

Actually, I expect this from Chuck. He always sees the glass half empty and insists his guests prove it's half full.

I switch over to NBC.

Patti Rutherford Rhodes is on with anchor Dan Callahan. Patti's a second term Democrat recently appointed, by the party, as character and policy assassin. Her job is to carve up Republican ideas and viewpoints as well as the members who come up with them. She's very good at her job. If Thomas proves himself too far outside the Democrat bubble, Patti's the one who'll point out his Achilles heel. I turn up the volume.

"I believe there's little doubt as to Thomas's affiliation," she's saying. "He's a Tea Partier through and through. Which is to say, he's a racist, he hates women, he wants to see the poor starve and the rich get richer and he wants our government to fail. I really don't know what Senator Feldstone was thinking."

"Whoa, Patti, that's a tad harsh don't you think."

"I'm just getting started, Chuck. This Thomas is a danger to us all, he's going to..."

I change the channel.

I can only handle Patti in small doses and I'm over my limit. I land on ABC where Host Roger Balcomb is questioning his guest.

"It seems we're starting to hear negative feedback from your own party, senator. Are you at all concerned about your choice of Thomas as the voice of the people?"

The camera pans to Senator Feldstone who chuckles then lights up the room with his Cheshire Cat smile.

"Not at all, Roger. Thomas was not my choice. He was a bi-partisan choice—the choice of congress and the people. We are honored to be working hand in hand with the republicans on a matter of such significance. I felt he handled himself magnificently in front of the press. I believe President Mays himself may even be a tad jealous." More chuckles followed by the smile.

"But his Tea Party remark, Senator. Does that not concern you?"

"Roger, Thomas has a limited memory capacity as you are aware. When he speaks of Tea Parties, he's talking about dumping

British tea into the ocean back in 1773. When you get to know Thomas as I do, you'll find him kind, affable, and well reasoned. A man who wants nothing more than what's best for this country. I believe that's what we all want isn't it Roger?"

"Senator, I wonder if I can entice you to come back on the program following Thomas's LTA speech for some follow up remarks?"

"Nothing would make me happier, Roger, I look forward to it. Meanwhile I believe we're in for a heck of a treat Friday night when Thomas gives his address before the nation."

I'm still holding onto the handful of hair I was prepared to tear out. The senator does this to me all the time—gets himself booked on a network news show without letting anyone know. I've scolded him for it but so far it hasn't taken. What are you gonna do—he's the senator. This time, however, he's done us no harm and possibly some good. He may have singlehandedly stemmed the rising tide of negative punditry. I think I'm proud of him.

I stare at the screen and slowly shake my head. I realize there's not a whole lot we can do about Chuck Mathison but the party powerful can sure as hell put a muzzle on Patti Rutherford Rhodes.

CHAPTER 20

I t's five thirty and I'm awake a full hour before my alarm is set to irritate me. I've been doing the twisted bedsheet, covers off, covers on, dance all night. Thomas wasn't home by the time I was ready for bed, so Annie offered to wait up for him. I reach over and touch the slumbering, sexy body next to me, which means Thomas made it home safely. Still, I'm antsy, so I get up and find the bathroom. I turn on the shower full blast and relieve myself while the water gets hot. Before stepping in, I turn it down a notch to avoid blistering. It takes a few moments for my skin to adjust to the heat, but once it does I stand limp under the spray, letting it warm my body and wake my mind. I soap up and rinse off, then do it a second and a third time; just to buy more time in my hydro-incubator. After twenty minutes and close to pruning, I step out of the shower and begin to dry off.

Maybe Thomas is right. Maybe working his t-shirts is the best course of action. It'll certainly keep him busy and perhaps deter his mind from succumbing to the stress and pressures that are on their way. Reporters and investigators are already pounding me and Feldstone nonstop, but we're pros and can probably handle it. Though our boy has proven himself thus far, we still have four days to go. Keeping him under wraps until then is by far the safest route. Not only will it eliminate gaffs and blunders, it'll heighten anticipation, much like the emotional build-up before an intentionally delayed rock concert. By Friday, DC will resemble a powder keg set to blow. I look in the mirror and begin to dry my hair.

I'm still not comfortable with Thomas's speech preparation routine, because there isn't one. He acts as if there isn't a speech. I've pretty much given up on the talking points ploy but would very much like to know what he plans to say. He's so damn close to the vest. I wonder if he knows my career hangs in the balance.

I turn off the bathroom light and creep back into the bedroom, fumbling for my workout sweats. I figure to go downstairs, brew up some coffee, and wait for the dawn. I dress carefully, managing to exit the bedroom without waking Annie, a mighty feat in itself. I tiptoe down the hall and consider checking in on Thomas, to see if he really did make it home, but nix the idea when I stumble and nearly fall on my face. It's too dark up here, I need light. I notice the glow from below and I head down the stairs.

Thomas is sitting at the pre-breakfast table nursing a tall, cold glass of milk. He must have heard me coming because he says, "Good morning, Hartford," before I step into the light. I good morning him back and head straight for the coffee machine. I'm not so much sleepy as in need of caffeine. The coffee maker is usually hot and bubbly and filling the room with aromatic smells by the time I get this far, but Annie's still sleeping and the machine isn't even plugged in.

"What time did you get in?" I mumble, trying to remember how to work the thing.

"Quite late, Hartford. It was well past eleven thirty. I had a most interesting day."

He looks at me as if I want to hear about it. Since I'm incapable of making conversation at this hour, I give him the stage.

Thomas gets up and wipes the slight milk mustache from his upper lip. He comes over, stands next to me, and says, "I have never before attended a show-of-trade, Hartford. Do you know of such shows?

"No," I say, trying to insert the new filter right side up.

"The auditorium was filled with numerous booths of all descriptions and sizes, Hartford. Every imaginable gift item was on display. It was an entrepreneurial paradise. Archibald and I were to deliver three boxes of Minuteman t-shirts to booth number four eighty-two in care of Ralph and Ida Watson. Mr. and Mrs. Watson had performed a most wonderful feat in setting up lights and display tables and mannequins for our goods. Alas, it was most disappointing when we were turned away at the front door."

I look up. "They wouldn't let you in?"

"The gentleman in charge would not allow our boxes to enter the premises through the front door. He required entry by way of the loading platform only, at the rear of the building. Archibald referred to him as a union prick. Do you know of union pricks, Hartford?"

"Sort of," I say. "Did you go around back?"

"Oh yes. We were required to return our boxes to Archibald's sports utility vehicle and drive around to the loading platform. Pedestrians were not allowed in this area, thus we traveled within a very long line of automobiles and trucks until our turn presented itself. We were quite surprised to discover there were four loading platforms available, yet only one was in use. I could only assume the three other platforms were inoperable."

I get the hot water to boiling and start to scoop the coffee in.

"Eventually we stopped in front of the lone operating loading platform and our turn was at hand. Archibald and I exited our vehicle and proceeded toward the rear for to retrieve our three boxes. We endeavored to place them upon the loading platform when a rather large union prick confounded our efforts. He claimed that only a proper union worker could do such a thing and that we must stand clear and return our boxes to our vehicle or else pay money to hell. Perhaps he was concerned for our safety."

I finally get the coffee to flow into the maker and am looking for my cup as Thomas drones on.

"After ten minutes had passed a different union worker came over to our vehicle and began carrying one box at a time to the loading platform. When he had finished his task, Archibald and I tried to mount the stairs to the loading platform in order to carry the three boxes inside the building but were again forbidden. A special union worker, we were told, was required to move our three boxes from the outside loading platform to the inside of the building. We were required to wait an additional fifteen minutes because the special outside-to-inside worker was on a break. Do you know of breaks, Hartford?"

I'm shaking my head, pouring my coffee.

"Eventually all three boxes were transported, by the well-rested union worker, from the outside of the auditorium to the inside of the auditorium and placed upon a four-wheeled cart. Archibald attempted to roll said cart to booth number four eighty-two but again was challenged, this time by two union supervisors who informed him that only a union worker could properly operate such a cart. Apparently neither of the two supervisors were skilled in this particular specialty. It required another twenty minutes to transport our three boxes to booth number four eighty-two. Do you know of union supervisors, Hartford?"

"Yes," I say, smiling and sipping, "I do."

"Are they physically incapacitated individuals, Hartford? Are they medically disabled?"

"Not all of them," I say, taking my third sip. "Why do you ask?"

"Because it required three union workers and two union supervisors to complete this task. I myself could have performed such duties in one tenth of the time. It would seem union people possess an abundance of time and manpower, Hartford, but little in the manner of efficiency."

I want to clue him in to public service unions, but my Blackberry rings. I look at the clock—6:07. What the hell? I click it on and put it in my ear.

"Hart," says Feldstone, "We need to debrief."

"Where are you, sir?"

"My office, where you should be. We need to powwow, boy. We need to strategize."

I hold the phone out and again stare at the clock—6:08. My head starts to slowly shake back and forth on its own; it's been doing that lot lately. I put the phone back to my ear and say, "On my way, Senator," and click off.

As I drive, I wonder why Feldstone wants to see me this early. I suddenly realize that he wasn't angry, he was excited. He had watched the press conference on TV and had seen our little Thomas shine. He now wants to milk as much PR out of this thing as possible. If I give him his head, he'll have Thomas on every news show and political talk-a-thon from now until Friday. My job, as always, is to bring him back to reality without pissing him off and getting me fired.

I arrive at six thirty. Jeannie isn't in yet, so I knock on the sanctuary door myself. I hear a muffled "Come in" and I enter chambers. Feldstone looks as if he hasn't slept in two nights, but has a smile on his lips and a skip in his step. I'll have to be careful in the way I prick his balloon.

"Hart," he says, "sit, sit."

I do, he doesn't. He remains behind his desk, pacing expectantly.

"Where is Thomas? Is he okay?"

"He's fine, sir."

"He shined, Hart; our boy really shined. He did us proud. I've had calls, lots of calls, calls from on high." He raises his eyes to the ceiling. "Everybody wants a piece of him." Feldstone stops pacing, stands tall, and beams. "And he's all ours." He rubs his big hands together and claps them once. "All ours, Hart. Oh this is gonna be good. This is gonna be so good."

He looks at me and notices I'm not mirroring his exuberance. He rears back on his heels and frowns. "What?"

"Well sir, it's just—"

"Just what?"

"It's just that Thomas is not a professional politician. He's just your everyday guy, he—"

"Did you see him out there, Hart, manhandling the press?" Feldstone has his chest thrust forward and both hands on his hips. "Did you see him eat their lunch for them? Nobody does that to the press; certainly not a novice. He's a natural, Hart. Our boy's a natural. He—"

"I don't know that he manhandled them as much as enraged them, Senator." They're gonna be all over that Tea Party remark."

"I'm sensing a whole lot of negativity here, Hartford. What's your game?"

Whenever you fail to agree with the senator he immediately labels you a double agent and tries to expose you. Maybe the p does stand for "paranoid."

"No game, sir. Thomas did well on his answers, I agree, but if you put him out there on the PR trail the press is going to hammer him. He's going to make mistakes. He's going to screw up; once, twice, maybe more, and after his Tea Party comment that's all it'll take. They'll crucify him."

"The Tea Party," Feldstone chuckles, "I thought that was cute. You should have dressed him in his outfit."

"Cute now, sir, devastating later. We still don't know his views: conservative, liberal, moderate. We do know that he's very passionate about his country and that's a good thing. However, I suspect he's equally passionate in his views on ways to fix it."

Feldstone puts his hand to his chin. He realizes his balloon has been popped but he's still intent on saving some of the air inside. He's simply incapable of hiding Thomas's light and his face time under a bushel.

"Senator," I say, "after the speech, after Friday night, you can parade him down Main Street in full minuteman regalia for all I care—I'll play the fife. We just can't do anything now, sir. Not until after LTA is wrapped up and in the can. You can see that."

He can't, but he nods his large, silver-haired head anyway.

"Okay, so where are you hiding him?"

"He's in a safe place. It would be best if you don't know where."

Feldstone doesn't understand words like "best if you don't know." He's spent his whole life in the loop; that's why he's been here for thirty-five years. He's about to challenge me, or most likely command me, when his office phone rings. Jeannie's still not in so he has no choice but to pick up. He puts the phone to his ear, ready to dismiss the caller and get back to me, when I watch his eyes go shiny and hear his breath turn shallow.

"Yes," he says, "thank you," and places the phone back in its cradle.

I can tell by his face all has changed. He stares at me flashing his Cheshire smile.

"That was the White House," he says. "The president wants to meet Thomas."

"When?" I say, trying to stay calm.

"Thursday, ten o'clock."

"Why?"

He remains silent. We both do. We stand for a while then plop down into our chairs with our minds spinning. Jeannie buzzes in to say she's arrived but gets no reply. We mirror each other's expression. Neither of us has a clue as to what the president wants with Thomas. We don't know if it's a good thing or a bad thing.

After a full five minutes of silence, I say, "Senator, I should go. I need to inform Thomas."

"Yes," he says without looking up, "go—inform."

After I clear the office suite and reach the hall, it occurs to me that Feldstone and I were so busy contemplating what the president might say to Thomas that we never considered what Thomas might say to the president.

CHAPTER 21

Thursday comes and I wake up refreshed and excited, packing a pure adrenaline rush. I don't know why—I couldn't have gotten more than four hours sleep. I glance at the clock, confirming the day more than the time; sure enough it's Thursday, June 16—meet the president day. I try to imagine how Thomas must feel—one-on-one face time with the most powerful man on earth. It's unimaginable. Thomas came to this city two months ago not knowing anyone, including himself, and now he's about to sit down with POTUS—quite a coup.

I jump out of bed wearing boxers, a Thomas tee, and a big grin. I'm happy for him, but probably more so for myself. I am, after all, the architect of his good fortune—I conceived it, strategized it, and implemented it.

Maintaining my smirk while brushing my teeth is difficult, but I manage. While rinsing I notice my eyebrow furrow is back and deeper than normal. I'm still smiling but I stop brushing and stare. The furrow remains. So am I happy or stressed?

Today my prodigy meets the president; tomorrow he gives a speech to the nation. I'm stressed.

My grin turns to frown and my furrow deepens. It's the unknown—Thomas is the unknown. You never put a witness on the stand unless you know exactly what he'll say. Thomas is about to appear before the president and the nation and I have no idea what he'll say.

I start to massage my forehead, staring intently at my reflection. Why am I worried? Thomas has already proven himself. He performed beautifully in front of the press, and aside from his Tea Party remark has walked a perfectly balanced line between liberal and conservative views. Nobody tore him apart. No one even stumped him. Why should anything change in the next two days? I stop the massage, relax my fingers, breathe, and take a step back. The furrow's gone. My grin returns naturally and I go to the bedroom to get dressed.

I skip down the stairs, excitement brimming with every step. I would love to be in Thomas's head right now. I reach the living room landing and turn toward the kitchen, then start to slow my pace. Eventually I stop. I feel my eyebrow furrow returning.

It occurs to me that I don't need to be in Thomas's head to imagine how he's feeling. I know exactly how he's feeling. It was on full display yesterday when I informed him he was to meet the president. He showed no feelings at all; no excitement, no jubilation, no joy, nothing. I take that back. He showed acceptance. I'm shaking my head—*acceptance*.

I clear my brain, don my faux smile, and stroll into the kitchen, where Thomas and Annie are sitting at the breakfast table sipping tea.

"What time's your meeting?" I say.

"Hartford," he says, "good morning. And I believe we both well know of our meeting time."

"Ten o'clock," I say. "Just confirming."

It's my job to get him there on time. Even though I won't accompany Thomas into the Oval Office, there's a fair chance I could draw some face time with the Commander-in-Chief and maybe even shake his hand. Thomas shows no excitement at all.

"You both have plenty of time for a nice hot breakfast," Annie says, standing up and walking toward the stove. She turns her head at the last moment. "Are you excited, Thomas?"

"As a mouse with an elephant," he says.

She laughs and he laughs and I laugh thinking, *What the hell does that mean?*

"Do you have any idea of what you will say to the president?" Annie says. "What questions you might ask him?"

"Yes, indeed," he says and then sips more tea.

"Anything you want to share?" I say.

"I would like to know why this president seeks to destroy the country I love."

Annie and I do a freeze take and stare at him.

"Your humor surfacing again, Thomas," I finally say.

He laughs. "Perhaps."

We both know our laconic houseguest well enough to realize this is all we're going to get for now. Maybe after the meeting we can regroup and elicit a blow-by-blow. Meanwhile, Annie serves up eggs and bacon and the discussion turns to t-shirts.

I blank out of the conversation and try to deal with my stress. The next thing I know, Thomas and I are on our way to the White House. My hands are jittery and my voice jumps an octave as we clear the security guard house and are ushered into the underground parking facility. We park and exit the car and are promptly directed to an elevator by an armed security guard. The elevator takes us to the main floor, where we step out onto the highly polished marble floor of the White House proper and come face to face with an intern named Darcy Hancock, our keeper. It's exactly 9:20. We're led into an oversized waiting room and offered a beverage of our choice. We decline and Darcy explains that we'll be escorted to the outer office at 9:55, depending on scheduling overruns. She bids us sit and make ourselves comfortable in two enormous brown leather chairs then quickly leaves the room.

A couple of uniformed military types sporting huge clusters of medals and ribbons sit across from us with cell phones attached to their ears. CIA is on our right—crewcut, dark glasses, fit; he sits perfectly motionless. An older man and woman are to his left, whispering softly to each other. They seem excited though a little sad. A thirty-ish woman in a business suit, stylish glasses, and tight hair is on our left. She never looks up from her laptop. I think about pulling out my Blackberry to fit in, but I don't want to confuse Thomas. I look over at him. He's staring straight ahead wearing his insouciant smile. Nothing seems to rattle this guy. We all repose in silence and anticipation while, one by one, we are fetched and led. Our turn comes at exactly 10:05.

Darby appears and motions us out of the waiting room, down the hall, and into a reception area just outside of the Oval Office. I figure on another bout of waiting but am quickly proven wrong as President Mays himself comes striding through the door. He dazzles us with his smile and immediately sticks out his hand to Thomas. Thomas smiles back, shakes the president's hand, then steps aside to let me in. I practically lunge forward, grabbing the man's hand and pumping it for all it's worth while gushing something about how glad I am to meet him, I'm his biggest fan and have all his CDs.

After embarrassing myself, I release my grip and allow the president to escape a step backward. He turns and enters the Oval Office, beckoning Thomas *and me* to follow. You couldn't have blasted the grin off my face. He leads us through the office and past his desk displaying the Presidential Seal. I'm like a bobble-head on a bumpy road. I try to spot the door which led to the Lewinsky scandal, but can't. I take in the flags all lined up behind the president's chair, the plush blue carpet with its tiny white stars, the many knickknacks displayed on tables and shelves, gifts from leaders all over the world, the portraits on the walls, price-less antiques dotting the room, the shear oval-ness of it all—It's surreal.

We enter the sitting room. The president indicates we should take a seat on the sofa across from the fireplace. His secretary, Mr. Marshall, asks if he can fetch us a drink, and we each decline, out of nervousness or fear. The president sits down in one of the large, overstuffed colonial high-backs closest to Thomas. The two of them smile at each other as if in competition.

"Well," he says, leaning forward and looking directly at Thomas, "I finally get to meet the man who speaks for America."

"Yes, Mr. President," says Thomas, "and I the man who leads my country."

"I must say, Thomas, I'm a little jealous. I've been informed that your listening audience is expected to be one of the largest ever for a major political event. I imagine Hartford, here, along with Harold Feldstone and his boys, have managed to put together one hell of a fine speech."

His presence and his smile leaves me speechless.

"No, sir, Mr. President."

He pauses so long I think he's not going to say any more, and then he adds, "My message consists of my words alone, Mr. President. Hartford and Senator Feldstone will hear them for the first time, along with Congress and the American people, tomorrow night."

The President's eyes dart back and forth between Thomas and me several times before settling on Thomas. "That's very bold of you, Thomas. Few of us would have the gumption to perform an address of such magnitude without professional help."

"And yet," says Thomas, "this is the way you choose to lead my country."

The president's smile disappears.

"Pardon me?"

"My country," Thomas repeats, "you lead it in a direction that we the people wish it not to go. Surely you have professional experts who would advise you differently."

"Now, Thomas," he says, his smile reappearing, "that is your opinion. Many feel, as I do, that history will prove we travel the correct course."

"Those with whom I have conversed do not feel this way. Past history shows our founding fathers, from their writings and teachings, clearly did not feel this way. Your own polls indicate the vast majority of the American citizenry do not feel this way. Hartford," he turns to me, "do you feel this way?"

My eyes are darting between the two men. I don't know whether I'm shaking my head or nodding it. I do know I'm too dumbfounded to speak.

"I do not understand," Thomas continues "why you seek to destroy the country I love."

The President's posture goes rigid. He sits up straight and loses his smile.

"Thomas, I believe you have been misinformed. My administration is one of the most caring and open administrations ever to serve the people of this great country. Do you not see that when the people suffer we step in?"

Thomas smiles politely and says, "No, Mr. President, it is *when* you step in that the people suffer." Thomas begins ticking off one finger at a time: "The bank bailouts, the stimulus bill, nationalization of health care, your jobs bill, the housing bill, bankrupt solar energy defaults—all abject failures. You spend the people's money quite recklessly, Mr. President."

President Mays glares hard at Thomas but doesn't respond. Thomas smiles at him as if they're both in agreement.

My mouth hangs opens wanting desperately to say something to stop the train wreck, but nothing comes out. I'm alternately checking the president and the door behind me, watching for The Secret Service, who are surely on their way.

I finally blurt out, "Thomas, this is The President of the United States, for God's sake!"

"Yes, Hartford, this I know." He turns to meet my eyes. "It is for this reason he must be informed. He is the only person who can effect the necessary changes."

I want to shout, "You don't inform the President!", but before I can get the words out the door flies open and Mr. Marshall, not the FBI, enters and quickly ushers us out of the Oval Office. Before the door closes I hear President Mays yelling into a phone or intercom, demanding to know who the hell set him up with that crazy little bastard and to get Studdeman in here on the double.

Thomas and I are immediately passed off to Darcy, who doesn't speak but leads us briskly down the hall and into the garage elevator. Once inside, the doors slide shut and Thomas turns to me and smiles.

"Perhaps President Mays will now reconsider his present course of action and change his ways in order to better serve the people," he says.

I'm too numb to speak.

We drive home in silence. My entire working life has consisted of one hard and fast rule: when climbing the ladder of success, do not piss off those on the rungs above you, and never, ever piss off the guy at the top. Yet that is what Thomas has just done. I should have seen it coming. I should have stopped it. I was so anxious to get into the Oval Office and meet the president I let down my guard. Now I'm a willing accomplice.

I wonder how quickly word will spread and how Senator Feldstone will take it. I wonder if Niles is cleaning out my desk about now and I wonder how long the unemployment line has grown. I look over at Thomas. He seems unaffected. He'd be twiddling his thumbs and whistling dixie were he the type. I'm lucky to keep the car on the road.

We pull into the driveway and Annie meets us in the garage with a nervous mantra of "How did it go?", first to me and then to Thomas. She gets nothing so she tails us up the stairs into the living room where she punches me hard on the shoulder and yells, "Hart, tell me what happened!"

I stare at Thomas and nod my head deferring to him.

"I thought it went quite well," he says.

"Tell me," she says, pulling him down on the sofa next to her. "Tell me everything."

I stare at the carefree little screw-up while my anger builds.

"Perhaps Hartford should speak," Thomas says. "I believe he holds a contrary view."

She switches her eyes to me and forcibly motions me to start talking.

I shrug my shoulders and try to sound casual. "Thomas angered the president and I've probably lost my job."

"Angered?"

"Royally pissed him off."

"How do you know that? Were you there, in the Oval Office?"

"Yes."

"How? What? Tell me." She stands up, marches over, and pins me eye-to-eye.

"Thomas asked the president why he was destroying the country."

"No!" Her eyes shoot to Thomas. "You didn't."

"I thought someone should ask," he says.

"Thomas," I shout, "why would you do that?"

"Either our president is being ill-advised or he is willfully leading us down a path to certain destruction. I wished to know which."

"And did you find out?" Annie says.

"Yes," he says, shaking his head sadly. "It is the latter."

We're both speechless—both helplessly staring at Thomas when my cell phone rings. Annie's eyes shift to me. I click it on, say hello, listen, and then hang up.

"Senator Feldstone wants to see Thomas in his office—now, alone."

We stare at each other then look back down at Thomas.

"News travels quite rapidly in our nation's capital," he says.

CHAPTER 22

'm still mad.

Glancing over at Thomas all nestled in the passenger seat and wearing that nonchalant smile of his should make it worse, but it doesn't. His presence comforts me. He has a way with right and wrong, justice and injustice, moral and immoral. When I'm with Thomas, their definitions seem clearer and less complicated. He both encourages my humanity and triggers my protective instincts.

"Thomas," I say, "don't let the good-old-boy persona fool you." He turns his head toward me. "With Feldstone and his lot, you're either with them or against them. Right now they see you as a loose cannon. You need to get back on their good side."

"Is this why Senator Feldstone wishes to see me, Hartford, to lure me back to his good side?"

"Well, in a manner of speaking, yes." I turn right on Independence Ave and speed up to forty. "He'll greet you warmly. Your confrontation with the president he'll treat as a small matter; probably won't even mention it by name. He'll offer you his friendship, his loyalty, and will expect the same in return. He'll present you with a proposal, a favor, to prove you're a team player. Should you reject his proposal, he and his boys will smear you from here to kingdom come."

"It sounds quite ominous."

"Don't treat it lightly, Thomas. These boys mean business and they have the clout and weaponry to carry out their threats."

"Do you know of jujitsu, Hartford?"

"Jujitsu—what, as in martial arts?"

"Yes."

"I know of it—I've seen my share of Chuck Norris movies. Why, are you a black belt or something? Should I be concerned for Senator Feldstone?"

"Jujitsu," he continues as if I hadn't spoken, "is a form of the martial arts which employs the strength of one's opponent in order to defeat him."

"Yes?"

He shrugs. "It may, one day, surface."

We ride the rest of the way in silence. The next words spoken are mine, wishing Thomas luck as he walks into Feldstone's den and closes the door.

I wait for over an hour, spending most of the time exchanging enigmatic glances with Jeannie while she deflects phone calls and takes down messages. I think about Thomas. It's ironic—less than two months ago I saved his butt from the campus cops, and now here he is, sticking mine in the fire. I should be mad as hell at the little screwup, but I'm not. I'm worried about him. I know what these guys are capable of—I've seen them destroy the powerful without an ounce of remorse; no telling what they'll do to the meek. The door opens and Thomas emerges cool, calm, and smiling as always. The only thing different about him is the sheet of paper he holds in his hand. I hear but don't see the senator. He didn't greet me when we arrived and he's not going to bid me farewell. I figure the paper Thomas holds is either my redemption notice or my pink slip. We both gesture a goodbye to Jeannie and step out into the hall.

Thomas hands me the paper but says nothing. I wait until we're out of the Russell Building and breathing fresh air before I look at it. It's the Democratic talking points with a few blatant add-ons. I shake my head. I knew this thing would eventually come back to bite me. It's an ultimatum: if Thomas agrees to incorporate the talking points in his speech, I'm back in the fold; if not, I'm looking to the Republicans for work. We make our way toward the mall.

"Lunch," I say.

"Oh, I dare not, Hartford. I must return to the shop."

Oh yeah, I forgot; the t-shirt priority looms.

"This meeting has already rendered me tardy," he says.

Re-arguing the point would prove fruitless, so I say, "Are you going to tell me what happened in there?"

"Why, it was just as you prophesied, Hartford. You know the senator quite well."

I nod slowly. "And the talking points: a token of your loyalty, the favor that puts us back on his good side?"

"Precisely," he says.

"What will you do?"

"There seems little punishment that can be inflicted on me, Hartford, but much can be imposed upon my friends."

Friends. He means Annie and me.

"I will give the decision much thought, Hartford. Meanwhile, I must tarry no more. My partner awaits."

He turns around and heads for the far end of the mall.

I spot two familiar oak trees across the way and unconsciously head toward them. Nestled between the two trunks and bathed in shade is the Thomas Bench, my bastion of solitude. I reach it, sit down, and begin to think things through. Thinking—I'm doing a lot of that lately. It isn't like me. I have no idea what Thomas is going to say in his big speech tomorrow night, and that isn't like me either. I know his words will be passionate, heartfelt, and born deep from within. Words that may mean little to some, but to Thomas will mean everything. Words that will invoke his passion, his patriotism, and his love for his country. Words that will speak disdain to those who wish to undermine or destroy her.

I'm shaking my head. Thomas is wrong when he says there's little they can do to him. They can discredit him by mocking his words as jingoistic prattle uttered by a naive, ill-informed little man. They can disgrace him by using his amnesia to label him ignorant and out of touch. They can dishonor him by using his unknown past and his missing surname, filling in the blanks to their purpose and to his chagrin. Yeah, there are a whole lot of things they can do to him.

And then there's his audience, those with whom he has connected. Those with similar ideals, similar passions, beliefs—Americans who also love their country, their liberty, and their freedom. How many of those will get crushed along the way? If Thomas stays the course I lose my job, but he loses his soul. Can I even let that happen?

It occurs to me that I might be smiling. I have to touch the corners of my mouth to make sure. What's wrong with me? Am I really willing to advise Thomas to blow off the talking points and my career in order to say what needs to be said? Willing to throw away my hard-earned status, my golden-boy reputation? And what good will it do? My sacrifice doesn't solve the problem, it just ends my career. If he leaves out the talking points he faces a smear campaign of gargantuan proportions. If he puts them in he corrupts his speech and loses his soul. Maybe it's not my butt in the fire after all.

I'm in crisis, in danger of turning into someone I won't recognize. I need somebody to step up and slap some sense into me—that would be Annie. I pull into the garage, jump out of the car, and dash up the stairs. As soon as I open the door I yell her name. It's overwhelmingly important to me that she be home at this very moment and she is. She turns and smiles. I want to embrace her but I'm afraid that might confuse things.

"Where is Thomas?" she says—the words every man wants to hear.

"He's at work. I dropped him."

"On the eve of his big speech."

"Go figure."

I ease down on the couch and pat the seat next to me. She comes over, sits down, looks me in the eye, and says, "What's wrong? Is it Thomas?"

I let out a sigh. "Of course it's Thomas. It's always Thomas."

"What have you done to him?"

"Nothing. It's Feldstone and the higher-ups, it's what they might do—what they *will* do." I look at her with what I feel is a massive dose of concern in my eyes. "He's in trouble, Annie, and there's nothing I can do to help."

She stares at me and then starts to laugh.

"What?"

"You want to do something to help someone other than yourself?" she says.

"Yes."

She holds her hands out palms up as if to say, Okay, lay it on me, but don't expect me to buy it.

"Feldstone gave Thomas a list of Democratic talking points to incorporate into his speech tomorrow night. If he complies then they ignore the president-bashing, leave him alone, and I keep my job. If he doesn't..." I shrug and hold my hands in a no-telling-but-it'll-be-bad gesture.

She laughs again.

"Annie," I say going a bit shrill, "this is serious."

"Hartford, do you have any idea what Thomas is going to say in that speech of his tomorrow night?"

"Not really, do you?"

"That speech is going to rattle up those boys so hard it'll be a wonder if half a dozen of them don't up and expire from heart stroke right there on the Senate floor. The inclusion or elimination of a few talking points won't make no never mind."

Annie sometimes reverts to her Georgia roots when she gets passionate.

"Feldstone and his boys," she continues, "have no idea what's coming at them. If I were you I'd call the senator right now and tell him he and his boys better get armored up cause all hell's about to come down on them. And that goes for the president, too."

"How on earth do you know these things?"

"Hart," she says, "what is Thomas doing right now?"

"He's out there selling his t-shirts."

"And what happens when he sells his t-shirts?"

Oh, good, twenty questions. "I don't know," I say, wondering why I needed Annie to be home so bad, "you tell me."

"He talks to the people," she says. "You've seen the crowds."

I glare.

"They've tripled in size since you were last there. Have you any idea what he says to the people? What the people say to him?"

"They ask about deepwater oil drilling, the Arizona immigration law, gays in the military, global warming, unemployment, shutting down Guantanamo, things like that?"

"You're wrong. Think about it, Hart. Who are the American people?"

I don't answer because I know she's not really asking.

"Three hundred million individuals," she continues. "How is Thomas or anyone able to speak for three hundred million individuals? He can't, no one can. Your friend the senator speaks for some. House members speak for some, the president for some, even the media—especially the media—speak for some. These people, these Americans who have the ear of such entities, have a name. I call them the squeaky wheelers. They have the ear of the government and the media precisely *because* they are squeaky wheelers. They typically come in groups, or committees, unions, or organizations of one kind or another. They usually rally around specific causes or issues. Reporters, newsmen, talking heads, opinion columnists, bloggers, tweeters, twitterers, Congressman, and even this president all focus on the squeaky wheel minority. What Thomas knows and what others have forgotten is that there are three other wheels on the cart and this much larger silent majority or moral majority or sleeping giant or whatever you want to call them can be awakened. Certainly by someone who knows how to connect with them.

And our friend Thomas knows exactly how. Not only that, but your employer, Senator Harold Feldstone, has kindly provided him a world stage on which to do it."

She still hasn't told me what Thomas plans to say tomorrow night, so I decide to take one more stab. "If he's not going to discuss oil drilling or over-spending or unemployment or global warming, what is he going to say?"

She smiles. "I expect he will use terms like freedom, liberty, American exceptionalism, free enterprise, entrepreneurialism, country first—words like that."

"So it's to be a 'rah, rah, wrap yourself in the flag' kind of thing."

"He'll also use words like wrongheaded, arrogant, self-serving, power-hungry, and out of touch with the people."

"I see," I say, thinking maybe I should put in that gird-your-loins call to Feldstone. "So this silent majority, this sleeping giant is made up of..."

"You've heard it before, Hart. They're your workaday people, your moms and dads, the gainfully employed, your legal immigrants and aliens, your hard-working, productive members of society. They're not activists, they're not revolutionaries or politicos. They're just grassroots people who expect their government to work for them by employing the principles and visions articulated in our Constitution and laid out by the men and women who founded this country. When government stops working, these people take notice and expect someone to put it right. If the president can't or won't do it then they'll find someone who will. When these people, these average American citizens, stop working and start forming up, it's time for those in power to watch their step. And they are forming up, Hart—these days, they're calling themselves The Tea Party."

"The Tea Party? The right-wing crazies, the outer-fringe haters, the racist rabble-rousers—*those* average American citizens?"

"They're none of those things, Hart, and you know it. The Democrats, the administration, and the media can smear and dismiss them all they want but it'll be at their peril. People like these and men like Thomas have one very important thing in common—they love their country and they will never let it be destroyed nor changed into something they and our founding fathers wouldn't recognize. You can roll your eyes and shrug it off all you want but these are the people for whom Thomas will speak tonight. These are the people he will energize and these are the people who will restore this country."

"Damn," I say, smiling at her. "Maybe you should give the speech."

I reach over and try to massage her shoulders, calm her down a bit, but she'll have none of it. I hear a car door slam and look at my watch.

"That'll be Thomas," I say, "Archie said he'd drop him."

Fifteen seconds later the doorbell chimes. No matter how many times I chastise him, Thomas will not walk into the house uninvited. Annie jumps up, runs to the door, and greets him with a long hug. Thomas has no words of greeting for the first time I can remember. He looks haggard.

"You probably need to get upstairs and rehearse," I say. "You're on in less than twenty-four hours."

He nods his head and says he would indeed like to go upstairs and perhaps lie down. He says he's rather weary and must contemplate a rather serious matter.

CHAPTER 23

There's just so damn much to think about: Thomas's speech, Annie's words, her warning, Feldstone's silence, the unemployment line. The complexity of it all, not to mention the implications, had my brain churning half the night.

So here I am, sitting up, staring at my bedside clock, looking at six a.m. on June tenth—speech day. I'm tired and frustrated and pretty much clueless as to what the next eighteen hours will bring. Annie's still asleep, so I slip out of bed quietly, shower and dress, hoping to meet up with Thomas downstairs at the table of truth. I plan to pin him down on content and elicit some straightforward answers. My concern is that he, too, has been up all night doing what he should have been doing all week—rehearsing—and, therefore, may also be done in.

When I reach the kitchen table there's no one there. His note tells me that he's gone to work. Speech day, and Thomas has gone to work—un-f-ing-believable!

I want to yell up the stairs to Annie—wake her up and demand her presence. Instead I go over to the coffeemaker and fix myself a cup. I sit down at the table of no-information to sip and think.

I think about that first tsunami wave, how it forms and builds to its peak and then comes crashing down with unimaginable force, decimating the nearest unfortunate village. That's what I'm watching now: a Thomas tsunami in the making. A wave of political change building to its peak. One that at eight o'clock tonight will either crest or fall flat. The village players are all frozen into stubborn intransigence, holding their ground. Feldstone is smugly moot, confident in his talking points threat. The president is incensed and missing in action, Congress is arrogantly complacent, and the press remains eternally hostile. Thomas's speech will either inspire millions or sputter and die.

If it inspires, the wave will crest and torrents of unhappy citizens will crash down, destroying the government's ill-gotten village. The corrupt, overspending, and bloated status quo will give way to the restoration of responsible government.

If the speech bombs, the good old boys will tighten their grip, grow bigger, stronger, fatter, and wield more power than ever.

Could all this really be contingent on Thomas's speech? I glance down at his note and get angry all over again. I take a couple of deep breaths and let them out slowly. Okay, I need to ease up. I mean look at his record—everything he touches turns to gold. Still the man refuses to prepare. So why am I mad? Good speech, the people win, government's reformed, the country reverses course and I lose my job. Bad speech, Thomas is squashed, the hopes of the people are dashed, big government gets bigger, the status quo rules, and I keep my job. I don't even know whose side I should be on.

In some ways I wonder if the talking points are the key. Annie believes they're unimportant and will have little effect, but I think the act itself is insidious. I believe the decision to interject them at all will affect Thomas's psyche and damage his inner being—like a crack in the dam.

My cell phone rings.

"Hello, boss," Niles says.

I wait for more but it doesn't come. I automatically transition into my silence game and then just as quickly cave.

"What's going on, Niles? What's up with Feldstone?"

After a long, unnecessary pause, because Niles is trying to be me, he says, "Well, Hart, he ain't humming *The Star-Spangled Banner.*"

"What is he doing? Asking for me?"

"No."

Again with the silence, then finally, "He's accepting good news only, Hart. Have you got any good news?"

Hart again, not boss. Things are changing.

"No," I say. "I don't know if the talking points will find their way into the speech or not. Tell him we'll all find out at eight o'clock tonight."

Silence again, and then, "Can't do it, Hart, the senator doesn't want to hear bad news." Another long silence and Niles clicks off.

I walk over for my third cup of coffee and hear Annie creaking down the stairs. About damn time. All this frustration is making my head swell. I need to release pressure. I need somebody to talk at.

My rant starts badly.

"How could you have let him go to work? It's the day of his speech for God's sake! He talks to you. You're supposed to be helping him. He's gonna screw this up, I'm going to lose my job, and we're going to lose this condo! Christ!"

The only thing I hold back is, *and it's all your fault*, but then that's implied.

Annie sits through my tirade, sipping her coffee and smiling— yes, smiling. She isn't really a button-pusher, but she enjoys watching me push my own. When I'm done, I stand there all puffed up and red-faced, daring a comeback.

After another sip or two, when she's sure I'm out of bullets, she says, "Thomas hasn't gone to work."

I grab his note, pugnaciously slap it down on the table in front of her, and glare.

"He and Archie have errands to run," she says. "They'll be back by noon."

"What errands?" I demand.

She shrugs. "I don't know, but when he gets back he and I are going to run one of our own—over to Macy's to buy him a suit and tie."

I don't totally deflate, but I do lose air as I plop down in the chair next to me. Of course he needs a suit. I've been completely oblivious to such details. I stare at Annie. What else has she been privy to while I've been tied up with procedures and powermongers? Are we really on track? Does she have this thing under control after all? Has my Annie prepared Thomas to give the speech of his life? I stare at her while she continues to sip and smile. I'm trying to decide if I should be happy or sad.

Annie and I are waiting in the living room all decked out in our finest. She in her simple black dress, with its spaghetti straps and matching three-inch heels, looking fabulous, and me in my black Armani suit and tie, which doesn't seem to fit as well as it once did. We simultaneously raise our heads when we hear footsteps on the stairwell. Thomas enters wearing his new Brook's Brothers suit and midnight blue tie. He looks almost present-century. We gather around the breakfast table and Annie pulls a bottle of wine from the kitchen cooler. I pour three glasses and my table-mates look to me for the honors.

"To our dear friend, Thomas," I say, holding up my glass. "May his words this night inspire all of America."

Annie raises her eyebrows and her glass—in pleasant surprise, probably, at the lack of sarcasm—and clinks in. Thomas nods a thank you and plinks his glass to ours. We drink fully and hardily and, lacking a hearth, set our glasses gently back down on the table. Thomas smiles brightly and wipes away his tears.

"Okay," I say, "let's do this thing."

We troop downstairs to the garage, pile into the Beemer, and drive to our destiny. I have a knot in my stomach the size of a hornet's nest, and I'm not giving a speech. I glance at Thomas through the rearview mirror and find him as unaffected as ever. Annie has chosen to sit in the backseat with him. He holds her hand in his and gently pats her arm, since she looks as if she might throw up.

After twenty-five minutes of heavy traffic we pull into a specially reserved parking space in the Capitol Building's underground garage and exit the car. We're a good two hours early so I expect the place to be mostly empty, but it's not. The garage is more than three-quarters full. We walk to the elevator, press number one, and ride up to the Capitol Building's main floor. The doors open onto the rotunda and we step out. Our eyes are immediately assaulted by the plethora of headlight beams shining through and reflecting off windows on all sides of the building. Cars are streaming forth from all directions in a build–it–and–they–will–come moment, which makes my stomach-knots tighten further. We make our way up the stairs to the Senate chamber, and I note the maze of electrical wiring along the way, twisting and turning like a giant anaconda escaping the utility room.

We enter the Senate chamber to a firestorm of activity. Last-minute adjustments to audio and video equipment are performed and tested by sound and lighting crews, but that's not what's causing the commotion. It's the huge number of attendees crowding the floor, nearly two hours early. House members and Senators, as well as invited guests, milling about in small groups engaged in lively debates, all speculating on Thomas's speech. No one immediately recognizes Thomas, probably because he's wearing a suit absent a three-cornered hat. Senator Feldstone spots us before I see him and calls my name. I acknowledge him with a wave and he and his two colleagues head our way.

"Hartford," he says grabbing and shaking my hand as if I'm not really on the outs. He turns to Annie. "Ahh, Ms. Anne, most enchanting, most enchanting. May I present Senator Ballingford and Congresswoman Pat Turner?" He then turns toward Thomas, thrusting out both hands in presenting fashion. "And this is Thomas."

The two Congresspersons eagerly shake hands with and gush over Thomas, all but ignoring Annie and me. Feldstone stares blatantly at me until he gets my attention. With his right hand low he gives me a furtive thumbs up. I smile and return it just as surreptitiously. I don't see any reason to burst his talking points bubble now, when in less than an hour Thomas will or won't do it for me.

The three of them continue to small talk with Thomas while Annie and I are left to ourselves. When they leave they do so in a high state of anticipatory fervor—a contagion that pervades the room. Others begin to notice Thomas and gravitate in our direction like hummingbirds to Bee Balm. We're never left alone again. Everyone wants a piece of Thomas—to shake his hand, hear his voice, complement his tie. He has accrued an amazing number of pre-speech groupies in a very short time. I wonder how the numbers will stack up following his closing remarks.

Eventually someone in uniform comes over and takes Thomas away. They lead him to the podium for audio and video adjustments, and then to a waiting room where he can sit and rehearse in peace. I won't see him again until showtime.

I glance at my watch, which shows 7:15—forty-five minutes until kickoff. The empty seats around us are starting to fill up. There are a lot of people here. In addition to the native senators and representatives, there's a large cadre of invited guests—campaign donors, CEOs, union heads, military brass, even a sprinkling of celebrities and athletes. I wonder who decided the guest list—I know neither Thomas nor I had been consulted. I do know of one VIP who'll not be in attendance—the President of the United States. A scheduling conflict had been cited, but Feldstone and I know better. I'm pretty sure, though, that President Mays will be glued to his TV set.

With Thomas absent our crowd of idolizers quickly dwindles to zero, and so Annie and I decide to find our seats. On the way we bump into Archie. I'm surprised but I guess I shouldn't be—Archie is, after all, Thomas's business partner. Still, for an event like this Archie doesn't seem the type. He grins at me and sets up for a fist bump.

I comply and he says, "Rather be home than here in this monkey suit, working."

"Working?" I say.

He pauses, looks back and forth between Annie and me, and says, "What, you don't know?"

My blank stare answers his question to the extent that he takes a step backward, slaps his right thigh loudly, lets a giant grin take over his face, then forms his hands into pistols and alternately fires his index fingers at both of us.

"Oh, hell," he says louder than necessary. "You two are in for some fun."

He starts to laugh as he turns away. He looks back over his shoulder and shouts, "Some damn good fun." He's laughing and shaking his head as he disappears into the crowd.

Annie and I look at each other cluelessly.

"Any thoughts?" I say.

"None."

So much for having it under control.

CHAPTER 24

We score good seats—close up, third row, with a clear view of the podium. Still, I'm shaking my head, with an "oh crap" running through it.

It's just a speech. How much damage can a speech do? My mind answers with an, "oh crap."

At length, the Sergeant-at-Arms comes up to the podium and asks everyone to please take their seats. I check my watch and note it's two minutes till eight. I wonder about protocol; is there to be a Pledge of Allegiance, an honor guard ceremony? It turns out there's only the Benediction by the Navy chaplain.

With my head bowed it occurs to me I don't even know who's going to introduce Thomas. I'm reasonably sure it isn't going to be me. I covertly raise my head, slightly open one eye, and look toward the Senate seats. It's not going to be Senator Feldstone either. He's sitting over there with his big silver head bowed low, praying hard. Before I can give it more thought, the benediction ends and the vice-president approaches the podium. It makes sense—the VP is the titular head of the Senate, and with the president in self-imposed exile he's top dog. He nods to a few individuals, clears his throat, and begins to speak.

"Ladies and gentlemen of the United States Senate and House of Representatives, honored guests, American citizens throughout the land, and especially our men and women in uniform serving this great country the world over, good evening. We come here tonight for a very special purpose. The United States government... needs to listen."

He pauses and lets go a toothy smile.

"The members of the Senate and of the House, the president, and the vice-president," he taps his chest, "have done an awful lot of talking over the past few years. Some would say 'blown a lot of smoke.'"

He receives a smattering of laughter and acknowledges it with another smile.

"It is now time for us to step back and turn over the microphone to you, the American people. It is time for us, in government to shut up and listen."

He turns left, takes three steps toward the side of the stage, holds out his right hand in gesture to someone we, as yet, cannot see, and says, "Welcome, Thomas."

The crowd goes wild, clapping, then standing, then clapping some more. There are no whistles, cheers, or squeals due to Senate decorum, otherwise there would have been. Excitement fills the room. Cameramen run out from their shadowed corners to kneel and crouch in front of the stage. Bursts of light from cameras as well as audience cell phones click and flash, adding a strobe-like effect to the mayhem. As Thomas approaches the podium, everyone in the room is on their feet in unrestrained applause. The decibel level is almost painful. The president has to be cursing his TV about now.

I'll have to hand it to Feldstone, this thing has turned into one slick production. Had there been a band, Thomas would have come out to a drumroll. They're treating him like a rock star instead of the people's representative—maybe he should have worn his minuteman outfit after all.

I'm shaking my head again. This time in amazement. Feldstone and his cronies have truly performed a political miracle here tonight, but it isn't just tonight—it's the whole production, the buildup, the misdirection, and manipulation from the start. They've managed to get Thomas to this point without a last name or a known background, without being chosen by the people but by the foxes, without a single in-depth interview or any inkling as to who he might be or in which political direction he might lean. That takes serious clout—or serious miscalculation.

I feel pain in my right hand and look down to see it clutched, vice-like, in Annie's two-handed grip. She's not seen Thomas perform in a room full of powerful senators, nor in a yard filled with hostile media, so she's petrified. I want to reassure her but I can see, as Thomas steps to the podium, he's about to do that for me. Thomas gingerly leans into the microphone and I recall Archie's words. I see the anxious look on Annie's face and feel the tension in her grip. What I can't see is fun happening here tonight.

"Good evening," Thomas says to the audience. He turns to the VP, "Thank you, Mister Vice President."

The camera people start to retreat, skulking away in a low crouch as if to avoid a helicopter blade, when Thomas stops them.

"Members of our Free Press," he says, "I wish you to remain a moment."

Some have made it back to their corners but most are still on the floor—a dozen or so. They stand and look at each other with wide-eyed, wildebeest stares, as if they've been cut from the herd.

"Please," Thomas says, holding out his hand and gesturing them to the center of the floor. His raised stage allows him to look down on them. "I will address the government of the United States, as is my purpose," he says, "but first I would speak with you, the ladies and gentlemen of the Free Press."

Now I'm thinking, *Maybe this will be fun.* Annie has released my hand and is leaning forward with her hands on her thighs, absorbing his every word.

"Our government, the legislative branch—these ladies and gentlemen before you," he says gesturing to the members of Congress, "the executive branch," he indicates the vice-president, "and the judicial branch have as their primary responsibility our protection.

They are tasked with protecting *we the people* from enemies both foreign and domestic. You," he points to the cameramen before him, "as members of the Free Press, are likewise responsible for our protection. You are tasked with protecting us from our government."

The men and women standing before him have no idea what he's talking about.

"The 'free' in Free Press," Thomas continues, "represents freedom from government interference, from government control, from government oppression. Your task is to expose those policies, laws, bills, executive orders, and appointments that result in excesses and abuses proving detrimental to *we the people*. In this effort I have observed great failure on your part."

The cameramen's eyes dart to the dark corners, looking for a place to hide.

"When you collude with government," Thomas goes on, "when you settle for quotes rather than for investigation, when you ignore truth and publish hearsay or spin more in line with your ideologies that with fact, you fail your country. A free press is a safeguard to the people. It works only if you perform your duties properly. Is it not well past time for you, the Free Press, to bring honor to your trade?"

Thomas pauses. He scans the wide-eyed faces before him and nods his head.

"I suspect that many of you feel I speak in error, my criticisms unwarranted. I have, after all, been in your fair city but a brief time. What could I possibly know of your trade? I will respond hereto, not in past illustration, but in future prognostication."

The cameramen relax, realizing he's not really speaking to them but to their bosses.

"I submit that the address I present here tonight, to every person in this chamber and to every person who watches and listens on their TV and their radio sets, will be heard plainly. Because I am a simple man and speak in simple terms, all will comprehend my meaning perfectly. Yet you of the free press with your editors and rewriters and analyzers will purposely distort and misquote my words. You will take them out of proper context to confuse and obfuscate. You will stretch them and bend them and twist them to correspond to your respective ideologies. You will dissect and disarrange my sentences, turning them quite unrecognizable. Not once will you refer to the Constitution, the visions and ideals of our founding fathers, our nation under God, freedom, liberty, or justice. Yet every word I utter will encompass all of these things."

Thomas steps back from the podium and takes a deep breath. He neither smiles nor frowns but hardens his face with purpose. He steps back to the podium and deliberately leans into the microphones.

"But I must also tell you this," he says. "There will come a time when you will quote my every word exactly as it is spoken. You will fill your newspapers, your magazines, your televisions and your radios with these same words, which you will repeat over and over again on a daily and even an hourly basis. Your quotes will prove accurate and constant. These things will happen as surely as the sun rises on the day."

Thomas again steps back from the microphone, scans the faces before him, nods his head and says, "Thank you, ladies and gentlemen of the Free Press, for your time and attention."

The cameramen look at each other briefly then turn and scurry back to their respective corners. No one remains to take pictures.

I have truly been enjoying myself up to now, but Thomas is starting to scare me. I know him to be a passionate man but I don't want him to go all zealot on me. Of one thing I'm sure: if this first ten minutes is any indication of the rest of his speech, the fallout from this night is going to be anything put pretty.

Thomas steps back up to the microphone and looks out over the audience. His eyes come to rest on the two large groups of senators sitting directly in front of him—Democrats in one section and Republicans in the other, separated by a chasm so deep and so wide that for centuries it has proven impossible to bridge. It's called "the aisle."

"And now, ladies and gentlemen," he says, "to the task at hand."

He looks toward the back of the chamber and says, "Archibald, I require your aid."

Thomas stands silent for two full minutes making everyone uncomfortable. Just as the din of whispers and murmurs begin to increase, Archie, followed by three other men—boys, really—marches down the infamous center aisle of the Senate. Each young man carries a number of folded t-shirts in his arms. The two gentlemen with red t-shirts stop, one at the bottom of the stairs and one at the top, facing the Republican side of the aisle while the other two, carrying royal blue t-shirts, position themselves in a similar fashion facing the Democrats.

"Friends bearing gifts, if you please," says Thomas, motioning to Archie and his crew to begin passing out the goods.

After ten minutes and a fair bit of commotion, every senator has a t-shirt—some holding them out and looking at them, others keeping them folded and laying in their laps, a few holding them up to the TV cameras. All are talking in low mumbles, breaking the formality of the moment.

"Members of the United States Senate," Thomas says, "if you would be so kind as to indulge me. Each t-shirt is of an innovative, one-size-fits-all variety. I would now request that each of you remove your coats and don your new t-shirts. They are designed to fit quite nicely over your shirt and tie."

Very clever. Normally, there would be no way you could induce a United States Senator to reduce himself to the level of wearing a t-shirt. These guys consider themselves the Lords of Congress, after all. But they've been put into a position where refusal would not only show poor sportsmanship in the face of a national TV audience, but would solidify their role as arrogant, overpaid, condescending elites. It's the ultimate in peer pressure. I lean back in my chair and chuckle, watching Senator Feldstone wrestle with the implications. *Damn, this is fun.*

I don't know who's the first to take off his jacket—it isn't Feldstone—but eventually, all one hundred senators remove their jackets and pull on red or blue t-shirts. To do so they all find it necessary to stand, creating even more chaos and commotion and providing the network a bonanza of camera play. When they're done, twenty-four cameramen pick up on fifty-one senators on one side of the aisle wearing royal blue t-shirts with large white letters that read *Democrat* across the front, and on the other side forty-seven senators wearing red t-shirts with the word *Republican* printed across the front. The two independents who sit on the Democratic side sport heather gray t-shirts that read *Independent*.

When they finish, they remain standing, looking around at their distinguished gentlemen compatriots and then peering across the aisle at their distinguished gentleman enemies.

Thomas's voice again finds the microphone.

"Senators," he says, "if you will please take your seats." As they start to sit down he says, "Except for Senator Turner and Senator Callahan."

Everyone's eyes go to Turner, a Democrat, and Callahan, a Republican.

"I wonder if I might persuade Senator Turner and Senator Callahan to exchange seats with one another."

The two Senators look at each other with expressions of horror. They probably don't know if it's even possible to cross the aisle, much less enter into the enemy camp. But then again, when confronted with peer pressure and TV cameras, they can hardly refuse. Reluctantly, donning big, fake, political smiles, they make a show of crossing over into hostile territory. Uncomfortable laughter is exchanged in passing.

Once they're seated in each other's chairs, Thomas calls the names of ten other senators—five Republicans, five Democrats—and asks them to do the same. Then another ten. Eventually half of the Democrats are on the Republican side of the aisle and half of the Republicans are on the Democrat side. The Senate chamber is a sea of alternating red and blue t-shirts. Surprisingly, they have all managed to cross without mishap.

"It seems," Thomas says, "the aisle has become both transverse and irrelevant."

The rest of the room begins to clap and laugh, pulling the Senators into the fray. Pretty soon the applause is running fun and loud, with all but a few Senators rising to their feet. Thomas stands calmly, showing his patented smile, until the noise subsides.

"Thank you," he says, and then, with his eyes back on the senators, "Now, I must reveal to you a secret. The shirts you wear are quite ingenious—they are what is termed 'reversible.'"

Someone lets go a low moan; I think it's Feldstone.

"Now," Thomas continues, "if each of you will remove your t-shirt and turn it outside in, and subsequently re-don your garment, our task will be at its end." There's hesitation so he adds, "The Free Press will be most grateful."

Again the entire Senate stands up and completes its task. When they are through, the one hundred Lords of Congress stand facing Thomas and the rest of the audience, wearing pure white t-shirts with alternating blue and red lettering that simply says *AMERICAN*, and underneath in smaller letters, *Country First.*

Thomas moves back up to the microphone. "We are all Americans," he says, gesturing to the room. "You are American lawmakers. Should you not toil together, Democrat and Republican alike, putting your country ahead of your party, ahead of your career? Is this not the way our founders intended? I, too, have a t-shirt."

Thomas steps from behind the podium and approaches the front of the stage. "This is a quote from King George III when he heard George Washington would turn down an offer of lifetime presidency."

It reads: If George Washington abrogates the presidency he would be the greatest man who ever lived.

"Country, party, self," Thomas says. "Many of you, I fear, have grown confused and reversed the proper order."

The chamber again bursts into spontaneous applause, but this time the Senate members fail to join in.

CHAPTER 25

A small cherry wood table stands to the left and three feet back from the podium. It holds an inviting pitcher of ice water, as evidenced by the little square ice cubes floating on top and the drops of condensation coating the outside. A glass sits next to the pitcher. Thomas takes the opportunity of this latest applause to step back and pour himself a drink. He takes a long swallow, savors it, then takes another. An excited audience completes its applause and waits in silent expectation for more; half in delight, half in dread.

Thomas steps back up to the microphone. He takes a deep breath then smiles.

"Tonight I have been called upon to speak for the citizenry of this country and to the arbiters of its government. This I cannot do—no man can. There exist three hundred million of us. All are individuals with individual thoughts, individual tastes, making individual choices. There are those of us who love this country. There are those who are indifferent to her. There are those who would change her completely and even those who would destroy her. Tonight I choose to speak for those Americans who truly love their country. I know not how to speak for the others."

Spontaneous applause ripples through the silence. Thomas steps back from the podium and pours another glass of water. He drinks it all and sets the glass down on the table. The applause fades but Thomas seems in no hurry to continue. He just stands there, perhaps collecting his thoughts. I see no evidence of note cards in his hands, so I expect him to begin frantically patting himself down in a where-did-I-put-them search, but he doesn't. The applause dies down and the chamber waits expectantly. But he just stands there. I think he's either regretting his past words or deciding how far to go with his next ones. Eventually he moves back up to the podium. I'm holding my breath and find myself with my hands on my thighs, out-leaning Annie, as Thomas smiles at me and begins to speak.

"As you all know, America began as a democratic republic. Our country took its first unsteady steps as an experiment—a truly bold experiment. No country had ever witnessed a beginning such as ours. This alone makes The United States Of America quite unique. Since this bold experiment has managed to produce the most powerful country the world has ever known, none could claim the experiment anything other than a glorious success. Why then, I ask, would we the people or you the government wish to disassemble such a system? And to what purpose? To mimic European, Asian, or Russian-style societies, conglomerations of 'isms' which have all seen failure in their own right? This makes no sense.

"All countries experience times of famine as well as times of plenty, regardless of their governmental makeup. Capitalism is no different. But, compared to all others, has it not proven itself the most successful and the most enduring of the lot? And this in spite of the constant erosion of our freedoms, our liberties, our pursuits of happiness; whittled away, thwarted and denied, bit by bit, year after year, until the country we inhabit hardly resembles the country we inherited. What of the visions of our founding fathers? Should we not be embracing our Constitution and the ideals established by our founders rather than turning from them?"

Thomas scans the faces of the senators before him. He switches his focus to the House members and studies their expressions. He turns to the nearest television camera and stares into it.

"We do not need you to transform our country, Mister President," he says. "We need you to restore it."

Another spontaneous applause takes up the silence and Thomas steps back for another drink of water. I'm thinking, *Christ, is there any piece of government he's not planning to skewer?*

"The most important role of government," he continues, reacquiring the podium and leaning into the microphone, "is to defend its people from enemies both foreign and domestic. This is a most difficult task, for I believe America will never lack for those who wish to do us harm. Vulnerability, however, does no always stem from a lack of military might. Financial weakness can prove equally disastrous. I believe our most dangerous adversary today lies within our own government. Search no farther than the once mighty USSR, or to Spain or Portugal or Greece, for your confirmation. Do we not presently travel the same road as they? Are our entitlements not unsustainable? Do we not spend more than we earn? Are we not burdened with an ever-increasing debt?

"I ask you: is our financial vulnerability due to this nation's inability to produce lucrative goods and services, or is it due to a bloated government's addiction to overspending? You, in this room, you, the duly elected representatives of the people, wish to blame a breakdown in the system, a failure of capitalism, of free enterprise, of entrepreneurialism, greed on the part of the American businessman. You do this while you, the arbiters of our government, wallow in its unrelenting growth, year upon year, program upon program, pension upon pension. I tell you in full truth that it was never meant to be this way."

Thomas leans back from the microphone and stands very straight, almost as if at attention. He looks down at his shoes. I don't know if he's thinking or praying. He abruptly raises his head and looks back at the audience. His smile disappears.

"I have spoken of capitalism," he says, "and I have spoken of debt. The two are mutually inconsistent with each other. Capitalism is the most prodigious wealth-producing system ever devised by man, and yet our government finds itself engulfed by the most massive debt accumulation ever achieved. How is this possible?"

He focuses on the Senate and points his finger at them. "You," he says, "you are the problem. And you," he waves his finger back and forth toward the House members, "and you, Mister President," he says, pointing directly at the nearest TV camera.

"With all of your posturing and all of your speechmaking and your complete inability to stand up for your country and its citizens, you have allowed a most insidious enemy to infiltrate your ranks. You have welcomed into our government the very antithesis of capitalism. You have praised it, embraced it, unabashedly curried its favor, and now you are dying from it. Worse still, you are taking our country and its citizens along with you. I have found it helpful to coin a word embodying the 'ism' of your undoing. I call it 'Unionism.'"

Good Lord, is he going to leave any hornet's nests unstirred?

"Capitalism is based on the free enterprise system," Thomas continues, "where an individual may take an idea or concept and turn it into a profitable business. An individual is thus free to profit or fail based solely on the merit of his idea, the quality of his business acumen, and the sweat of his brow. Should success grace his doorstep, he is free to hire employees. He is free to pay said employees by way of mutual agreement. He is free to release such employees if they fail to meet his standards. These same employees, by mutual agreement, are free to accept positions from whom they please and are free to resign positions as they choose.

"Capitalism under such tenets has proven itself extremely efficient, highly competitive, and enormously productive. Free enterprise, based on individual achievement, thus compliments our constitutionally guaranteed rights to life, liberty, and the pursuit of happiness.

"Unionism is in direct contrast to capitalism. A union is the opposite of an individual. Unions do not create businesses. They do not hatch and incubate ideas or concepts. Unions do not persevere through difficult times, risking all of their worth on the chance of a successful outcome. Unions are equipped to do none of these things. Instead they invade and imbed themselves in business only after it has become successful.

"Business owners do not, at present, maintain overstaffed departments because of exceptional workmanship. They do it because to fire a union worker brings threats of slowdowns, work stoppages, and strikes. Union workers are promoted based on seniority, not on merit, making personnel cuts in staff even more inefficient. Everything from pay to work hours, duties, and frequency of breaks is negotiated—not by the individual but by the group, which means by union negotiators. Every area of possibility is stipulated, from whose job it is to pick up a piece of paper from the floor to who's job it is to drop said paper into the trash receptacle. Unions by their very nature are less efficient, less competitive, and less productive than their non-union counterparts. This is why union shops in the private sector have been in steady decline since the 1930s. To this day their numbers are at an all time low. This is also why the unions have invaded the public sector—your sector.

"If we would all don our thinking caps I believe we would discern other reasons why. In the public sector there is no competition, no requirement to earn a profit or make a payroll, no chance of going out of business, and no concerns over cutbacks in staff or workers, because government never shrinks or stands still—it does naught but grow. Is this not then the perfect home for greater inefficiencies, lesser production, higher wages, and glorious benefits? And with you, our congressmen, our elected officials, happily embracing such overabundance, why should they desire to go elsewhere?

"Groups are quite pleasing to politicians; certainly as compared with individuals. Individuals with their individual ways, individual thinking, ever making individual choices, require much work by politicians to garner their votes. For it must be done one person at a time. But a group, especially a large group such as a union, may already be persuaded to vote for the politician that butters their biscuit. Is this not a most attractive situation? Not only can a union provide votes, a union can contribute campaign dollars, can offer demonstrations of support for the candidate of choice, as well as tactics to smear his opponent. In addition they are allowed paid time off of work to do all of these things. The politician has only to offer favorable collective bargaining outcomes to union negotiators. Thus, it seems, everyone emerges victorious. Everyone except the American taxpayer, who must pay the toll.

"This country was built on individual rights, not on collective rights. A universal health care bill has already been passed into law, yet you, the government, have found it necessary to grant over a thousand waivers to various groups and businesses so they may ignore such a law. Is this the kind of government you have become? The kind that favors one over another? Are we no longer a country of laws but of men? Are there now those who are, indeed, above the law?

"You must realize that unionizing our public sector is unsustainable folly. Many states, due in no small part to public sector union pensions and favors, are either already penniless or well on their way. Union bosses colluding with career politicians is clearly disastrous. Why would you allow such a thing? Does not our national government carry a truly massive debt already? So massive that we spend hundreds of billions of dollars every year just to sustain its interest? Are we not already to our bursting point with overstaffed workers and redundant programs?

"Government coffers depend on the successful production of its people. Production comes from competitive, efficiently run businesses started by individual entrepreneurs with better ideas and innovative concepts. If we thwart these entrepreneurs, if we taint their enterprises with collectivist demands of excessive salaries and exorbitant pensions, if we overburden them with numerous government rules and regulations, do we not kill the golden goose? Is this what our founding fathers had in mind? Is this the way it was meant to be?"

Thomas raises up as tall as he's able and glares at the Senators and House members before him.

"I am here to speak for Americans who love their country, so hear me now. We the people do not wish more entitlements. We do not wish more programs, more bills passed, more government regulations implemented. We do not wish a government who would carry us, or feed us, or shelter us, or cure our ills. We do not wish a government who would lead us by the hand like small children, nor one that expects us to follow it lamb-like to the slaughter. We would, instead, have a government which allows us our pitfalls as well as our bounty. We would have a government which would not lead us down the path as a group but would stand up for us as individuals. A government which would defend us from our enemies and not become one. A government which would ensure that our freedoms, our liberties, and our pursuits of happiness remain unfettered. The government envisioned by our founders. Is this so much to ask?"

Thomas stares again at the members of Congress. He then shakes his head and answers his own question.

"I think not."

The applause, once again, is deafening, even though many congressmen are sitting on their hands. Thomas takes the opportunity to step back and savor more ice water. I assume it's over, as more and more of the audience rise to their feet and ratchet up their applause. Thomas sets his glass back down on the table, turns away from the audience, and pulls off his t-shirt. The clapping lulls a decibel or two as the people watch his actions. He calmly turns his shirt inside out and pulls it back on. He turns and steps back up to the podium before anyone can read what it says. He seems quite oblivious to his actions as he leans back into the microphone and begins to speak.

"Now I would speak not for but *to* the people. Ours is purported to be a government of the people, by the people, for the people. This makes 'we the people' the last bastion of our protection. If government and the Free Press fail in their duties then 'we the people' must protect ourselves. Fortunately, we still hold fast to the most powerful arrow in our political quiver—our vote. Many of us, however, use it foolishly or not at all. Many, perhaps all, of our political difficulties could be solved by an informed voting public. We the people, by our vote, determine the quality of the executive branch, the legislative branch, and, indirectly, the judicial branch. If the Free Press insists on distorting or burying the truth, you must uncover it for yourself, and with the information age in full turn, this task should hardly prove a difficult one. We have squandered many of our precious rights and freedoms thus far; let not the right of the vote be next."

Thomas looks up with this last and arches his eyebrows. "Think you this sacred safeguard not in jeopardy? How then can a nation which leads the world in advanced computer sophistication fail to tally votes either quickly or accurately? What excuse can be offered for persons returning from the grave, characters from cartoon films, and those who have never existed at all casting their votes with impunity? When proper identification is required to purchase a fine brew, to lease a post office compartment, or to enter a moving picture theater, why can this same verification procedure not be employed in matching a name to a voting roll? How is it proper for voting districts to be realigned willy-nilly, favoring one party over another? These improprieties corrupt the most important power we the people have left to us. If we squander such a right we will have lost all. Government by the people will cease to exist.

"If we vote for good, honest people then we will retain good, honest government. Vote for the dishonorable, the dishonest, the power-hungry, the corrupt, the ideologically extreme, the incompetent, the career-minded, the extravagant and...well...as you see. Even our pioneer ancestors could detect a slimy snake oil salesman when they encountered one. Are we not capable of doing the same? Your television set is a wonderful invention, but basing one's vote on a candidate's paid advertisement is surely a recipe for disaster. Should we really believe that watching an incumbent office-holder move toward the center of the political spectrum just before re-election is an indication of a change of mind or a change of ways? We the people must inform ourselves of a candidate's voting record—nothing less will suffice. Should we fail in this simple task then we will surely deserve the government that we get and can thus blame no one but ourselves."

He stands straight, drops his hands to his sides, and completely takes me by surprise when he says, "Ladies and gentlemen, I have nothing more to say. A good evening to you all."

He catches everyone off guard, so much so that no one even applauds, and the room lingers in silence. It's enough for one brave soul, seated in the visitor's section, to break with decorum, stand up, and shout out, "Thomas, we can't see your t-shirt."

Thomas smiles for the first time in a long while. He remains behind the podium for a minute, teasing us. He then abruptly steps to the side and walks forward to the front of the stage. He pulls his t-shirt taut so it can be read by all.

A snake in the grass you'd always been when you
come to my door in the rain
You say you've changed so I let you in,
your face shows hurtin' and pain
you drink up my beer then give me a yell
as you steal my ole Dodge Ram
"A snake in the grass I always was
And a snake in the grass I am!"

Snake In The Grass
Lyrics by Lightiker Rawlings

First there's silence. Then giggles, then chuckles, then raucous laughter with full applause that rocks the house. Thomas bows and takes his leave well before the noise dies out.

CHAPTER 26

The fallout is instantaneous. Before ladies can find their gloves, political shrinks are analyzing, talking heads are blathering, and spinmeisters are in full spin. In specially appointed media rooms, news anchors are primped and primed and sent scrambling for their marks. From where Annie and I sit we see a big screen TV suddenly come to life, showing a CNN anchorman interviewing a speech expert who is already dissecting sentences and enumerating the times Thomas used the phrase "we the people."

We watch for a few seconds and then begin to file out with the others. Everyone's chattering, some in frenetic, hand-gestured speak, others in hushed, conspiratorial tones. I glance over at the senator section and find most have removed their t-shirts and slipped back into their jackets. A few are carrying their jackets draped over their arms and proudly strutting their new slum wear. One elderly statesman has put his jacket on over his t-shirt, leaving a good ten inches of visible hem-line. I make him for a front page headline: *Senator Silliness on parade.*

I finally spot Feldstone. There's no sign of his t-shirt, so I figure it's found the nearest trash can. He's speaking with two colleagues in overly heated terms, gesticulating with harsh, brash moves. I can't hear the words but I don't need to. The senator is not happy.

I'm slowly shaking my head and looking back at an empty podium. *And so it begins, the instigation of a political crucifixion.*

I wonder if I should go backstage and attempt to round up Thomas. One look at the overly attentive security detail guarding all entrances to the back rooms tell me no. Annie suggests we go home. She feels Thomas may need some time to himself, and besides, she had earlier bought him a cell phone and taught him how to use it. Her cell number is on his speed dial. She says he'll call when he's ready.

So we head home. We discuss the speech on the way and unanimously decide it beat our expectations all to hell. It was like nothing we've ever experienced before: inspiring, insightful, honest, refreshing, and harsh—especially harsh. From experience, I know that powerful people don't accept "harsh" well.

I'm worried. We both are. To the average American watching it on TV, the speech had to have been spectacular; to the average statesman, sitting in the chamber, mighty humbling. I wonder how they'll bill it: "Thomas Dresses Down the Senate." I chuckle. But making sport of senators, challenging the president, and blasting the media have consequences. There will be a price to pay, and I'm not sure Thomas can afford it. Still, Annie and I find it impossible to keep the grins from our faces. Let's be honest, our Thomas has rocked the planet with his little show-and-tell.

I press down on the accelerator. I need to get home and turn on the TV. Maybe I'm overreacting, maybe it's not as bad I think. I pull in the garage, dash up the stairs and flick on the tube. It's worse.

I go to MSNBC to get the worst of it over with. Their prime-time anchor is interviewing a popular pundit who's going after Thomas personally. He speculates on how anyone with only two months of "consciousness" could possibly write such a speech. The t-shirt shenanigans, he says, was pure showmanship done for effect. If the American people wanted that kind of tomfoolery in their political leaders they would have voted in the Ringling Brothers.

I switch to Fox for the softer side—ironic, huh. Their anchor, Will Bryan, is talking to one of their regular pundits eliciting his take on the speech. He absolutely loved it, thought it was high time someone set the media straight, even though Fox is the media. He loved the Senators-in-t-shirts bit and thought it rather fun to take the Lords of Congress down a notch. He thought Thomas connected beautifully with mainstream America and had truly captured the voice of the people.

I go to ABC and freeze up, shocked to see Senator Feldstone's giant head fill the screen. This isn't possible. I just watched the man walk out of the capital building ranting and raving, mad as hell.

It hits me. The senator had promised Roger Balcomb a follow up interview after Thomas's big speech. ABC must have caught up with him before he got out of the building and held his feet to the fire. Reading his face I'm pretty sure they've picked a bad time to interview the Senator. I turn up the volume and step in closer.

"So, Senator, what do you think of your boy, Thomas, now?"

I note even Roger's standing a couple steps back as Feldstone tries to smile but can't pull it off. His face is as red as a hydrant and he looks like he's about to blow. He glares hard at Roger.

"We were had, Roger, we were duped, deceived, lied to. I will personally be conducting an investigation into this matter first thing tomorrow morning with my chief of staff. We *will* get to the bottom of this."

"You mean Hartford Keepe."

"Yes, I mean Hartford Keepe." He hisses my name.

"Tell me Senator, what did you think when Thomas accused..."

"Roger, I'm cutting this thing short. I have a meeting."

The senator abruptly stands up, pulls off his microphone, and throws it in the chair. He turns and stomps down the hall.

"A meeting," Roger shouts running after him, "at this hour? What kind of meeting?"

I don't know what I expected. Thomas did come down hard on just about every facet of government. Naturally they're gonna go into lockdown mode if only to spitball a strategy. When they come up with one, though, they're gonna come out swinging.

Since I didn't get an invite to the meeting, I have no place to go so I switch back to MSNBC where Chuck Mathison is talking to, who else, Patti Rutherford Rhodes. There's not a muzzle in sight. The two of them are smirking at each other like the original I-told-you-so twins.

"So, Patti," Chuck is saying, "what do you think of Senator Feldstone's prodigy, now?"

"Well Chuck, I tried to warn them but nobody wanted to listen. I told them Thomas was a Tea Party plant all along but they all wanted to buy into this innocent, man-of-the-people, nonsense."

"I'll bet their listening now, Patti."

"They'd better be. This man is dangerous. He wants to take our government apart plank by plank, department by department. He doesn't care how many jobs are lost or how many Americans go hungry. In his address he denigrated every part of our Democracy from the press to the president. I believe he would do away with government altogether if given the chance." She puts her finger to her chin. "And this is the man chosen to speak for the America people. Can you believe it?"

" I imagine Senator Feldstone is fit to be tied."

"Let's not be too hard on the good senator, Chuck. I understand it was his chief of staff, Hartford Keepe, who put this thing together. I'm sure Senator Feldstone was taken in just like the rest of us."

"You weren't, Patti. I think it's very fortunate that the American people have watchdogs like you who can ferret out and expose scoundrels like Thomas and his cohorts.

"You know, in his speech, Thomas insisted that we are harboring enemies within our borders who would do us harm. I believe he was right, Chuck. It's people like Thomas who would do us harm. He and his ilk would destroy this government and allow people to run rampant in the streets. It's people like Thomas who would allow hunger and disease to infect the poor while fat cats on wall street refuse to pay their fair share of taxes. If this country is destroyed from within, it will be because of people like Thomas."

And that, I decide, is enough Patti Rutherford Rhodes.

I run through CNN, CNBC, CBS, then NBC. Most emulate MSNBC, but with less sarcasm and rancor. They tear into the speech more than they tear into Thomas. Still, they do just what he said they'd do: they either misquote or dismiss everything of consequence, and not once do they mention the Constitution or the founding fathers. As the night wears on, their rhetoric is filled with less truth and more equivocation, until eventually, just as Thomas warned, I can't recognize the speech they're criticizing. When I look up at the clock I see it's after two a.m. and still no word from Thomas. That's when I notice the blinking red light on the answering machine which wasn't there before.

I stand up, walk over, and hit the play button.

"This is Thomas," it says. "You shall see me and hear my words this Monday next. I must abstain from communication until such time." It clicks off.

"Hartford." It's Annie, from upstairs. She had given up on the news after MSNBC and taken to her bed in exhaustion. Her sonic ears, however, never shut down. "Is that Thomas?"

"He left a message," I yell. "He said we would see him on Monday and that he would be out of touch until then."

There's silence.

Finally, in panic, "Hart, quick, you need to come up here."

I race up the stairs to the bedroom. Annie's holding the remote, pointing it at the TV.

"Wait," she says, "let me rewind."

She goes back about forty-five seconds and then clicks pause. She's on a local station that's playing an excerpt from one of the national news streams. A familiar anchor is talking to Katie Kattzman of the DC Morning Show. Katie is known as the "Enquirer" of the DC airwaves. She usually features celebrity has-beens, scandal-ridden politicians, and Washington socialites on their way down.

Everyone calls her Katie Katt and knows she comes with claws and hiss.

"I don't want to see her," I say, turning to leave.

"Yes you do, watch." She hits play.

The anchor's talking, "You've managed quite a coup, Katie. How on earth did you do it?"

"He called me," she says, "right out of the blue. I have, as I'm sure you know, an exclusive interview Monday morning at eight o'clock with the infamous Thomas. We've extended our time block and are giving him an entire two-hour slot. You don't want to miss this."

Annie pauses the TV and looks at me. I'm still staring at the frozen screen.

"Our Thomas?" I say, knowing that it has to be.

She nods. "I guess this is what he meant by 'we'll see *him* Monday' and not the other way around."

"Why…" I say, unable to get past the shock. "Why her?"

"I don't know. Something's not right." She picks up her cell phone and stares at it. "I just wish he'd call."

"Have you called him?" I say lamely.

"At least a hundred times, it goes straight to voicemail. I leave the same message every time—'Call me, please.'"

This is bad. Thomas has scheduled himself on the worst "got-cha" show with the worst "gotcha" host in television history. This, while most of the media are already out to bury him. What was he thinking? I take the remote from Annie and go over the segment another half dozen times trying to make sense of it. Finally, I, too, surrender to exhaustion and frustration and take to bed alongside Annie. I lie there trying to think it through but sleep forces my eyes shut and quickly puts me under.

I awake in ten minutes, which turns out to be eight hours. I hear Annie's voice from the bathroom, talking on her cell, so I yell, "Is that Thomas?"

She clicks off and sticks her head out the door to explain that it was Archie, who seems to know nothing about Thomas's whereabouts. I immediately figure he's lying and wonder if the FBI left me any waterboarding equipment in the conference room.

I suggest we jump in the car and go Thomas-hunting, but Annie will have none of it. She says she needs to be here when he comes home. She can't keep the Kleenex from her eyes. I wonder if she gets this way when I don't show up on time, but I doubt it. Let's face it, Annie's highly attuned to her female instincts, and they're telling her something's definitely wrong. Who am I to dismiss such concerns?

Truth be known, I'm not taking it so well either. I wonder if Feldstone and Niles have Thomas tied up in the basement of the Russell building and are methodically cramming talking points down his throat.

I finally manage to convince Annie to take a walk with me and breathe some fresh air. She reluctantly agrees, pulls on her sweatshirt, and grabs her cell. We go out the front door, turn left, and start walking. It seems more than a mere stroll. I figure we'll stop on the way at one of the delis or breakfast spots for coffee and bagels, but that's not in the plan. We walk briskly and purposely toward the Capitol Park grounds.

We enter the park to the usual smattering of Saturday morning tourists meandering in random patterns about the campus. There's one obvious difference, however: there are a whole lot of them. Annie seems not to notice. She turns left and heads straight for the mall. The number of tourists increases dramatically as we get closer. I notice a lot of these people—most of them, actually—are wearing Thomas t-shirts. The colors vary, the quotes change, but there's a little Minuteman logo at the bottom corner of every one. I look over at Annie and see the hint of a smile for the first time since last night.

We continue down the mall at a fast clip, her leading, me following. Eventually I'm able to realize her goal—Thomas's shop.

Her pace picks up the minute she sees it. Hundreds of people are concentrated around the kiosk. The place is closed so they're not buying, but they're standing around, congregating in twos and threes and fours, discussing, bantering, debating one another. No one's shouting or arguing, they're just talking, communicating. We keep walking, heading straight for the center of the fray. Once we reach the front of the kiosk, we stop, stand there, and listen. There are small groups of people all about us, most wearing Thomas tees and all discussing last night's speech.

Words and phrases like, "unbelievable," "fantastic," "spot on," "man of the people," and "I love this guy," are being bandied about—that last one coming from me. I look again at Annie, who's in full smile, absorbing the mood and the words like a cat in the sun. I touch the corners of my mouth and discover I'm smiling too. This is quite the change from all the TV and newspaper negativity. I wonder if these people represent mainstream America or if they're just the fringe, the Tea Partiers. Then I wonder if the Tea Partiers represent mainstream America. If this is so then mainstream America is about a hundred and eighty degrees out from DC America, free press America, and Senator Feldstone's America.

I reach out for Annie's hand and feel her warmth. I look at her. She is truly basking in the glow. I suggest we sit and stay a while but then realize all of the benches are occupied. She smiles and points to an empty one up the hill some twenty yards away. It surprises me since this will take her out of, well, the glow. But as she pulls me along I realize it's the Thomas Bench she seeks.

And that's how we spend the rest of the morning, our lunch time, and the whole of the afternoon: avoiding negative news and watching American citizens practicing their freedom of speech, right here, on the Capitol grounds in the good ole USA.

CHAPTER 2

'm up early, down the stairs, sitting at the kitchen/news table with coffee in hand by 6:31 a.m. I have the TV on Fox News and the Sunday paper laid out in front of me. Fox and panel are embroiled in an all-out Katie Katt speculation bout. What will she say to Thomas? How will Thomas respond? How quickly and severely will she emasculate him?

Katie is known for digging the dirt, and, though no one knows Thomas's past, I wouldn't put it past her to have uncovered something scandalous—and if not uncovered, fabricated. I watch as the ignorant chatter drones on and eventually moves to a discussion of the great divide: government, the media, the fringe activists versus the American majority. The former hates Thomas; the latter loves him. I glance down at the paper and read the headline:

Thomas Speaks But Does Congress Listen?

I peruse the article and it, too, is all about Thomas—not his speech, but about what Katie Katt will throw at him, about why he accepted the gig in the first place, and about what he expects to gain from the deal. I scan the rest of the articles on the front page, all of them all about Thomas. I hear the stairs creak and glance at the clock—7:15. I look toward the living room and see Annie shuffling my way. She's wearing her PJs and robe with sloppy socks and no slippers. She's had a rough night. I know the TV and newspaper aren't going to make things better, so I pick up the remote and point it at the set, but she sees me and shakes her head.

"I have to hear it sooner or later," she says. "I can take it. Besides, tomorrow I get to see how he looks."

"Did you try his cell again?"

"No. He's not going to answer. We'll see him when everyone else does—on the Katie Katt Show."

Her eyes are red and puffy. She's been doing a lot of crying. I think she might start up again so I say, "I'm sure he was required to sign a contract with the DC Morning Show. It probably restricted any contact with the outside world."

"We're his family," she says.

"Not to them. I'm Feldstone's Chief of Staff. I'm probably at the top of their 'don't call' list."

I stand up and open my arms, figuring she'll wave me away since I've never stood up and opened my arms before, but she doesn't. She walks directly into my hug, puts her arms around my waist, lays her head on my shoulder, and slips into a soft cry. I hold her for a long time, longer than I can remember ever holding her before, until the sniffles go away, and then I hold her for a little while longer. She eventually begins to make little ease-out movements, so I reluctantly let her go.

Even though she said those things about the news, she still won't look at the TV or the paper. I suggest a movie but she shakes her head at that, too.

"What then?"

"Let's go back to the park," she says. "We can stop at Jerry Dale's for breakfast."

She's hungry, I'm hungry, this is good, so I say, "When?"

"As soon as I change." She throws me the hint of a smile, the second one in two days, and heads up the stairs to the bedroom.

Breakfast at Jerry's is always delicious, and this time even more so. Cream cheese on whole wheat bagels for Annie; eggs, bacon, hash browns, and a waffle with strawberry topping for me.

We leave Jerry's with broad smiles and satisfied tummies, but as we approach the Capitol grounds our mood shifts. The change is obvious. If yesterday was "discussion," today is "demonstration." There are at least twice the number of people on the mall today, but they're not in small groups anymore. They're divided into two large crowds, each numbering in the hundreds. One group distinguishing itself by a plethora of Minuteman t-shirts, the other by large signs and loud chants.

"Thomas doesn't speak for me," reverberates throughout the grounds.

The signs are mostly homemade, although some are printed. The printed ones say "Workers Unite" in purple letters on white backgrounds, with a bold SEIU at the bottom of each one, which explains the chant. The homemade signs are larger and more confusing. Annie's favorite says "Impeach Thomas, Now." It's hard for me to choose. There's "Go home Thomas—if you can find it," "Tom, Tom, The Capitalist's Son," "Thomas who?", and "T-shirt Tommy," to name a few. People are yelling and screaming at each other, but I see no fisticuffs yet. It seems we've stumbled upon the nastier side of freedom of speech.

Annie turns to me and suggests we take in that movie after all, and as we do an about-face her cell phone rings. I'm afraid she'll rip her pocket off trying to get it out of her jeans. Her whole being lights up as she holds the phone to her ear. She says hello and her face crumbles.

It's Archie, checking to see if we've heard from Thomas. It seems the shop is open today and his famous partner has pulled another no-show, so he needs help. A certain gleam finds Annie's eyes as she relates Archie's dilemma.

It sounds crazy but I suddenly hear myself saying, "Let's do it. Let's go sell Thomas t-shirts." At this point, I'll do anything to keep a smile on that woman's face.

So for the rest of the afternoon and well into the evening, Annie Green and the Chief of Staff to the honorable Harold P. Feldstone sell Minuteman t-shirts at a kiosk on the mall of The US Capitol. America's entrepreneurial, free enterprise spirit in action.

CHAPTER 28

Monday morning takes forever to get here. I don't sleep and neither does Annie. We both did our toss-and-turn, bed blanket tug-of-war most of the night, so by six thirty we're wide awake and exhausted. I elect to get up while Annie stays put searching for lost sleep. I leave the bathroom, ease down the stairs, and reach the kitchen table still wearing my boxers and Thomas tee. I immediately turn on the TV.

The cable stations are continuing their all-Thomas, all-the-time programming, and now the networks are catching up. The Katie Katt interview speculation game is in full swing. An expert on CNN is convinced that Thomas isn't going to show and that Katie Katt has invented the whole thing to boost ratings. I switch to Fox and listen to a discussion on whether Thomas will backpedal on some of his more extreme views. They seem especially adamant that he take back his criticism of the free press.

I walk over and start the coffee machine. While it prepares to percolate, I step outside to retrieve the paper. By 7:03 I'm back, sitting at the kitchen/breaking-news table with coffee, paper, and a bagel in hand. It feels a little like Super Bowl Sunday without the beer and pretzels.

Annie walks in but I fail to hear her. Her unkempt hair, tattered robe, and groggy eyes reflect her mood. She looks lovely. She zones in on the coffee machine, asking if I want breakfast. I suggest that she sit and savor a cup or two and then we can decide if we're hungry.

By the time she lights, I've perused the front page of the paper and found it, like the TV, filled with anticipation and speculation. It seems that Katie Katt has put this town on its edge. I'm hoping she's not putting us on along with it.

We're still twenty minutes away from the start of The DC Morning Show—or, as some call it, "The Katt Show"—but I click over to her channel anyway. And—surprise, surprise—they're doing a pre-show buildup with Katie Katt and a panel of Thomas experts. The three pundits are sharing their wisdom with Katie. One thinks Thomas is coming on TV to defend his speech and make a book deal. Another suspects he's going to apologize to Congress, the media, and the president for his remarks. The third one believes Thomas has caught the fame bug and is eager to extend his fifteen minutes. Katie Katt is positive Thomas is coming on the show to meet her.

Annie gets up and starts breakfast while the four sages on TV manage to slow down time. We tolerate the ignorance as long as we can, but eventually our attention strays. With me in my paper and Annie in her frying pan, the clock strikes eight before we're ready. Our heads jerk toward the TV and our ears pick up on the words "DC Morning Show with host Katie Kattzan" blaring from the speaker. Annie hurries over to the table and sits down. I automatically grab the remote and turn up the volume, though it's plenty loud already. We both lean forward, trying to control our breathing.

Katie Katt, all two hundred pounds of her, bounces out onto the set wearing a pink flowered muumuu and a giant grin.

"Everybody," she says, "he's here, right here on my show, yes, he is, so let's not waste any time. Please, give a nice warm welcome to our very special guest—Thomas!"

Clapping, cheering, and whistling erupt from the TV speakers, though we can't see the audience because the cameras are aimed directly at the side curtains. Nothing happens for several long seconds and then, suddenly, Thomas struts out onto the stage. The audience notches up the noise and the camera pans to Katie Katt, registering both surprise and relief, and then it returns to Thomas. At least I think it's Thomas.

A man wearing a t-shirt, jeans, and Reeboks swaggers over to Katie Katt. Talk about a jolt, the camera should have been panning us. Annie and I sit there drop-jawed. We've known Thomas his entire present-memory life and we've never seen him dress or walk this way. His t-shirt isn't even a Thomas tee. And then there's the way he stands, the way he moves, the insolent expression on his face. I recognize the man, but It makes me wonder if he has a slovenly twin.

He shakes Katie Katt's hand instead of kissing it and sits down on the couch next to her, absent a wee bow. He casually crosses his leg, ankle to thigh, and leans back in a slouch.

"So, Thomas," Katie says, and before she can go on he interrupts her.

"It's Tom," he says, "Tom Montgomery."

Somebody on the set actually squeals. Annie and I barely hear it because we're too busy sucking in air and fighting off hyperventilation. Stunned is not strong enough—numbed on our way to paralysis is more accurate.

Once Katie Katt finds her voice she says, "You know your last name."

"Absolutely, it's Montgomery, Tom Montgomery. I'm from a little town in northern Maine called Kosinage." He pronounces it K -sin-age. He leans back and smiles into the camera. Kattie Katt remains helplessly mute so he says, "So, you bought the whole Thomas bit, did you?" He chuckles. "I guess everybody did."

The camera pans to Katie Katt for a response but gets nothing, so it pans to the studio audience and shows a bunch of silent, wide-eyed, open-mouthed spectators.

"I did it on a dare," Tom goes on, "a bet. Everybody in Kosinage was in on it. Nobody thought I could pull it off, but then..." he throws his hands out in font of him, "here I am."

Katie Katt, with her hands over her chest trying to control her heartbeat, pants, "A bet—a bet over what?"

"Over whether a good ole boy from a small burg in Maine could get his fifteen minutes of fame." His smile goes big. "I won." He shrugs his shoulders. "Never figured on all this, though."

He stands up, turns, and points both his index fingers, pistol-like, at Kattie Katt.

"So," he says, "now you know, gotta go."

"What?" She mumbles. "Where?"

"To collect my winnings, of course." He winks at the camera, turns, and walks off the set.

It's apparently the jump-start Katie Katt needs. She hops to her feet, shouts, "Wait!", and rushes after him. The fixed studio cameras follow the action through the exit curtain as best they can—first Tom, then Katie Katt, then an empty curtain waving in the breeze. It eventually pans to a stunned audience and then back to an empty couch, hoping someone will come back and entertains us. Nobody does.

CHAPTER 29

If we were numb before, now we're vegetables. Our brains won't think and our mouths won't speak; our arms and legs have gone completely limp. I guess we're fortunate our lungs still breathe and our hearts still beat, because every other part of us is stone cold dead.

Annie comes out of it first, mumbling something unintelligible. Thirty seconds later I respond with, "What?"

"He's lost his formal speech," she says more slowly.

"That's what you're worried about?" I say, jumping up, rage curing my paralysis. "His speech? Did you hear what he said?"

"Calm down, Hart, I'm right here."

I try to calm down and succeed only in lowering my shrillness half an octave.

"How could he? How the hell could he? He deceived us. No, he betrayed us, all of us. Damn him!" I shake my head and throw her an accusing look. "I can't believe you're not furious."

"I'm upset," she says, "disappointed, sad. I just can't help thinking there's more to this. That—I don't know—that it's not over."

"Well, it sure as hell's going to be over when they catch him. And believe me, they will catch him. Talk about your tar and feathers. Anybody who supported him, cared about him, embraced his words—they're done, discredited, humiliated. Don't you see,

Annie? He destroyed more than himself today. He destroyed everyone who believed in him, in his speech, in the restoration of this country. He'll become the Bernie Maddoff of politics."

"You never believed in the restoration of this country."

"Not until Thomas came along I didn't. He changed me."

She gives me a skeptical look but I don't see it. I'm too busy pacing, shaking my head, trying to clear my brain. I stop and put my fists to my temples to quell the anger or maybe to keep my head from exploding.

"I suppose it could have been worse," I say. "I guess we were lucky we found him out when we did."

"We didn't find him out. He confessed on his own, and not to us, to the nation. It begs the preeminent question." I stare at her and she says, "Why?"

"Oh, that's easy, he said it himself. He wanted the spotlight, the fame, he wanted to show us how clever he was. Hell, he was getting paid for it, remember? He's off to collect his winnings."

"It just isn't like Thomas," she says.

"There is no Thomas," I practically yell—*do* yell.

"Do you really think they'll go after him?"

"I guarantee it. They're organizing a posse as we speak. This is one time the Feds and the media will work hand-in-hand. They're both after the same thing—Tom Montgomery's neck in a noose."

"Will he do jail time?"

"Jail time?" I lower my voice but not my anger. "They'll fit him with an iron mask and put him in a dungeon if they can—after parading him down Main Street in a steel cage and flashing his mug shot with the words 'Scammer, Deceiver, Impostor' on every TV screen and newspaper in the land. Damn right he'll do jail time. He lied to us Annie."

"The Enquirer lies every day, politicians lie all the time, even the president lies."

I'm nodding my head slowly while not saying, *My, poor, sweet, naive Annie.*

"Legally they'll get him for lying under oath, at the Senate hearing and when he was vetted by the FBI. That's how they'll charge him, anyway, but he'll be condemned for deceiving the United States government as well as the American people."

"They won't find him," she says softly.

I stare at her.

"Annie, they have his name, first and last, his hometown, his last known location—they know where he's going. I'm sure the media has already unleashed an army of investigative reporters. Feldstone, with the president's backing, has probably already assembled the top FBI SWAT team in the country. Oh they'll get him, even if they have to extradite him from Peru."

I plop back down at the kitchen/bad news table and put my head in my hands. I take a deep breath and feel the cold mist of disappointment and hopelessness envelope me.

"I thought he was my friend," I say. "I can't believe I fell for it."

"We all did."

"Yes, but I'm a pro. I'm supposed to be able to read people, to ferret them out, to call them on their lies, their deceptions. It's what I do, it's my job, it's who I am. How did I miss this?"

"Hartford."

"Yeah."

"What if they don't find the town?"

"Annie, we've been over this. They've got the resources, they..."

"What if there is no town called Kosinage? What if..." she pauses and takes in a deep breath, "there is no Tom Montgomery?"

I freeze up and look into her eyes. I think I see past the desperate. I think I see something more, and then I get hold of myself.

"Of course there's a Kosinage and of course there's a Tom Montgomery. *Thomas said*—" and suddenly I stop talking.

"Yes, that's right, Thomas said...And yet there is no Thomas." She smiles and takes my hand. "You believed in him, Hart. I believed in him. Maybe it's time to keep believing. You know who Thomas is—he's your friend."

She squeezes my hand and stares into my eyes.

"Could it be," she says in a voice just above a whisper, "that there is no Tom?"

I sit here trying to get my head around the incomprehensible and can't. I finally retort with the only thing that comes into my mind.

"Why?"

"To protect us—you, me, Archie, his friends, his supporters, those who love this country."

"How is making us look like gullible fools protecting us? How is delivering the greatest speech I've ever heard and then turning around and invalidating it and himself protecting his supporters?"

"They were going after him, Hart. The smear campaign was already in high gear. You said so yourself. Thomas had criticized the media, the Congress, the president to his face. Look what they did to Reagan, to Quayle, to Bush, to Palin, to anyone who questions their actions. Thomas did much more. He not only criticized them, he chastised them, and he did it in front of the world. His speech was incredible, the people loved it, they loved him. A man of the people, who had the audacity to love his country and to want to try and save it. He was a threat, Hart, a big, bold threat. The irony here is that it was they who pushed him into the spotlight. They were the ones who offered him a stage on which to shine. Don't you see? They have no choice now but to destroy him."

"Why not stand up to them, fight 'em, take their best shot. We'd support him."

"Hart, he's not stupid. He knows what happened to the others, to Bush, to Palin. Their reputations suffered death by a thousand cuts. That's how they do it, you know. And those two had credible backgrounds, a history of government service, stellar reputations. Thomas has no reputation and no background at all, he's a blank page; one which his critics would love to fill in. They'd have no trouble dicing him up and serving him raw."

I don't have to urge her to continue, she's on a roll.

"So what does he do? He pulls out a classic sports tactic—you should know. He pulls out the old rope-a-dope. He makes a bet, not with some boys in a bar, but with himself. He bets that if he shows surrender or even vulnerability his enemies won't back off but will come at him even harder with everything they've got. That they'll try to squash him in the public square while the entire nation watches. He's baiting them, Hart."

I shake my head, partly in astonishment, mostly in confusion. "But—why?"

"Because he can't defeat their thousand cuts. He needs to goad them into putting all their efforts into one, giant, decapitating blow."

"What does it matter, a thousand cuts or one decapitating blow—either way they destroy him."

She smiles. "Did you notice his t-shirt during the Katie Katt interview?"

I think about it but my brain is busy synapsing around her last words.

"Some kind of Martial Arts thing," I say.

"It said, *Hong's Martial Arts Club,* with, *we specialize in jujitsu,* printed underneath. Ring any bells?"

I keep shaking my head, this time to clear it, and some recall returns.

"A sport where a participant uses the power of his bigger, stronger opponent to defeat him," I say.

"Exactly. I believe Thomas's confession, through his alias, Tom Montgomery, was done purely to gin up hatred from his enemies. I believe when their wrath reaches the proper level he plans to use it against them. I think they're playing into his hands." She picks up the remote and points it. "Shall we view the fallout?"

A smile, something absent my face the past hour, reappears. The two things I've been loath to do—pick to up a newspaper or turn on a TV—suddenly becomes necessary, even desirable. I nod and she hits the power button.

MSNBC and Chuck Mathison fill the screen. It seems he's hit the trifecta. He's assembled a discussion panel featuring Patti

Rutherford Rhodes, Senator Harold Feldstone and Attorney Logan Duckworth. What we have here is the Jerry Springer News Hour.

"I'm going to start with Patti Rutherford Rhodes," says Chuck, "with the same question I asked her last time. What do think of Thomas, or should I say, Tom Montgomery, now, Patti?"

Patti is practically drooling with delight.

"Well Chuck, I really feel for the American people—especially those naive souls gullible enough to be taken in by this Tom Montgomery..."

"We were all taken in, Patti."

"No, not all of us, but you're right, a lot of people were and I hurt for them, Chuck."

"Senator Feldstone." Chuck switches over while Patti tries to replace her grin with a look of concern.

"I suspect you must be feeling especially ill used. Do you think your chief of staff, Hardford Keepe, was in on this?"

"We don't know that, Chuck, but yes, I am devastated. I'm an honorable and a trusting man, always have been, and this Tom Montgomery both lied to and deceived me. I don't know what this world is coming to. It makes my blood boil. We're wrapping up our internal investigation as we speak. We should have some answers for you soon and when we do, believe me, the guilty parties will be held accountable."

"Speaking of holding people accountable," Chuck says, "we are fortunate to have with us on the panel, Mr. Logan Duckworth, attorney extrordenaire—welcome to the show, Logan."

"Thanks, Chuck, happy to be here."

"So tell us, has this Tom Montgomery broken any actual laws and will he do time."

"I should say so, Chuck. You can't go around lying to people, pretending you're someone you're not. There are penalties to be paid."

"He didn't just lie to people," Patti jumps in, "he lied to congress, the president and the entire United States of America. They should lock him up and throw away the key."

"Unfortunately if you're not under oath you can say pretty much anything you please."

"Can't yell fire in a theater."

" No, you can't do that, Patti, but I wouldn't worry about it. They have plenty on which to convict Tom Montgomery. Just the fact he concealed his true identity has implications under the law. But where they have an open and shut case and where they'll convict him, is in the FBI vetting session and the confirmation hearings. Both of those instances involved an administered oath. He'll do jail time for that alone." Everyone around the table takes a moment to trade gleeful smiles.

"I'm told no expense is being spared in an effort to capture Tom Montgomery," Chuck says. "They're calling him a national security threat. I think this headline says it all."

He holds up a copy of The New York Times: ALL OUT MANHUNT UNDERWAY FOR TOM MONTGOMERY—THE MAN WHO EMBARRASSED A NATION.

I'm shaking my head. *Man, I hope Annie's right.*

I switch through a dozen other news channels, finding an aura of smug anticipation emanating from the faces of pundits and talking heads throughout the networks as they speculate on the certain demise of the man. Only on Fox News do I detect a note of anything but joy—disappointment, perhaps, as they try to rationalize Mr. Montgomery's actions. Not one station, pundit, or panel comes anywhere close to offering Annie's rope-a-dope theory. There's hardly a mention of Thomas by anyone. They're all too busy trying and condemning Tom Montgomery.

We're both desperate to hear from Thomas, but as the morning wears on our expectations wane. I don't go into work and nobody calls to ask why. Either they're too busy licking their wounds or I've been fired. The television continues to turn out talking heads, Tom experts, and all-star discussion panels, who carry on incessantly about that lying, guilty-until-proven-innocent Tom Montgomery and his inevitable apprehension. The local news rears its head every half hour to give us a blow-by-blow of the preparations taken and resources assembled in pursuit of the culprit.

Neither the Feds nor the national media have yet placed boots on the ground in Northern Maine, but the state cops have been alerted and are scavenging for clues at this very moment. I'm sure they have standing orders not to shoot anyone until the FBI shows up. The first wave of media is expected to be on location by tonight, while the others won't land until Sunday morning. This tells me that nothing of any consequence will happen until at least Sunday afternoon. So I turn off the TV, flash a charming smile at Annie, and suggest we go out for a late breakfast.

We walk to a small diner three blocks from our house, hearing dribbles and snippets of talk on the street, all of it about Tom Montgomery—that dirty rat. Once we reach the restaurant and sit down, I want to continue my discussion with Annie but the owner has the TV turned up so loud we can't hear anything else, and, based on the expressions around the room, nobody wants to.

We scarf down our food quickly and escape to the outside. We're bound and determined to avoid TVs, radios, and newspapers for the rest of the day. I think neither of us wants to be brought down by the negativity. Even though Annie's theory garners us a measure of hope, it's still just a theory—one in which we are the only believers. By mid-afternoon we wander onto Capitol grounds and find ourselves sitting, once again, on the Thomas Bench. It seems apropos.

We sit awhile without speaking, enjoying the flora and fauna. The people are few in number, with no discussions or demonstrations in sight. I look toward the kiosk to see if it's open and it is. Not much of a crowd, though; a handful of tourists looking but not buying. I turn to Annie.

"Okay," I say, "tell me exactly how the media is playing into Thomas's hands."

She looks at me and smiles; beautiful, smart, insightful—I need to marry this woman.

"Let's go back to his speech," she says, "when he chastised the media."

"Okay, loved it, especially when he accused them of twisting and distorting his every word—which, of course, is what they did."

"Yes, but after that."

I have to think. "Sure, he claimed they would quote him word for word, time and time again, as surely as the sun would rise on the day—a bit dramatic, I thought."

"And now?"

I should be getting annoyed, leading me point by point like a two-year-old, but I'm into the game.

"And now?" And it hits me. "Oh my God. you're right. They're quoting him verbatim, word for word, over and over again, but they're not quoting Thomas—they're quoting Tom."

"Because," she prompts.

Okay, now I'm getting irritated. The old Hartford would have blown up at this point, but the new Hartford says, "Because Tom Montgomery is saying what they want the people to hear."

"Exactly."

I look around for my gold star but don't see one, and Annie continues.

"Thomas was a threat. In his speech he spoke the truth. They needed to discredit the speech which means they needed to discredit Thomas. With no race card to play they were probably preparing to deal the too-dumb-to-take-seriously card when Thomas offered up the lying-cheating-scoundrel card in the form of Tom Montgomery. It was too good to pass up. It was nearly perfect."

"Nearly?" I say.

"There's a problem, a paradox. Thomas is a smart, honest, humble man who loves his country and wants to do right by her. Tom is a greedy, dishonest sleaze. They've endorsed the sleaze."

"I don't follow. They're out to get Tom Montgomery, they want to hang him up by his thumbs, to lock him in a cell and throw away the key."

"Only because he was once Thomas," she says.

It's getting too complicated, too convoluted, I can't get my head around it so I just nod.

"I think he's trying to teach them a lesson," she says.

"Them, who? The media, the government?"

"The American people; the rest are beyond help. If we're right," she kindly adds me to the team, though she's the only Sherlock here, "and there is no Tom. If Thomas is, indeed, validated, then the fall these guys are going to take will make our temporary setback feel like a hiccup."

"Explain—please," I say.

"Okay." She spreads her hands and rests them on her knees. "There is a Thomas, he's real, and he's not stupid."

I nod.

"Tom Montgomery is not real. Tom is a lesson."

I nod again but not in understanding.

"I know that Thomas has recovered his memory or at least some of it."

Shocked, I say, "When?"

"Sometime prior to his speech, maybe even the night of his speech."

I'm without words, trying hard to digest hers. She takes my silence as license to continue.

"Thomas shoulders a heavy burden. He must prove to the people, beyond a shadow of a doubt, that he is who he says he is. To do this he must rely on the media."

"Wait a minute," I hold up both hands. "The same media who thinks he's Tom Montgomery; the media that's out for his scalp."

"A difficult task," she says.

"Not difficult, impossible. But let's move over to the *why* for a second. Why would Thomas do such a thing? I mean, he's not an office-holder protecting his fiefdom. He's not even a candidate. Why fight this fight?"

"He loves his country, Hart, he wants to save it, to restore it. He didn't accept your LTA offer out of friendship alone. He saw it as a way to inspire others, those who feel as he does. But he realized that there are powerful forces out there, those who would practice the politics of personal destruction—those who would smear him, who would attempt to discredit his words, his honor. For his speech to have impact Thomas knew he had to neutralize the smearmongers."

"That's what this is all about? Neutralizing the smear machine?"

Annie smiles and nods her head. "I think so, yes."

"Wow." I'm now shaking mine.

"What?"

"It can't be done. Reagan, Quayle, Bush, Palin—all of them power figures and they couldn't do it. Is Thomas to succeed where everyone else has failed?"

"He's not stupid, Hart."

"I think it's going to take a lot more than 'not stupid' to pull this off."

She crosses her arms over her chest and sits up straight. It's her "conversation over" posture. She looks quite cute sitting there all rigid and huffy, but it isn't helpful and it isn't what I want. I screwed up when I challenged her precious Thomas, but I couldn't help it. I want to hear her story. I need to know how she sees this thing playing out. It's just that I doubt I can restrain myself from poking holes in her theory.

"So can we continue?" I say.

"I don't think so, Hart. I think it best I keep my theories to myself for the time being and we watch this thing play out separately."

"Okay, fine, have it your way. But I'll tell you right now no-body's that smart. Nobody can predict the actions and tactics of a vast national media, five hundred thirty-five members of Congress, and the President of the United States—especially someone who's been absent his memory until just a few days ago."

She stands up, hands on her hips, and glares at me.

"Has it ever occurred to you that Thomas may have had more than just a passing interest in early American history? Could it be that he has also studied world history, particularly political world history, and has learned that those in power, when threatened, act in a similar and predictable fashion? Could Thomas be an expert on such things?"

Her body language, the blazing eyes, the thin, compressed lips, the defiant posture, tells me her thoughts are more than speculation. I don't want to fight with her, especially when she's fighting for Thomas; it's un-winnable. But I also don't want her to get her hopes up too high just to have them dashed all to pieces as this thing plays out.

"I'm sorry, Annie. I know Thomas is smart. He's my friend, too, but how does anyone prevent one's enemy from smearing him? Especially when one's enemies consist of the most powerful people on earth?"

She huffs once, then sits back down next to me, maintaining her stare, searching my eyes for, I'm sure, some smidgen of sincerity.

Finally, she says, "You do it by having your enemies—those who want to smear you, demonize you, destroy you—reverse course. You have them validate you."

"Oh," *crazy woman*, I think but don't say. "Is that all?"

"That's all." She says in a soft, condescending tone which tells me that's also all I'm gonna get.

We walk home in relative silence. The few words we do speak are not about Thomas, which is the one subject we both want to discuss. Once we arrived at the condo, Annie goes upstairs to do some cleaning and calm her psyche, and I settle onto the living room sofa, switch on the TV, and pretend to watch baseball. I hate baseball.

Once I hear the vacuum cleaner start up I click over to CNN. The anchor is saying that there is no town called Kosinage in northern Maine nor in any other part of the state and that there has been no word on the whereabouts Mr. Tom Montgomery. The man seems to have completely vanished.

A grin finds my face. I have to tell her even though it'll blow my baseball cover. I wait for the vacuum cleaner to shut down and I yell up the stairs.

"Annie, you were right. The town of Kosinage doesn't exist." Silence, so I add, "How did you know?"

She comes down the stairs softly and perches on the next to the last step with a smile.

"How do you spell Kosinage?" she asks.

Oh, goodie, the teacher's back. "I don't know: K-O-S-I-N-A-G-E?"

"The French were early settlers to Northern Maine, French speaking Acadianes, actually. They would have spelled it: C-O-Z-E-N-A-G-E, with a short 'o'—Có-zen-age."

"Fine, but there is no Cozenage, Thomas made it up. Again, how did you know?"

"It's in the dictionary. As a noun it means: a deceiver. I knew there was no Cozenage the minute I heard Thomas say it."

I knew there was no Cozenage the minute I heard Thomas say it, I want to mimic her in my sarcastic falsetto voice, but I know better, so I say, "Tell me, then, why are you wasting your talents as a lowly t-shirt rep while I am Chief of Staff to one of the most powerful senators in the country?"

"Because," she says, "that's what you think you want to be." She smiles, walks over and gives me a peck on the cheek.

Something in our banter, my stupidity or her brilliance, softens the anger. We're talking again. Not about Thomas, but about everything else: her career, my career, our relationship, the future. We skirt the *m* word but admit to having grown closer over time, especially over the time Thomas has been in our lives. The possibility of longevity and even permanence in our relationship has never before been discussed, perhaps it never existed, so I take this as a good sign. We go out for a nice dinner of steak and wine. We come home, watch non-news TV, and drink more wine. We make gentle, passionate love and fall asleep. The name *Thomas* never enters the evening.

CHAPTER 30

I wake up at 7:31 a.m. and Annie is missing. I sit up and listen. I hear mumbled, half-muted voices emanating from the kitchen: either she's watching TV news or Thomas has returned home. There would have been shrieking had Thomas returned home. I quickly put on my robe, brush my hair and teeth, and hurry downstairs just in case. Annie sits at the "hoping for good news" table, sipping hot tea.

"Anything?" I say, stealing a glance as I traipse past the TV toward the coffee maker.

"It's circus-world," she replies. "They're trying to unravel the non-existent-town riddle. They've interviewed Katie Katt on at least five different channels. She knows nothing, but then we all knew that. Reporters have zeroed in on a county in northern Maine called Cozen County, with a 'C.' It encompasses a goodly number of small towns and villages." She smiles at her use of the word *goodly*. "It's like a scavenger hunt out there—reporters, cameramen, camera-women, anchors, anchoretts, all going full tilt in opposite directions. Come watch, it's fun."

I pour my coffee and come watch, sitting down across from her. The TV is on NBC News, showing the anchor talking to his man on the scene who stands proudly in the little village of Washburn. The reporter is very excited waiting to interview a woman who knows a man who used to fish with a fellow named Tom. She's pretty sure that his last name sounded something like Montgomery. They're following the story closely and will bring us further breaking news as it develops.

"It's like this on every channel," she says, "even Fox."

"So nobody has a clue?"

"Nobody has a clue."

"Is Thomas in Maine?"

"Something's in Maine."

I pick up the remote and switch to another channel—CNN, I think. Their reporter is in the extreme northern town of Caribou, talking with three locals at their favorite watering hole. They claim that Tom Montgomery is a regular there and comes in all the time. They know nothing about a wager he might have made but they expect him to walk through the door at any minute. They've been drinking since four thirty a.m.

I switch to another channel. Annie winces when I do.

"What's wrong?"

"Nothing." Her cheeks flush. "It's just...I don't want to come across some news station showing Thomas in handcuffs, bordered by to two gloating, black-clad FBI agents."

"I think the FBI is still in Augusta."

"Okay, then Thomas in handcuffs, flanked by a grinning, pot-bellied sheriff and his snaggle-toothed deputy."

"You said they won't find him. You said he isn't there."

"I know what I said, Hart. I hope I'm right."

I look at her and see the tears start to well. She looks away.

"Annie," I say, "you're right. I know you're right."

She looks at me and a teardrop escapes the corner of her eye and runs down her left cheek. She allows me to brush it away.

"But what if I'm not? What if..."

I gently place my finger against her lips. "You're right Annie. I know it."

She leans into me, sniffling a little while I hug her. Her hair tickles my cheek and brings a smile to my lips, and I stiffen. She feels the tension and leans back wiping her eyes. She looks at me but doesn't question. She stands up and walks over to the stove.

"How about some eggs?"

I nod and attempt to recover my smile and mood, but it isn't happening. I switch the TV back to Fox and turn down the volume, figuring we can tell the tale by the antics of the players. I know you can't rely on that Fox News Alert banner. That thing never leaves the screen.

She burned the eggs, so we eat our toast in silence because and I think that's the way she wants it, but midway through my second piece she says, "We need to talk about it, Hart. Talking helps."

"Even negative talk?"

"Everything, I want us to consider everything."

I stare at her.

"Everything, Hart. I mean it—out with it."

"Okay." I place both hands on the table in front of me and spread my fingers. "If things are as you say they are, and so far they have been, then there could be a problem."

She looks at me over her teacup with arched eyebrows, a signal I'd better continue.

"We assume there's evidence out there that validates Thomas's existence, correct?"

She nods her head.

"This evidence is what the FBI and the media are searching for, though they don't know it."

She nods again.

"Okay, let's say the FBI comes across the evidence first. They'll likely confiscate whatever they find and truck it back to Langley. There, they'll go over every shred meticulously, studying it, categorizing it, and filing it before writing it up in a detailed report. If this report does, in fact, prove the existence of Thomas and the non-existence of Tom Montgomery then it also proves that no crime has been committed." She again arches her eyebrows at me. "In other words, Thomas never lied to anyone and Tom lied only to Katie Katt and her viewers, something she herself does every day." Annie continues to arch but her eyes grow uneasy. "The report goes to Justice and from there it's shared with congressional intelligence committees. Since no crime has been committed, there is nothing that requires them to share the facts with the media or the American people. The report, therefore, may never see the light of day and Thomas's identity may never be validated. It happens all the time."

She frowns. She's thinking and frowning and staring at me. "What else?" she says.

Because I don't know when to stop, I say, "What if one of the more liberal TV stations uncovers the truth?" I hold my hands out. "Same thing, they never bring it to light. They bury the story. Thomas remains a fabrication and Tom Montgomery is listed as 'whereabouts unknown.'"

She slowly shakes her head. "I considered that—so did Thomas, I think. It's a calculated risk, but when it comes to the media, ideology would hardly trump a news story of this magnitude. Also a news organization would not be allowed to confiscate information. The press are like crows once they uncover a big story, they start squawking their pointy little beaks off so that by the time they're done every news crew in the country is on site."

"Good point," I say.

"But the FBI," she says, "that worries me."

Suddenly Fox News interrupts their panel discussion for breaking news just in. They take us to Carl Castle in the field.

"We have breaking news," Carl says. "It appears to be more than just rumor. In the town of," he glances down at the paper he's holding, "Quimby, located in North Cozen County, a woman, Mrs. Lila Senkowski, has positively identified Tom Montgomery from a newspaper photo shown to her by local law enforcement. He is said to reside in a cabin discovered some five miles west of town. Our crews are on their way to the scene as we speak."

"Law enforcement," I say. "Did you hear?"

Annie nods her head. I know the image of Thomas in handcuffs is flashing through her mind.

"Some news teams are probably already there," I say. "Can we switch channels?"

She nods again and I start to surf. I hit paydirt on my fourth try—CBS. Their reporter, a pretty young girl in a yellow sweater and fur-topped boots, is positioned in the middle of a narrow dirt road bordered on both sides by dense woods. Directly behind her stand two impenetrable police officers—they look like state but could be county. In the far distance, through the trees, I can barely make out a wooden structure, most likely the cabin. I look over at Annie. Her shoulders sag but her breathing seems normal. A look of relief finds her face as we both realize the cops would have already checked the premises, and had Thomas been there he would have already been apprehended and paraded in front of the cameras. The reporter confirms this as we watch.

"This is as close to the cabin as we are allowed," she says. "The county police assure us there is no one inside and that the integrity of the cabin's contents must be preserved. Sheriff Tanquera says they are working closely with the FBI, who are presently en route from Augusta, Maine, the state capital. He expects them here within the hour."

I look again at Annie. She wears an expression of consternation.

"Law enforcement," she says, "they beat the press."

I nod.

"This thing will never see the light of day," she says.

I pick up the remote and switch to another station. It shows a news crew arriving—a reporter and cameraman exiting their van and rushing toward the cabin, only to be stopped by Sheriff Tanquera. Two other news vans pull up behind them.

"Look," I say pointing at the screen, "news teams are coming in from all over. By the time the Feds get there the place'll be knee-deep in overly aggressive reporters all demanding answers. Somebody will have to say something."

"Perhaps," she says in an optimistic tone, while her face shows otherwise.

I switch back to Fox. The talk has moved from the inevitable apprehension of Tom Montgomery to the possible treasure trove of damning information within the cabin. Speculation runs the gamut from Tom the war veteran suffering from post-traumatic stress disorder to Tom the con-man and criminal mastermind bent on embarrassing a nation. They all seem confident that a thorough search of the premises will yield the information necessary to not only capture the fugitive but to rightfully condemn him for his guile and treachery.

CHAPTER 31

I suggest we go out for a late breakfast and Annie agrees. We take our time. We walk to Stan's Bagel Bin, a little bagel place several blocks away, and sit outside for some fresh air. I order cream cheese on white and she chooses low fat margarine on multigrain. We speak of unimportant things, small talk about nothing, anything to change our focus. It doesn't work. In the middle of our conversation, she pulls out her cell and dials Thomas's number. A monotone voice asks her to leave a message.

Sadness dwells. She fumbles with her phone and drops it trying to put it back in her purse. I look at her face and sense an emotional breakdown. My face reddens and I start to get angry at Thomas. She loves him and he loves her. Why won't he call?

Her cell rings. She fumbles for it, almost dropping it again. She gets it open but in her haste accidentally hits the speaker button. She puts it to her ear. The voice on the other end, clearly heard by both of us, makes everything else irrelevant.

"I trust you have not been taken in by the glib Mr. Tom Montgomery," it says.

"Thomas," her voice is filled with such relief and her face shines with such delight that my throat lumps up.

"My apologies to you both. My time has been fully occupied with being, as you say, 'on the lam.' I can speak but briefly. I am well and quite safe. Trust your instincts, Miss Anne, for this journey rapidly approaches its end. I expect it to be a just and proper one. I call today but to urge you to worry not and to convey my love to you both." His voice is replaced by a click and then silence.

Annie lets the phone fall to the table as she drops her face into her hands and begins to cry. She cries for a long time. I don't try to comfort her for there's no need. These are tears of joy and relief. I'm doing my best not to cry along with her.

Our walk home is different; all has changed. It no longer matters to Annie about the FBI, news reporters, or detailed reports. It matters only that Thomas is alive and safe. I don't believe I've ever seen her this happy. I guess I should be jealous, but then I'm feeling pretty much the same way. Unlike Annie, though, I do worry about the FBI and the fallout yet to come.

She doesn't want to go home and she doesn't want to sit still, so we continue walking—walking and enjoying the day. We skip the Capitol grounds and head directly into Georgetown, affording us less politics and more shopping. She isn't actually in the buying mood, she just wants to stroll the sidewalks and shop the windows.

It's almost dusk by the time we reach the condo, so whatever has happened on the Thomas front has happened already. We need merely to go in, switch on the TV, and find out what it is. I figure Annie has had enough drama for one day, so I stay clear of the remote. I'm surprised when she picks it up, points it toward the TV, and presses the power button.

She switches to NBC, a station she knows for sure is on location. By the images on the screen it seems every TV station and newspaper crew in the country are on site. Hundreds of reporters line the dirt road to the cabin. Many more are scattered throughout the woods, looking for a way in. They're all stymied, however, by at least fifty or sixty FBI agents. Some are carting papers and files from the cabin and stacking them in one of the three white windowless vans parked in front. Most are acting as security guards keeping the media at bay.

"Looks like it's going according to plan," I say.

Annie nods.

"One of the few times the press could and would print the truth," I say, "and the FBI won't let them near the place."

She looks over at me. "Will it ever come out, Hart?"

I think about it. The Feds complete their findings, they present their report to Justice, Justice finds no laws have been broken—the whole thing becomes a political football. Releasing the information would require Senate and probably presidential approval. There is absolutely no friggin' way.

So I say, "It's possible."

She switches back to Fox. She's just in time to see the ever-present Fox News Alert Banner, only this time it means something.

"Turn it up," I say, and she does.

Ben Gleason is speaking with Rick Dickson and Dick Scott on primetime news. It's unusual, because Gleason left Fox some time ago to form his own show. He's excitedly waving around a sheet of paper he claims is the print-out of an email he had received earlier in the day. It's from the publisher of The Mountain Courier, a small local newspaper in Cosen County, Maine. He was initially contacted by phone, Gleason says, then followed up by said email. It seems The Courier's reporter—singular because there's only one—had actually been the first person to discover Tom Montgomery's cabin. The same woman who had identified Montgomery's photo to the local police neglected to mention that she had done the same for the Courier's reporter some two hours earlier.

My eyes meet Annie's in shared hope. I turn up the volume and we lean in closer. The gist of the email is that the reporter, Lawrence Takin, had arrived at the cabin with a pen, a yellow-pad, and his cell phone camera, well before anyone else knew anything about it. He knocked on the door, which slowly swung open to his action. He called twice and got no answer, so he entered the cabin and found a most fascinating conclusion to our present-day national mystery.

Gleason stares hard into the camera and says, "Let me repeat that: A most fascinating conclusion to our present day national mystery."

He goes on to announce an exclusive interview with reporter Lawrence Takin tonight, only on the Fox News Channel. He also throws in a teaser saying, "Mr. Takin has taken hundreds of photos at the scene which, when viewed, will explain everything."

"Ladies and gentlemen," he says, "I beg of you, tune in to Fox News at eight o'clock tonight. Trust me, you do not want to miss this."

I look over at Annie with a big smile on my face. "I doubt he had to ask for viewers," I say. "Everybody with a TV will be watching Fox News in about," I look at the clock, "two hours."

She starts giggling as she raises her hand into a way out of character high-five position. I slap it and start laughing uncontrollably. We sit there at the good news/LOL table with shaking bellies, in unbridled mirth, until our sides start to split.

We flick through several more stations. Most have already heard the Fox News announcement, but no one has a clue as to what's about to come down. I even consider calling Feldstone with a heads-up but know full well it would be more about gloating than informing. Annie's desperate to call Thomas again, but I caution her to wait until after the interview. We can't be completely sure until it's all out there.

I start pondering on all the things that can go wrong because that's what I do. Number one: can the Feds nail this Lawrence Takin and seize all his info for interfering with a federal investigation? I don't think so, since he was at the cabin well before the FBI got there and sealed things off. Two: can they charge him with breaking and entering or even simple trespassing? Again, I don't think so. The owner would have to file charges, wouldn't he? And in this case, Takin did exactly what the owner wanted him to do. In addition I'm sure the FBI warrant was under the name of a Tom Montgomery. This cabin belongs to a Thomas somebody else. I expect some smart lawyer could even make a pretty compelling case against the FBI for storming the wrong cabin.

The one remaining gap is Lawrence Takin himself. Can the FBI detain him as a person of interest? Maybe, but they'll have to find him first. I suspect Fox News has him in some safe house in an extremely secure area waiting for eight o'clock tonight. I doubt even the FBI would storm a coast-to-coast television station once the cameras start rolling.

Damn, I'm thinking, while checking the corners of my mouth for an up-turn. *I believe Thomas has got 'em!*

CHAPTER 32

Annie and I decide to give it a rest for the next two hours and eleven minutes. I choose to go down to the basement and tinker with the BMW, cleaning and polishing since I don't do under–the-hood work, and Annie decides to spiff up the condo, dusting and vacuuming. We're both trying to kill time and thwart anxiety, but neither of us will admit it.

Eight o'clock comes right on time. The TV is already on, so I have only to turn up the volume. Rick Dickson and Dick Scott are sitting across the table from Ben Gleason and a young kid of fifteen who's probably twenty-one and who can only be Lawrence Takin. Lawrence has a white box and a laptop on the table in front of him. The laptop, I assume, holds the hundreds of photographs promised.

Rick introduces everyone then turns to Lawrence and says, "Before we get started, please tell our viewing audience why you have chosen Fox News and particularly Ben Gleason to present your story."

Lawrence sits up very straight, his head swiveling about, eyes darting everywhere at once. He seems truly excited to have made it to the big time. He speaks with the exuberance of an Idol wannabe.

"I thought, you know, we'd just print it in the Courier like always," he says, "but Mr. Canton felt we needed wider distribution. Mr. Canton says we'll be breaking about the biggest story in my lifetime." He smiles and his cheeks go red. "So Mr. Canton calls you guys."

"But why Fox, why Gleason?"

"Mr. Canton felt that Fox News would put everything out there, you know, wouldn't hold anything back, being all fair and balanced and letting the people decide. Mr. Canton contacted Mr. Gleason because everybody knows he's an honest guy. He's going to tell it like it is."

The camera shows Rick, Dick, and Ben, beaming. Their bright smiles and white teeth light up the set and partially blind the audience. The camera pans to Gleason for comment.

"What can I say? The kid has taste—eat your heart out, O'Reilly." He stares into the camera and puts on a serious face. "I've seen the information young Lawrence, here, has in store for you and all I can say is that the truth shall set you free. Hold on, America, you're in for a heck of a ride."

Gleason stands up and takes a few steps to the center of the set. He pauses, puts his face into the camera and says, "Mr. President, shall we consider this a teachable moment?"

He walks over, rolls out one of his signature blackboards, and wheels it to the center of the stage. He angles it so the audience and camera can see.

"These are the facts," he says.

He produces a long, fat stick of chalk and writes the following:

There is no Tom Montgomery

There is a Thomas: Thomas P. Boyd

Thomas was a war hero, a history professor, and a circuit lecturer

Thomas survived a tragic accident 29 months ago which killed his wife and left him with intermittently occurring amnesia

He leaves number 5 blank, steps back and looks at his handiwork. He turns and smiles into the camera. "Would you like me to explain?" he says with a grin.

The audience breaks into a cacophony of claps and cheers as the camera pans to Rick and Dick, who are collectively and animatedly nodding their heads.

"Lawrence," Gleason says, "the pictures please."

Lawrence brings over and opens the white box filled with pictures. Each photo has a magnetic back affixed to it. Gleason turns to the blackboard and reads number one.

"There is no Tom Montgomery."

On cue, Lawrence hands him the photo of Tom Montgomery that had recently graced the front pages of the DC Sentinel. Gleason slaps it on the blackboard next to Tom's name.

"This is the photograph shown to Lila Sandowski by the local cops, which led to the discovery of the cabin in the woods. This same photo was shown to Lila Sandowski several hours earlier by our intrepid young reporter here, Lawrence Takin. Lila recognized the man in the photo, not as Tom Montgomery, but as a man whose name she did not know. A man who lived a hermitized existence somewhere west of her village of Quimby. He used to buy vegetables and fruits from her garden. She was convinced his cabin was close by because the man always came on foot."

Lawrence hands Gleason a picture of the cabin sitting all by itself in the woods, absent police or reporters. He slaps the photo on the board next to Tom's picture and goes to number two.

"There is a Thomas: Thomas P. Boyd." Gleason reads. "Thomas was a history professor and lecturer. The *p* stands for patriot." Gleason pauses and smiles. "Honest to God, Thomas's middle name is 'Patriot.'"

He is handed a picture of Thomas taken during his speech to the nation. He places it on the blackboard next to Thomas's name and reads number three.

"Thomas was a war hero, a history professor, and a circuit lecturer. Born in 1946, Thomas was a Vietnam vet who served with the Army Rangers. He was awarded both the Purple Heart and the Silver Star for his service. He was married to Mary Breeze, a middle school teacher. Thomas was a history professor at Cumberland Junior College in Augusta, where he taught early American history. He was such an avid history buff, in fact, he and two of his fellow professors formed a group called the Minutemen. They would dress in colonial clothing and present lectures on our founding fathers and on early American life. They were quite popular on the junior college and high school lecture circuit."

Gleason placed three more pictures on the board next to number 3. One was a county records document that showed ownership of a log cabin by one Thomas Patriot Boyd. One was a letter addressed to Mr. Thomas P. Boyd inviting him and his compatriots to lecture at DC Community College in Washington, D.C. The third was the photo of a military citation awarding him the Silver Star.

"Thomas survived a tragic accident 29 months ago which killed his wife and left him with intermittent occurring amnesia," Gleason reads.

"Two years and five months ago, Thomas and his wife Mary were involved in an automobile accident. Mary was killed and Thomas was critically injured. He incurred multiple injuries to the face and head, requiring extensive reconstruction and plastic surgery. After a prolonged stay in the hospital he was released, but continued to experience extensive headaches and periodic bouts of amnesia lasting one to three months at a time."

Gleason places the picture of the newspaper article detailing the accident, a picture of the medical record summary, and a picture of the death certificate of Mrs. Mary Breeze Boyd next to number 4. Gleason picks up his chalk and begins to write next to number 5. He speaks each word as he writes it.

"Thomas...is...exactly...who...he...says...he...is."

He clicks the chalk against the blackboard at the end for emphasis. He spins around and glares into the camera. He bounces the chalk from one hand to the other, then holds it still, clutching it with both hands as he leans in closer.

"Thomas Patriot Boyd addressed this nation on April sixteen of this year. His words were spoken from the heart by a man of the people, whose mind and memory had been reconfigured by tragedy thus giving us a unique perspective of our present day way of life by a man from the past. He spoke in formal tongue, a side effect of his accident. Nothing was contrived, nothing plotted, nothing faked. Thomas spoke as a man who loved his country. He spoke for all Americans who love their country. He spoke against those who would do her harm. He chastised us, he urged us, pleaded with us, he cautioned us. He put the onus on 'we the people' to take back America—to restore her to her original purpose and promise as laid out in our Constitution. It was the greatest speech I have ever heard. Thomas P. Boyd stood up for us. Perhaps it is time 'we the people' stand up for America."

Gleason moves the picture of Thomas giving his speech to the nation down to the fifth spot and puts it next to Thomas's name. He then turns and walks over to the table, picks up the t-shirt lying there, neatly folded, and slips it on. He turns with a grin and faces the camera. His shirt reads:

"A long habit of not thinking a thing wrong
gives it a superficial appearance of being right."
Thomas Paine

There is a small minuteman silhouette in the bottom right-hand corner.

"I wonder where Thomas Patriot Boyd is now?" Gleason says. "I hope we hear from him soon. We need such men."

With that he thanks Lawrence Takin, acknowledges Rick and Dick, and signs off the show. Annie and I sit in frozen silence, staring at the screen.

"Wow," I finally say.

She reaches over, takes my hand, and nods silently.

"Everything we hoped for," I say.

"And more," she agrees.

"Well, you've been right all along, Annie. Want to take a shot at the aftermath?"

"Aftermath?"

"You know, the about-to-be, the endgame, the happily ever after."

She stares at me. "I suppose that would depend on 'we the people,' now, wouldn't it?"

My turn to nod silently.

CHAPTER 33

Monday morning I'm up with the sun but still fail to beat Annie down the stairs. I hear the clinking of china, teacups, and saucers, and so I hurry on with my robe, brushing my teeth and patting down my hair in a rush to join her. I figure she has the TV turned on and is immersed in the Thomas P. Boyd aftermath, but, surprisingly, I find her sitting at the tea table, contentedly sipping and smiling, a look of lost thought on her face. She sees me and lights my morning with her smile, so I go over and collect a kiss before making my way to the coffee machine.

"No TV?" I say.

"We'll get caught up in it soon enough. I thought we should embrace the morning, enjoy the sunrise."

"Better still," I say, inhaling the smell of coffee while taking my seat across from her. "How about some fresh air and exercise? A morning walk to further seize the day?"

She nods and proceeds to not ask about work, allowing me to maintain my if-they-want-me-they-can-call-me stand. We finish our stimulants in tranquility and go upstairs for our walking clothes.

We leave through the front door and Annie takes my hand as we start down the porch steps. I'm already aware of a lightness in my step, and now there's a warmth in my heart. An air of hope permeates our conversation as we speak of the future, both ours and the nation's.

Out of habit we turn left toward Capitol Park grounds. We no longer wish to avoid the seat of our government. Quite the opposite. We wish to embrace it, to challenge it, to restore it. We walk confidently and comfortably, holding hands in harmony with each other and perhaps many more. We stroll and chat and laugh and eventually find ourselves on park grounds staring at the Thomas bench. We look at each other and without words walk over and sit down.

I lean back and look up, taking in the green leaves of late spring and a sky of clear blue. My eyes scan the grounds, admiring the expertly manicured lawn and artfully trimmed shrubbery. Throngs of people grouped in twos and threes and fours roam throughout the mall. They're animatedly talking to one another with excitement in their voices and purpose in their movements.

"Look," Annie says, pointing, "a Thomas t-shirt." Then, "Another, and another."

There are dozens of them, hundreds—maybe thousands.

"They can't all be tourists," she says, now standing up on her tip toes. "Look, they're gravitating toward the mall, toward Thomas's shop."

I stand up, too, but not on my tiptoes. I see the crowd drifting toward and gathering down by the kiosk.

"They will be much disappointed," comes a voice from behind me, "for, alas, it is early in the day and we are not yet open for business."

"Archie?" I say turning, knowing damn well it isn't Archie but my mind unable to grasp the truth.

Standing before me is Thomas Patriot Boyd. I reach out to hug him but am entirely too slow. Annie charges forward, latching her arms around his neck in an instant, squeezing him for all she's worth. I'm not jealous, I'm impatient—wanting my turn.

After the hugging and the handshaking and the hugging some more, Thomas is allowed to escape a step backward. We stand and stare at him as he does us. Nobody has the words. We embrace the silence and bathe each other in smiles and happiness. Finally, I break the quiet.

"Thomas," I say, happy to speak his name again, "you have your memory back—Congratulations."

"Indeed, I fear not, Hartford. I have been able to recall the location of my dwelling only. From there, through accident reports, newspaper stories, and most especially letters written between my wife and myself, have I been able to ascertain much of my past. Dr. Alex Greenberg, the psychologist who attended me following the accident, has been most helpful. I have no memory of the accident nor the death of my beloved wife, Mary."

Thomas swiftly brushes his eyes with his sleeve and continues.

"Dr. Greenberg regrets to inform me that my condition may remain thus for the foreseeable future. He claims my mind may continue to obstruct such painful memories in defense of my sanity."

"You have retained your formal speech," I say.

"Yes, Hartford. I am told I was on my way to Colgate Junior College when the accident occurred. I was donned in my minuteman outfit at the time, rehearsing my speech on early American life. When I awoke in my hospital bed my speech was as you hear it today. The good doctor assures me it may gradually change, much like a man from the state of Georgia losing his southern drawl after dwelling in New York City for too long a time. As for now, well, I can assure you I am no Tom Montgomery." He grins. "My manner of speaking at present feels quite natural to me, and any other way of communicating, quite uncomfortable."

I'm feeling a bit uncomfortable myself so I blurt out, "Well, at least you won. Congrats on that."

"What might I have won, Hartford?"

"You beat them, you shut them down, to the victor go the spoils."

I hold my hands out in a double low-five. Thomas just smiles and says nothing.

"Are you going down there?" I point toward the kiosk. "They're all waiting for you."

"Why no, Hartford, I am not—and they are not. Miss Anne, I believe Hartford is under a misconception."

"Hart," she says, taking an unseen cue, "Thomas didn't do this to become the leader of a movement."

I stare at her. I've worked with people all my life. People who want nothing more than to control and manipulate the masses. They call it leadership. Most would sell their souls for the opportunity that Thomas is passing up.

I turn to him. "Then why put yourself through all this? Why fight the smearmongers?"

"Someone must halt their tactics, Hartford, their 'smear machine,' as you call it. Otherwise, how can good men and good women fairly vie for elective office?"

"But it's not your fight. If you're not going to run, if you're not going to enter the fray— what does it matter?"

"It matters to them," Annie says, pointing down the hill at the crowd. "To us, to everyone who heard Thomas's words and believed in them. It matters to all of us who love America and would restore her to her original vision and purpose. We're talking about the politics of personal destruction, Hart. Both parties have employed it for years. They learned long ago that if you destroy the man personally, you discredit his words, dishearten his supporters, and cripple his cause, all at the same time."

"But by inventing Tom Montgomery didn't Thomas discredit himself?" I expect him to say, *I'm standing right here, Hartford,* but he doesn't.

"Yes he did," Annie says, "in order to pull them in for the kill. He disappointed his supporters, true, but only for a brief time. His actions served to embolden his enemies, revealing them in all of their hate-filled glory. They showed themselves willing to do anything and everything to destroy Tom and Thomas. Tom Montgomery was created to allow 'we the people' to clearly see the system manipulators, the men behind the curtain—to unmask them, to expose their core. That's exactly what happened. The people saw that this media and this government had no qualms in destroying a man whose only crime was to love his country and be trusted by its people."

"The window of opportunity shall eventually close," Thomas says. "Memories die. We have but little time."

"How much time?" I say.

"I expect the coming election in November is our most promising chance to place good, honest Americans in office without the accompaniment of an organized smear campaign. Beyond that, I believe, those that can will revive such tactics and begin again."

"So we need to get to work."

"Yes indeed, Hartford. That is your work—down there."

I look toward the steadily growing crowd down by the kiosk, but I'm not ready to leave. I'm not ready to walk away from my friend. I search for a diversion to delay the inevitable and find it right in front of me.

I point to his t-shirt and say, "That's not a Thomas Tee."

He stretches it out so we can read it. It's a quote, but not one that can be attributed to Thomas and his unique memory.

"There followeth after me today
A youth whose feet must pass this way.
This chasm that has been naught to me
To that fair-haired youth may a pitfall be.
He, too, must cross in the twilight dim;
Good friend, I am building the bridge for him."
Will Allen Dromgoole

Annie and I stare at him, her head cocked to one side.

"I feel it quite appropriate," he says and grins. "It speaks to our obligation as a nation as well as our purpose. George Washington, John Adams, Thomas Jefferson, James Madison—these men not only established a nation, they cherished and upheld its principles and promises and passed them along to their offspring. Are we not obligated to do the same, to pass along a strong and viable United States of America to those who follow? Are we not tasked as keepers of the flame? Will we not forsake our children, our God, and ourselves should we fail?" He wipes his sleeve across his eyes. "And yet, I believe we will endorse failure in every manner possible should we continue on our present course."

All's quiet until Annie says, "Can it change?"

"Most assuredly," he says. "The people may change it if they are willing."

"Those people?" She points to the crowd which continues to build.

"This country is made up of two kinds of people," he says. "Those that wish for someone to lead them and those that wish for someone to stand up for them. Those people," he motions to the crowd, "the Tea Party people and others with similar values, I believe, constitute the majority of American citizens. They do not wish to be led. They wish to be represented, to be stood up for. I have been afforded the privilege of standing up for them before Congress and the president. It is now time for them to stand up for their country."

I stare at him and he stares back.

"They could surely use your help, Hartford."

"And you, Thomas?" Annie says. "What is to become of you?"

"I know who I am. I know where I dwell. I shall return home to my passion—my study of American history. Perhaps I shall obtain a dog." He grins. "Hartford," he says, "this is for you."

He hands me a soft package wrapped in brown paper.

Thomas ushers us go, to join the throng, to begin the restoration. Annie remains rooted in place, then lunges forward for a last, long hug. She finally lets him go and lets me in.

We turn and walk slowly, hesitantly, reluctant to leave. I look back at Thomas standing by his bench.

"Hartford, Miss Anne," he shouts spreading his arms wide, indicating the exuberant stream of people filling the mall. "This is the way it was meant to be!"

I nod. I wave. I make it all the way down to the edge of the crowd before looking back and finding him gone.

"It's okay," Annie says, taking hold of my hand and showing me her brightest smile yet, while her tears flow freely. "We'll see him again. We'll stay in touch. For now we need to become 'we the people.' We need to restore a nation. Thomas has provided the spark, we need now to build the fire."

She pulls me into the fray. I put my other hand in my pocket and wrap my fingers around something that isn't supposed to be there: Thomas's cell phone. I slowly shake my head. We won't stay in touch. We won't see him again.

Suddenly I hear my name. Someone in the throng has recognized me, not as Hartford Keepe, political Golden Boy, but as Thomas's friend. Others turn toward me and start to crowd in. They're all shouting questions, desperate to know of Thomas: is he safe, have I seen him, talked to him, will they see him again? I remain silent, not sure what to reveal. They move in closer, surrounding me, urging me, hungering for any bit of information on Thomas.

Annie responds, "Thomas is well, we have spoken with him." Seeing their thirst for more she says, "He even gave Hartford a gift."

All eyes go to the package I have clutched in both hands. The package is their link to Thomas. They need to see it, to examine it, to uncover its message. More than one voice cries out for me to open it. The people move closer, some jostling me from behind.

I rip it open, dropping the paper on the ground. It's a t-shirt—who knew. Before I can read the quote someone shouts, "What does it say?" then, "Hold it up," then, "Put it on!" The crowd starts to back away, affording me space. I put on the t-shirt and turn in a slow circle, affording all but me a look at the message. Everyone's looking at me and smiling. Not because of my golden boy status, mind you, but because I'm a symbol of something bigger than myself. This is new to me. I might like it.

I stop turning. The crowd breaks into applause and cheers. I look down at the t-shirt and try to read the words upside down, but it's difficult. I sense a presence in front of me and look up into Annie's smiling face. She reads:

"America is what 'we the people' make it.
Always has been. Always will be."
Grandma Moses
(slightly altered in a way, I believe, she would approve)

I feel proud, patriotic. I feel the corners of my mouth for an upturn.

It's there.